PREGNANT BY THE COLTON COWBOY

BY
LARA LACOMBE

MILLS & BOON

First Published in Great Britain 2017
By Mills & Boon, an imprint of HarperCollins*Publishers*
1 London Bridge Street, London, SE1 9GF

© 2017 Harlequin Books S.A.

Special thanks and acknowledgement are given to Lara Lacombe for her contribution to *The Coltons of Shadow Creek* series.

ISBN: 978-0-263-93038-2

18-0517

Our policy is to use papers that are natural, renewable and recyclable products and made from wood grown in sustainable forests. The logging and manufacturing processes conform to the legal environmental regulations of the country of origin.

Printed and bound in Spain
by CPI, Barcelona

Lara Lacombe earned a PhD in microbiology and immunology and worked in several labs across the country before moving into the classroom. Her day job as a college science professor gives her time to pursue her other love—writing fast-paced romantic suspense with smart, nerdy heroines and dangerously attractive heroes. She loves to hear from readers! Find her on the web or contact her at laralacombewriter@gmail.com.

This book is for Elizabeth, friend extraordinaire.

Chapter 1

The rain started just as Maggie Lowell finished the last entry in the account book. The drops fell in a gentle patter, but a quick glance at the dark sky outside made it clear the sky wouldn't stay peaceful for long. Time to go home.

She quickly packed up her laptop and papers with one hand and pecked out a text to Mac with the other. All done. Everything looks good.

Maggie normally didn't come to a client's home to work on their books, but she made an exception for Joseph "Mac" Mackenzie. He was impossible to refuse—always smiling, always kind. He'd been one of her first clients in Shadow Creek, and he hadn't hesitated to promote her bookkeeping services to all his friends. Since Mac was a deservedly popular man, it hadn't taken long for Maggie to build a solid roster of clients. Mac's actions had essentially ensured her success here, and Maggie never forgot it. Dropping by his ranch to work on his books every quarter was a small way to repay him for his kindness.

And if she happened to run into Mac's son, Thorne, while she was at the ranch? That was just a bonus.

Maggie glanced around as she left the office, hoping to catch a glimpse of Thorne while she made her way to her car. The rich scent of horses and hay hit her nose as she stepped into the barn, and one of the animals whickered softly in response to the sound of the office door being shut. There was no sign of Thorne, but it was clear he'd been there recently—a set of wet boot prints marred the otherwise clean floor of the barn, and since Mac was in San Antonio on business, the prints could only belong to Thorne.

Would she see him as she dashed to the car? The thought made her heart flutter, and a sense of anticipation warmed her limbs. Even a drive-by sighting of Thorne was better than no sighting at all.

Maggie knew her crush on Thorne was irrational, but she couldn't help herself. The man was her personal catnip, and every time she saw him she fell a little bit more in love with him. How could she not? His smile lit up a room, and when she saw those dimples in his cheeks she went weak in the knees. His light brown eyes were full of a quiet intelligence that drew her in and made her want to learn more about him. And the fact that he had the body of a man who made his living working with horses didn't hurt, either. His long, lean frame filled out a pair of jeans in all the right places, and his dark skin contrasted nicely with the light blue work shirts he often wore. Thorne Colton was the total package, and ever since she had first laid eyes on him, Maggie had thought of little else.

She harbored no illusions about Thorne's feelings for her. He had inherited his father's impeccable manners and he always treated her with respect, but Maggie knew she wasn't the kind of woman Thorne dated. He was horses, hard work and sunshine, and she was… well, truth be told she was more of an indoors girl. They had very little in common, but that didn't stop her inner thirteen-year-old from letting out a squeal of delight any time he was near.

She debated lingering in the barn for a moment in the hopes of seeing him, but decided against it. She had her pride, after all.

Maggie hugged her computer bag close and dashed to her car, diving into the driver's seat with more momentum than grace. She deposited the slightly damp bag in the passenger seat and grabbed a handful of napkins from the console, then set about patting herself dry. The water was cold and she shivered slightly, but she told herself to enjoy the sensation while it lasted. Summer came quickly to Shadow Creek, Texas, and she knew in a few months she'd be begging for the relief of a cool rain.

Feeling slightly less waterlogged, she stuck the key into the ignition. Hopefully the storm wouldn't affect traffic too badly. Her stomach growled in agreement, and she began to mentally review her dinner options as she turned the key.

The engine whined in protest, and thoughts of food vanished as Maggie focused on the car. "Not again," she muttered, pumping the gas before giving the key another turn. The red sedan had been a steady and reliable workhorse for the past several years, but it was starting to show its age. A few months ago, the mechanic had advised her to start looking for another car, but Maggie had yet to find the time. Besides, she had faith in the old man. Surely they could go a few thousand more miles before she had to say goodbye?

As if in response, the engine emitted an alarming grinding noise that sounded like rocks slamming together. It shuddered, causing the whole car to vibrate, and then stopped with a pitiful wheeze.

Great. It seemed her cheerful red stallion had finally given up and died.

Mother Nature apparently sensed the loss, as the sky opened up in earnest. The torrential rain pounded the car in a deafening onslaught and Maggie sighed, dropping her head to lean against the steering wheel. *It just keeps getting better...*

She indulged in a moment's self-pity, then fished out her cell phone and called for a tow.

"It's gonna take a while," the dispatcher informed her. "The ranch is outside the town limits, and we've got a lot of calls ahead of you. The weather is slowing us down."

"That's fine," Maggie said. "I'm not going anywhere."

She hung up the phone and eyed the computer bag in the passenger seat. Maybe she could get some work done while she waited...

She pulled the bag into her lap just as the passenger door opened and someone plopped into the seat. Maggie let out a squeak of alarm and jumped, her hand scrabbling for the handle as she pressed herself against the door.

"Hey there." Thorne's deep, calm voice filled the

car, and Maggie's body recognized him a split second before her mind caught up. Her muscles relaxed and a swarm of butterflies took flight in her stomach as her body celebrated its proximity to his.

Her breath gusted out in a shaky sigh. "Hi, yourself."

"I'm sorry—I didn't mean to scare you." He took off his brown, rain-spattered cowboy hat, careful to keep it level so the water trapped in its folds didn't drip onto her seats. It was a thoughtful gesture, one that Maggie appreciated.

"It's all right," she said, offering him a smile. "You startled me more than anything."

"Everything okay? I noticed you've been sitting here for a while now. Are you having trouble with your car?" His light brown eyes were full of concern and her stomach did a little flip. Thorne had noticed her. More importantly, he cared enough to check on her. Maybe she wasn't so invisible after all.

Maggie reined in her imagination before visions of flower arrangements and bridesmaid dresses crowded out rational thought. "Yeah," she said, focusing on his question. "My car won't start. I've called for a tow."

Thorne nodded. "I'd offer to take a look at it for you, but I don't really know much about fixing cars." He sounded a little apologetic, as if his lack of mechanical acumen was a personal failing.

"Don't worry about it," Maggie said. "My mechanic told me a few months ago I should start looking for a new car. I guess I can't put it off any longer."

"Guess not," he replied. He was quiet a moment, his expression thoughtful. "Would you like to wait inside?"

She considered the offer. It would be nice to have

a little more room for her laptop, and the air inside the car was getting a little stale. But she didn't know how Mac would feel about her hanging out in his office after hours. He had no problem with her working there while he attended to other matters on the ranch, but he might not appreciate her taking up space when she wasn't balancing his books.

"Do you think Mac will mind if I use his office?"

Confusion flitted across Thorne's face, then realization dawned. "Probably not," he said. "But what I meant was, would you like to wait with me? I live in the apartment above the supply building attached to the stables, and I was just about to head upstairs and start dinner. I've got enough to share, and I bet you're getting hungry."

She was, but Maggie doubted she'd be able to eat in Thorne's presence. The idea of sharing a meal with him in his apartment both thrilled and terrified her. What if she said or did something embarrassing? She'd never be able to live it down.

Thorne mistook her silence for reluctance. "Come on," he coaxed. "I don't bite." The corner of his mouth turned up in a grin, and Maggie's heart thudded hard in her chest. Did the man have any idea what he was doing to her?

Probably not, she thought with a mental sigh. He wasn't the kind of man to deliberately taunt a woman, and given his down-to-earth attitude and old-fashioned manners, he likely didn't even realize how attractive he was. His apparent ignorance of the effect he had on the opposite sex was just another one of his appealing qualities, and Maggie felt her worries recede as her desire to spend time with him grew.

"Are you sure you don't mind the company?" She didn't want to intrude on his personal time, even though her sense of curiosity demanded to learn more about Thorne and his life. What did his apartment look like? Was he a good cook, or would he order pizza? Most important, did he have a girlfriend?

"On the contrary, it'll be nice to have someone to talk to while I eat. I usually only have the TV for company."

That answered her question about the girlfriend, and Maggie couldn't help but smile. "I know what you mean," she said.

He turned his head and frowned out the window. "I don't think it's going to let up anytime soon. Want me to go grab an umbrella so you don't get too wet?"

It was a sweet offer, but Maggie shook her head. "Thanks, but I won't melt. Besides, that's not really fair for you to make two trips in the rain just to spare me a few drops."

Thorne lifted one shoulder in a casual shrug. "I don't mind." He glanced over, eyeing her up and down appraisingly. Even though there was nothing suggestive about his gaze, Maggie still felt a chill as goose bumps popped out on her arms. "I don't think you could get any wetter, though," he said, a smile tugging at that delectable mouth of his.

She glanced down at her still-damp shirt and pushed a scraggy tendril of hair out of her face. "I think you're right about that." She shook her head, trying to see the humor in the situation. Of all the times for Thorne to notice her, and invite her in for a meal, no less! Why couldn't this have happened when she looked more like a woman and less like a drowned cat? *Doesn't matter*, she told herself sternly. *There's no help for it now.*

"Ready to head inside then?" His voice was warm and inviting and Maggie nodded, happy to have an excuse to leave the claustrophobic confines of the car. It would be so much nicer to wait for the tow truck inside. But now that she was looking forward to dinner with Thorne, a not-so-small part of her hoped the tow truck driver would take his time in driving out to the ranch. After all, it wasn't every day she got to share a meal with the object of her affections.

The man in question put his hat back on and turned to face her. "Race you to the door?" Even in the dim light, Maggie could see the flash of mischief in his brown eyes. She felt an answering tug low in her belly and nodded, already groping for the door handle.

"You're on."

Thorne slid to a halt a few steps behind Maggie, grateful her back was to him so she didn't see him slip on the smooth floor of the supply building. He righted himself just as she turned around to give him a triumphant grin, and his heart thudded hard in a rhythm that had nothing to do with his near wipeout and everything to do with the woman standing in front of him.

She is so beautiful.

It wasn't the first time he'd had the thought, and he knew from experience it wouldn't be the last. But Maggie looked especially lovely tonight, despite her rumpled clothes and dripping hair. Any other woman would have looked soggy and bedraggled, but Maggie looked even more appealing. His eyes traced a tendril of blond hair that clung to the curve of her neck, and he wished he could follow the path with his fingertip.

Or his tongue.

Shaking himself free of the thought, he focused on her face and her big blue eyes, which sparkled with amusement. "I figured you'd be faster, seeing as how you chase down cows for a living." She tilted her head to the side with a teasing smile.

Thorne removed his hat and brushed the raindrops away with the side of his hand. "In my defense," he grumbled, "I'm usually on a horse." And he usually wasn't distracted by the sight of her curvy backside in front of him, her clothes clinging to her frame like a second skin…

This was a bad idea. But as soon as he had the thought he dismissed it. He couldn't very well let Maggie sit alone in her stalled car while a storm raged—his father had raised him better than to ignore a woman in need. And while he might like to get to know Maggie on a more personal level, he had to keep things platonic. She was his father's bookkeeper, and Mac wouldn't appreciate him hitting on someone who worked at the ranch, even though she wasn't really an employee. His father would still view it as mixing business with pleasure, and given Thorne's parentage, it made sense the man had strong feelings on the subject.

It was no secret his mother, Livia Colton, had seduced Mac and then broken his heart. Thorne didn't know all the details, but his mother was a devious woman who stopped at nothing to get what she wanted. Mac had been a handsome man—he still was—and Thorne figured he'd caught Livia's eye. Livia wasn't one for delayed gratification, nor was she willing to let a little thing like her marriage vows stop her from having fun. He didn't know what spell she'd cast to get Mac to do what she wanted, but he was the product of that encounter.

In his more cynical moments, Thorne wondered why Livia had continued the pregnancy. He'd never bothered to ask, but he figured she must have thought Wes Kingston, her husband at the time, was the father. Of course, that little assumption blew up in smoke as soon as he was born and people got a look at the color of his skin. His skin color wasn't as dark as Mac's, but anyone could see he didn't share the pale shade of his brother River. It didn't take long for the rumors to start about his parentage. Knowing he was the topic of gossip had stung, and Thorne had found it was easier to spend time with Mac and the horses while he was growing up. The ranch had been his safe space, free from whispers and rude stares.

As he'd gotten older, Thorne had been curious about Livia and Mac, but he knew better than to press for details. Mac never talked about it, and no amount of pestering was going to get him to open up about the experience. Thorne figured his father had his reasons for keeping things to himself. Some things were better left unsaid.

He pushed aside the image of his father's frowning face and gestured for Maggie to precede him up the stairs that led to his apartment over the supply building. He was careful to keep his eyes on the floor and off her, a task that proved rather difficult. She stopped when she reached his door, and he tugged his keys free from his pocket to let them both inside.

Thorne walked in first and flipped on a light, his

eyes doing a quick scan of the apartment in search of any grievous messes that required immediate attention. He hadn't exactly considered the state of his home when he'd issued the dinner invitation, but he was relieved to see the place didn't look too bad. An empty glass sat on the worn wooden coffee table and his denim work jacket hung on the back of a chair, but other than that his apartment was fairly clean. It was a testament to how much he worked as opposed to any great housekeeping skills on his part, but no matter—the effect was the same.

Maggie hung back by the still-open door, appearing suddenly shy.

"Everything okay?" Was she having second thoughts? He couldn't blame her if that was the case. They exchanged pleasant greetings every time their paths crossed, but they were basically strangers. It made sense she might worry about being alone with him in his apartment. "Would you rather I ordered a pizza and we sat in the office?" They'd still be alone together, but sitting there would keep things from feeling so…personal.

"I'm fine," she said. "I just don't want to drip water all over your floors."

"Don't worry about it," he quickly assured her. "Let me grab you a towel so you can dry off." He trotted down the hall to the bathroom and grabbed fresh towels from the cabinet, then returned and handed one to her. "Here you go."

Maggie took it with a smile. "Thanks." She began to dab at her face and clothes and he did the same. The towels quickly grew dark as they soaked up the rain, but Thorne was feeling drier already.

Thorne gestured down the hall. "The bathroom is the door on the right, if you'd like to freshen up a bit."

"I will, if you don't mind."

He shook his head. "Not at all. I'll just get things started in the kitchen."

Maggie moved past him and he caught a whiff of her scent—vanilla and coconut, like some kind of exotic, intoxicating drink. Thorne was suddenly very aware of how he must smell after working with the horses all day—sweaty, stale and probably on the stinky side. Too bad there wasn't time for a quick shower before he started cooking.

But Maggie didn't appear to be bothered by his eau de livestock odor, so he shrugged and stepped into the small kitchen. *Besides*, he told himself as he gathered plates and silverware from the cupboards, *this isn't a date or anything*.

And wasn't that just too bad? He couldn't deny that Maggie had captured his heart from the beginning. He'd met her when she'd started doing the books for Mac, and it hadn't taken long to fall under her spell. But it wasn't just her appearance that drew him in. It was the way she looked at him, as if she saw him for his own sake and not as an object of speculation or gossip. His siblings and Mac were the only people to treat him like a normal person instead of a walking scandal. The fact that Maggie didn't appear to be fazed by his unorthodox roots and Livia's many crimes made her even more attractive, and he'd spent many an idle moment wondering what it would be like to get to know her better.

Maybe he could start tonight. It was the best chance he'd had in a while to really talk to her. Usually when she came out to work on Mac's books, Thorne was called away to a far part of the ranch to fix a fence or round up a stray calf. This was the first time in months he'd seen her for more than a minute, and he should make the most of it.

The table set, he opened the fridge and stared at the shelves with a critical eye. What to fix for dinner? Normally, he didn't give the subject much thought but tonight was different. He wanted to make something nice that Maggie would enjoy, but not something with especially romantic overtones—he didn't want her to think he was coming on too strong. Since he didn't exactly have a fridge full of oysters and chocolate-covered strawberries, there really wasn't any danger of giving off the impression he was trying to woo her with food. But he did need to come up with a decent meal, lest she think he survived only on TV dinners and the odd PB&J.

Which wasn't too far from the truth, but still. He had his pride.

Thinking quickly, Thorne reached into the fridge and gathered up the ingredients to make a simple quiche, depositing them on the countertop. He set the oven to preheat, then rolled up his sleeves and got to work chopping vegetables.

"Can I help?"

Thorne jumped at the sound of Maggie's voice. The knife in his hand slipped, the sharp edge of the blade scoring the pad of his thumb. He dropped the offending tool with a muffled curse and stuck his thumb in his mouth, easing the sting of the cut with his tongue. He'd been so engrossed in his task he hadn't heard her walk in behind him, and now he looked like a clumsy oaf.

Maggie's eyes were wide with concern. "I'm so sorry—I didn't mean to startle you!"

He pulled his thumb out of his mouth and examined it. "Don't worry about it," he told her. The cut was deep enough to bleed freely, but not so bad as to require stitches. It was more of an annoyance than anything else.

Before he could protest, Maggie grabbed his hand a pressed a wad of paper towels to his thumb. There was nothing remotely sexual about her touch, but a thrill shot through his limbs from the contact. She bit her plump bottom lip as she stared down at his hand, and she was standing so close he could feel the heat coming off her body. She was so focused on his hand he was free to study her face, and he traced the lines of her features with his gaze. Her eyelashes were still a little spiky from the rain and her cheeks held a soft pink glow that reminded him of the color of sunrise. There was a light dusting of freckles across the bridge of her nose, something he'd never noticed before. And this close, he could see the faint laugh lines at the corners of her eyes and mouth.

Her vanilla-coconut scent filled his nose and went straight to his head, making him feel a little dizzy. He wanted to lean forward and bury his nose in her hair, to drink in her perfume until it filled his lungs and saturated his senses. He leaned forward without realizing it and would have done it if Maggie hadn't lifted her head and met his eyes.

Surprise flashed in her bright blue gaze as she realized how close he was. She sucked in a breath, and a look of such naked yearning appeared on her face Thorne found himself reaching for her instinctively.

It was clear she wanted him, and his body rejoiced at the realization. There were a million reasons why this was a bad idea, but he ignored them all. He wasn't interested in thinking right now—he only wanted to feel.

His free hand found her cheek and he touched her gently, silently asking permission. She leaned into his touch, closing her eyes for a second as if savoring the contact. His heart started to pound, the blood whooshing in his ears as he bent his head, already anticipating the sweet pressure of her lips against his own.

He forced himself to go slow, to take his time. Thorne had fantasized about kissing Maggie ever since he'd met her, and he wanted this moment to be perfect for both of them. No matter what his hormones demanded, it wouldn't do to rush into the kiss. He wanted to give her time to change her mind, if that's what she wanted.

He needn't have worried. Maggie dropped his injured hand, grabbed his shoulders and stood on her toes, pulling herself up to meet his mouth. Her lips were warm and soft against his, and he tasted the subtle, waxy flavor of lip balm as he angled his head to get a better fit between them.

She made a soft humming sound and he smiled against her mouth, happy to hear she was enjoying this as much as he was. The pain in his hand receded as he focused on the woman in his arms. He'd wanted her for so long, but given his family history he had never dared to think she might want him back. He tried to lose himself in the moment but his worries swirled in his mind, a distracting chorus that prevented him from truly connecting with Maggie.

Livia's criminal actions had cast a shadow over

Thorne's life, leaving him feeling dirty and ashamed. Maggie was bright and good and kind, the type of woman who deserved a man with a decent family, a man she could build a life with and not have to worry that the sins of her mother-in-law would come back to haunt her own children. Livia had made a lot of enemies, and Thorne knew people weren't ever going to forget her crimes.

Disappointment was a small weight in Thorne's stomach. No matter how much he liked Maggie, no matter how good it felt to hold her, to kiss her, he needed to let her go. The people of Shadow Creek already looked down on him, thanks to his connection to Livia. He didn't want Maggie to be painted with the same brush. She didn't deserve to be the object of gossip, and if anyone learned of his interest in her, she'd be the talk of the town in no time. And not for the right reasons.

He eased back, slowly breaking the kiss. She stood frozen for a moment, her eyes closed and her lips pink and swollen from his attention. It was almost enough to make him throw caution to the wind and reach for her again, but he ruthlessly stomped on the urge. Maggie might not be thinking about her reputation right now, but he was.

She opened her eyes and he saw the question in the bright blue depths. Thorne cleared his throat, searching for the right words to explain why he'd pulled away.

"I'm sorry," he began.

She cut him off, her words lightning fast in the small kitchen. "I'm not."

Thorne rocked back on his heels a little, unsure of

what to say next. If Maggie didn't consider this to be a bad idea, maybe he was overthinking things...

She stared up at him, her eyes blazing with a heated arousal that stoked the fire of his need. "What's wrong?" she asked softly. A flicker of doubt crossed her face. "Did I do something to upset you?"

"No!" His denial was instant and fierce and he felt himself reaching for her, wanting to erase her worry. He softened his voice and tried again. "No, you did nothing wrong. It's just... I'm worried. For you."

Her eyebrows drew together in puzzlement. "What do you mean?"

Thorne reached a hand up to rub the back of his neck, feeling his skin prickle with embarrassment. How to explain his concerns without sounding like an egocentric ass? *My reputation, my family, my problems. My, my, my.* She was going to think he was too wrapped up in his own life, but really, he just wanted to protect her. He heaved a mental sigh and nearly shook his head. This was why he preferred the company of horses. Conversations with people were just too complicated.

"You know who my mother is," he said, risking a glance up. Maggie nodded, but she still seemed confused. "You know what she did."

"Sure," she replied slowly. "Everyone does. But what's that got to do with you?"

"People talk," he said simply. "They've done it all my life, and they're not going to stop. Especially now that Livia's crimes and escape from prison have provided new fodder for them. You don't want to be associated with me."

Understanding dawned in her eyes. "You're trying to protect me from town gossip." He nodded, happy she had caught on. Now she would put some distance between them and he could go back to cooking. They could pretend like this had never happened. The thought sent a pang through his chest, but it was for the best. He could relive the magic of their kiss when he was alone.

He reached for the knife, intent on picking up where he'd left off. But Maggie's hand on his made him freeze.

"It's sweet of you to worry for me." She rubbed the pad of her thumb along the side of his hand, her touch simultaneously featherlight and electrifying. "But I'm a big girl, and I don't care what people say."

Thorne swallowed hard, trying to dislodge the sudden lump in his throat. The blood in his body was rapidly racing south, making thought and speech difficult. "You don't?" he asked stupidly.

Maggie shook her head and moved her hand up his arm, trailing her fingertips along his skin in a teasing caress. She placed the palm of her other hand on his chest, directly over his heart. Could she feel it speed up in response to her touch?

"So if that's the only thing stopping you…" she trailed off, her suggestion clear.

"You're sure?" His voice sounded hoarse even to his own ears. He held his breath as he waited for her response. It had been so long since he'd connected with a woman, and the revelations about Livia and her subsequent trial, imprisonment and recent escape had made him feel more alone than ever. Maggie was exactly what he needed right now, but he wasn't going to soothe his own soul at the sake of her feelings.

Maggie nodded, her eyes shining brightly with an emotion he couldn't name. "I'm sure. I like you, Thorne," she said, sounding a little shy.

Her confession washed over him, breaking down the last of his resistance. He closed the distance between them and captured her mouth again. She reached up and clasped her hands behind his neck, returning his kiss with equal fervor.

Moving carefully so as not to break their connection, Thorne reached down and hooked his hands under the curve of Maggie's bottom. He hitched her up, smiling against her mouth as she let out a little "oof" of surprise. She recovered quickly though, throwing her legs around his waist and locking her ankles together. The change in position afforded him new access to her body, and his blood heated in anticipation as he registered the warmth of her core.

With Maggie in his arms, Thorne headed for the bedroom. Her body bounced against his sensitive groin with every step, turning the short trip into a seemingly endless stretch of exquisite torture. By the time he made it to the room he was nearly blind with need, and he rammed his shoulder hard against the doorjamb. He grunted in annoyance and felt the vibrations of Maggie's amusement in his chest.

"Are you okay?"

Thorne deposited her on the bed, then stepped back to toe off his boots. "Never better," he said, the pain of the blow already forgotten. He paused, hands on his belt buckle. "Are you?" Was she changing her mind?

Maggie smiled and reached for him. She slipped her hands into the back pockets of his jeans and pulled him closer, urging him forward until his thighs hit the edge of the mattress. "Oh, yes," she said softly. "I'm right where I want to be."

Chapter 2

Three months later...

"Doing okay in here?"

Maggie looked up to find Mac standing in the doorway of his office, his light brown eyes friendly and warm. She nodded, but the sight of him made her stomach drop. *He looks so much like Thorne!*

Hoping her distress didn't show, she offered him a small smile. "I should be done soon, and then you can have your office back."

"Oh, I'm not worried about that." Mac propped his shoulder against the door frame and crossed his arms over his broad chest. "I just wanted to check on you. You seem a little...off today."

Apparently she wasn't as good of an actress as she'd hoped. "I appreciate your concern, but I'm fine," she said. "Just tired. Work has been keeping me busy." It was the truth—mostly. She had been feeling exhausted lately, and to make matters worse, she'd been dealing with a constant, low-level nausea that had turned her off most food. She made a mental note to schedule a doctor's appointment soon. Having dealt with endometriosis for the last fifteen years, Maggie was used to a certain amount of regular physical discomfort. But she knew from experience it was better to try to get ahead of the problem than to wait and allow it to get worse.

"Staying busy is a nice problem to have, especially when you work for yourself," Mac joked.

Maggie nodded again and leaned back a little in the chair. "It definitely is. I'm not complaining, believe me."

Mac studied her for a moment, his gaze searching as if he suspected she wasn't telling him the full truth. His scrutiny was kind, and under other circumstances, Maggie probably would have opened up to him. But not this time.

"I'll let you finish up," he said, pushing off the jamb and straightening. "I hope you know that if you ever need a sympathetic ear, I've got two."

"Thanks, Mac." Tears prickled her eyes and she blinked hard, turning back to the computer in the hopes of hiding her reaction. She heard his footsteps as he walked away and let her shoulders slump. Mac was a sweet man but she couldn't talk to him about her problems.

Not when they all centered around his son.

Thorne hadn't said one word to her since that night three months ago, unless you counted *hello* and *goodbye* and "let me find Mac for you." And she didn't.

Those were the polite sentence fragments strangers used, not the language of two people who had shared their bodies with each other.

Even now, a shiver of arousal tripped down her spine at the memory of that night. Being with Thorne had been amazing. Their chemistry had been electric, with none of the awkward fumbling that often accompanied her first time with a man. She and Thorne had moved in a seamless rhythm, as if they had read each other's minds and knew exactly where to touch, how to move to give and receive pleasure. She'd never felt such a profound physical and emotional connection with a man before—being with Thorne had truly rocked her world.

Which had made it all the more painful when he'd pulled away from her in the days after their encounter.

It had been three months since that night, and in all that time, they'd only exchanged a handful of words. Her calls to him had gone unreturned, and when she'd dropped by the ranch to talk to him, he'd been "too busy" to see her. Maggie hadn't been expecting a proposal or a declaration of undying love, but she didn't understand why Thorne was giving her the cold shoulder. At first, she'd thought he was feeling shy. After all, things had gotten intimate very quickly and it was possible he was a little unsure of how to act now that the nature of their relationship had changed. But every time Maggie saw him he seemed to go out of his way to avoid talking to her. It didn't take long for her to get the message that he wasn't interested.

Ordinarily, she would let it go and try to move on with her life. But Thorne's current behavior was so at odds with the way he'd treated her that night that she couldn't stop wondering where things had gone wrong.

Had she said something? They hadn't really done much talking, but perhaps she'd made a comment in an unguarded moment that had rubbed him the wrong way. If that was the case though, why hadn't he bothered to tell her? She felt a flare of irritation that straightened her spine. If Thorne was upset with her, the least he could do was respect her enough to tell her why. This wasn't junior high; they were both adults, and he needed to act like one.

It was the lack of closure that bothered her the most. If she knew what he was thinking, why he had changed his mind, it would be easier for her to move on. But his silence only provided space for her imagination to run wild, conjuring all sorts of explanations for his sudden reversal. She was tempted to force the issue, to grab his arm the next time she saw him and drag him into an empty room so they could talk. She deserved to know why he was treating her like a stranger! But something told her even if she did manage to catch Thorne alone, he wouldn't open up to her.

"It's better this way," she murmured. After their night together, her crush on Thorne had morphed into a full blown infatuation. Even now, her heart ached at the thought of what might have been between them and the relationship they could have built together. But she deserved better than to be treated like a mistake. She deserved a man who wasn't ashamed to be with her, who was proud to stand by her side and wanted to be a part of her life. She had hoped Thorne was that man, and it would take time to deal with her disappointment at finding out he wasn't. At least she had found out his true feelings for her before she'd fallen all the way into the emotional quicksand of love. His silent rejection hurt, but she had learned a valuable lesson. The next time she met a man, she wouldn't be so quick to involve her heart.

Working quickly, she put the finishing touches on Mac's books and shut down her laptop. She really needed to talk Mac into moving his records and paperwork to a digital filing system—that way, he could simply email her the information and she wouldn't have to come out to the ranch every few months. Although it was nice to get out of Shadow Creek and to see the horses and cattle up close, with her growing client list she simply couldn't afford the commute time.

And if she was being truly honest with herself, she didn't want to risk seeing Thorne.

She put on a brave face every time their paths crossed, which fortunately wasn't often. But it was hard to pretend like nothing was wrong, and it was equally difficult to keep her anger and frustration bottled up inside. She wasn't sure how much longer she could hold her tongue, and the last thing she wanted was to make a scene at Mac's ranch; she couldn't let her personal problems interfere with her professional duties.

"That's what I get for mixing business with pleasure," she muttered to herself. Lesson learned.

Maggie rose and slid the computer into its bag, then glanced around to make sure she'd gathered up everything. The place was orderly as always, the afternoon sun glinting off the metal handles of the filing cabinets that lined the far wall of the office. Maybe it was a little ridiculous to ask Mac to change a system he'd spent twenty years using, but in the end it would make his life easier.

Change was good, even though it was sometimes difficult.

She stepped out of the office into the barn and took a deep breath. Even though she was a city girl, Maggie had always loved the smell of a barn; the sweet scent of hay, the warm whiff of the horses and the potent tang of manure all combined in an instantly recognizable and deeply appealing aroma. Being in the barn, even if only for a few moments, had a relaxing effect on her.

At least, it normally did.

For the first time, Maggie wrinkled her nose at the familiar odors. Something seemed off about the smell—the hay emitted a sickly sweet fume that nearly gagged her. And the horse sweat had a musky tang that turned her stomach. But it was the scent of apples that sent her running out of the barn in search of fresh air; something about the combination of food and manure curdled her earlier cup of coffee and caused bile to rise in her throat.

She took a deep breath and was assaulted this time by the smell of fresh-cut grass. But at least it was better than the olfactory overload of the barn. Shaking her head, Maggie headed for her car. Its pearlescent white paint sparkled subtly in the sun, a contrast to the dull red of her previous ride. It still felt a little strange to walk out of a building and not see her old sedan waiting for her, but she had to admit, the new car smell was pretty nice.

A movement by the trunk caught her eye and she glanced over in time to see a bird take flight from her trunk, squawking in protest. That in itself was not unusual, but something still seemed strange...

Maggie slowed her pace and squinted at the trunk,

trying to put her finger on what she was seeing. Finally, it hit her—the air above her car was shimmering, bending and moving in the liquid, languid dance of heat. She normally saw it in the summer, when the superheated asphalt seemed to melt the air above the road. But why was it happening now?

As she watched, a thin tendril of smoke curled into the air, the wisp so fine she would have missed it if she hadn't been looking. Realization and shock slammed into her, followed quickly by disbelief. Her car was on fire! But how was that possible?

She glanced around the yard, searching wildly for something she could use to douse the flames. There was a water trough just inside the barn and she ran for it, dropping her computer bag in the dirt.

"Help!" Her mind raced as she searched for something, anything she could use to carry water back to her car. She needed the fire department, but they would take too long to get here. Maybe she could dump enough water on her trunk to put the fire out before it spread? But why was it on fire in the first place? Cars didn't spontaneously ignite…

"Help!" she yelled again. Where was everyone?

"Maggie?" She heard her name, barely audible over the rush of blood in her ears. There was a bucket sitting a few feet away, full of grain. She dumped it out and scooped up water from the trough.

"My car," she yelled, not bothering to look back. "Call the fire department!"

She ran back outside, water sloshing over the sides of the bucket and soaking her clothes. Smoke was pouring out of her trunk in earnest now, the stench of it filling the air and burning her nose. There was a shout behind her but before she could respond, the world exploded in a ball of heat and light.

Chapter 3

Thorne reached the barn door just in time to see Maggie's car explode.

He caught his breath and threw up a hand to shield his face as a ball of fire shot into the air. A loud boom shook the building, startling the horses inside. A chorus of panicked whinnies rang out, but Thorne couldn't spare a moment for them.

He had to find Maggie.

The stubborn woman hadn't listened to him when he'd called out to her. *And whose fault is that?* he thought bitterly. He hadn't exactly been treating her well lately.

His heart in his throat, he scanned the dooryard for Maggie, straining to see through the smoke that now obscured most of the area. He considered calling 911, but by the time the ambulance arrived Maggie might be dead. There was no time to waste. He stepped into the yard and immediately started coughing as the thick, black fumes filled his lungs. He pulled a bandana from his back pocket and clamped it over his nose and mouth, but it didn't help much. He had to find Maggie and get them both out of here, the sooner the better.

"Maggie!" He shouted her name, hoping she would hear him. But his stomach dropped as time ticked by without a response.

Was she dead? Just the thought made him want to vomit, but he had to consider the possibility. She'd been standing awfully close to the car when it exploded. He could still see her, arms wrapped around the bucket of water as she charged forward to save her vehicle. If only he'd been able to stop her!

He scanned the ground, his growing panic making it difficult for him to see. *Oh, God, please let her still be alive!*

"Thorne!" He heard his name from the direction of the barn but didn't stop searching. "Thorne, come back! It's too dangerous!"

"Help me find Maggie!" She was still here, he knew it. And he wasn't leaving without her, no matter how much smoke filled the air. The car was a raging inferno now, and the sparse patches of grass near the dirt of the drive were turning black from the heat. It was only a matter of time before a spark caught one of the nearby buildings on fire…

The cries of the horses grew louder, and Thorne realized the other hands were busy moving them out of the barn. Good—that was one less thing to worry about.

He staggered through the smoke, tears streaming

down his cheeks. An odd shape on the ground caught his eye, and he turned, blinking hard and squinting to focus.

It was a shoe.

"Maggie." He tried to shout her name, but the smoke and his fear caused his throat to lock up. He ran over to find her lying on her back, her eyes closed and her face too pale for his liking.

For a split second, he froze, fear locking his muscles into place. She was so still… He'd never forgive himself if she was dead. If he hadn't treated her so badly after their night together, she would have listened to him, would have waited for him to catch up instead of running headlong toward danger by herself. This was all his fault…

His hand shook a little as he reached out and gently placed his fingers on her throat. Her pulse beat sure and strong, and the breath shuddered out of his lungs in a gust of relief. She was still alive!

Moving quickly, he ran his hands along her body, feeling for any damp spots that would indicate blood from an injury. When he came up dry, he hooked his hands under her arms and dragged her across the yard. They made it to the relative coolness of the barn just as a fire truck turned off the main road and came screaming up the drive to the dooryard.

The firemen wasted no time attacking the blaze. Under other circumstances, Thorne would have been right in the middle of the response, helping the other ranch hands with the horses and telling the firefighters what he knew about the situation. But he wasn't about to leave Maggie's side.

Someone knelt next to him but Thorne didn't bother

to look over. His eyes were glued to Maggie's face, searching for a sign of awareness, a flicker or a twitch that would indicate she was regaining consciousness.

"What happened?" Mac spoke calmly amid the chaos, and the tension in Thorne's chest eased at the sound of his father's voice.

"Her car exploded." Thorne still couldn't believe it. Cars didn't just explode in real life—that was the stuff of movies. Something was definitely off here, but he couldn't worry about it right now.

"It exploded?" Mac echoed in disbelief. "How in the hell—"

"I don't know," Thorne said shortly. "But I watched it happen." The scene was burned into his brain; Maggie, her body limned in bright light for a split second as the fireball formed, then obscured by a cloud of smoke. It was a terrifying image that would live on in his nightmares for the rest of his life.

Mac gently placed his hand on Maggie's forehead and she moaned softly in response to his touch. "I can stay with her if you want to check on the horses," he offered.

"No." Thorne didn't bother to elaborate, but he felt his father's gaze cut over to him in surprise.

There was a brief silence between them as Mac digested his response. "I see," he said finally, his tone carefully neutral.

The wail of another siren cut through the air, and an ambulance pulled up behind the fire truck. Mac stood and began waving his arms, signaling for the paramedics. They arrived a few seconds later, arms laden with supplies. Mac took a few steps back to allow them access to Maggie, but Thorne couldn't bring himself to move away. He tried to make himself as small as possible so he wouldn't interfere with the medic's exam but he kept a tight grip on her hand. *Please be okay, please be okay, please be okay...* What he wouldn't give to see her open those big blue eyes!

"How long has she been unconscious?" asked one of the men.

Thorne jumped at the question, trying to get his brain back on track. It felt like it had taken him forever to find Maggie, but it couldn't have been more than a few minutes. "Uh, maybe ten minutes?"

The medic nodded and placed a blood pressure cuff around her upper arm. He and his partner moved in a kind of synchronized dance, passing each other instruments and supplies with very little dialogue between them. It was clear they worked well together as a team, and it reminded Thorne of the easy back and forth that developed between a horse and his rider, when man and animal spoke the same language, if only for a little while.

Maggie stirred under the medic's attention and began to shake her head back and forth. "Stay still for me," one of the men commanded. The pair of them worked to secure a foam collar around her neck and her eyes flew open in shock.

"What's your name?" the EMT asked. He gave her a second to respond, then asked again. "Can you tell me your name?"

Thorne held his breath, silently urging her to speak. Was she simply too dazed to answer, or was something more serious going on?

After an endless silence, she spoke. "Maggie." Her

voice was weak and scratchy, sounding as if she'd screamed herself hoarse.

The medic nodded. "That's great, Maggie," he said encouragingly. "Can you tell me where you are?"

She frowned slightly. "Mac's ranch," she said slowly. "I was working on his books." She paused, and Thorne could tell by the expression on her face she was replaying her memories, trying to piece together what had happened. Then everything clicked into place, and her confused expression morphed into one of anxiety. "My car!" She tried to sit up, but both medics held her down.

"Whoa," said one of the men. "Try not to move, please. You may have a spinal injury."

She let out a small sound of distress that sliced into Thorne's heart. "It's okay, honey," he said, speaking before he could think twice about it. Given the way he'd treated her lately, she probably wouldn't take comfort from his presence, but he had to try. Seeing her lying on the ground, bruised, battered and scared, triggered a wave of regret so strong it threatened to overwhelm him. He'd spent too much time pushing her away because of his fears—he owed her more than that, and he wasn't going to waste another minute before trying to make amends.

She glanced over at him, her eyes wide with fear. He saw her body relax as she registered his proximity, and felt something in his own chest ease. "Thorne?" She sounded lost and a little unsure, but he detected no anger in her voice.

It was better than he deserved.

"I'm here," he said, pushing aside his bitter self-recrimination. There would be time for that later—right now, he had to focus on supporting Maggie.

"Was anyone hurt?"

He shook his head, marveling at her question. Even in the middle of her own troubles, Maggie was concerned for others. "Just you," he said softly.

The medics counted to three in low voices; they rolled Maggie onto her side and slipped a long board under her, then rolled her to her back again. They secured her in place with thick black straps at her forehead, shoulders, knees and ankles, and one of the men moved to her head while the other knelt by her feet. In one smooth motion, they lifted her off the ground.

"Thorne!" The change in position seemed to startle her—she thrust a hand out, searching the air for him.

He jumped to his feet and jogged after the medics, catching up to them at the ambulance. He slipped his hand into hers and she squeezed hard, causing his bones to grind together painfully. "Please don't leave me," she called out, a hint of desperation lacing her words.

Thorne didn't bother to ask permission; he climbed into the back of the ambulance and slid along the bench seat until he sat by Maggie's head. Her head was immobilized on the board, so he leaned forward until his face was directly over hers. Her blue eyes were bloodshot, but her gaze was steady as she stared up at him.

"I'm here," he said, repeating his earlier assurance. He swallowed hard, trying to calm his frayed nerves. "You're going to be okay." Was he trying to convince her, or himself? She looked fine to his untrained eye, but the medic's comment about a possible spinal cord injury made his guts cramp. He didn't want Maggie to see his fear though, so he tried to give her a comforting smile.

"I'm scared." The words were no more than a whisper, but Thorne heard them loud and clear. *Me, too,* he thought. Her confession made him feel a little bit better, as if they were working together as a team. A spark of confidence kindled to life in his chest, and his worries began to fade as he focused on being strong for Maggie.

He squeezed her hand gently and leaned down to speak into her ear. "It's all right," he said softly. "I won't leave you."

Not this time...

Maggie shivered slightly in the cool air of the hospital room. The thin cotton johnny they'd given her was practical for the staff, but it did little in the way of providing warmth.

Or modesty.

She tugged the mint-green blanket higher on her lap and tucked the edges under her legs. Fortunately, Thorne had stepped out of the room when she'd been asked to change, and he hadn't seen her out of the bed since. Not that it mattered. He already knew what she looked like naked.

"Are you cold?"

She jumped a little at the unexpected question. Thorne had been sitting silently by the bed since she'd returned from getting a scan, unmoving except for the gentle rise and fall of his shoulders with every breath. At first, she'd found his presence awkward and uncomfortable. She was not in the mood to discuss their one-night stand. But after a few moments, she realized Thorne wasn't here to talk. And as the silence in the room had continued, her agitation had gradually faded until she'd almost forgotten he was there.

Truth be told, she was surprised he'd noticed her movement. He'd spent the past three months doing a bang-up job of ignoring her, so why should now be any different?

She bit her lip to hold back a sarcastic response and settled for a nod.

"I'll see if I can find you another blanket." He rose from the chair and lifted his hands over his head in a quick stretch. Maggie followed the motion with her eyes, noting the flex and play of his muscles under the blue cotton shirt he wore. All at once, she was assaulted with the memory of his strong arms banded around her, the feel of his work-roughened hands on her body. She flushed, and was grateful his back was turned so he didn't see her reaction.

His boot heels tapped against the tile as he walked out of her room, and Maggie let out her breath in a sigh. Why was he still here? More importantly, what was she going to do about it?

She knew why he'd come to the hospital, of course. After all, she'd practically begged him to, the way she'd grabbed his hand like he was some kind of savior. The explosion of her car and the chaotic aftermath had left her terrified and vulnerable, and she'd latched on to the first familiar face she'd seen. It was kind of Thorne to indulge her moment of weakness, but now that the situation was under control, he no longer had to stay. He was probably itching to get back to the ranch to assess the damage and make sure the horses were okay, and as soon as he returned she would suggest he do so. Mac likely needed his help cleaning up the mess, and it would be easier for the both of them if they no longer had to tiptoe around each other.

A steady click announced Thorne's return and he slipped into the room carrying another blanket. Without saying a word, he walked over to the bed and carefully spread it across her legs.

The fabric was surprisingly warm and she burrowed into the heat, fisting her hands in the waffle-print of the weave. She felt like she'd been run over by a truck, and her bruised and battered body welcomed the warmth. It soaked into her muscles, dulling the sharp edges of her aches and pains. "Thank you," she said.

He nodded. "Is it helping?" His voice was slightly scratchy from disuse, and it brought back another memory from that night—or rather, the next morning, when she'd woken to find him watching her, an unreadable expression on his face. When she'd met his gaze, she'd seen a flash of something she'd sworn was love in his light brown eyes. But it was there and gone in the space between heartbeats, and as she'd watched, he'd thrown up a wall between them.

"I should make coffee," he'd said, his voice rough with the morning. Innocent words, and yet Maggie had known in that instant the magic they'd shared the night before had not survived to see the dawn.

"It's not too hot?" His question cut through her unhappy reverie and she blinked to find him staring down at her, his eyebrows furrowed slightly in concern. "The nurse took it out of some kind of incubator. It felt pretty warm to me when I was carrying it."

"No, it's perfect," she said. *Time for him to go...*

Just as she opened her mouth to suggest he leave, the door swung open to admit her doctor.

"I've got test results," he said, holding up a manila

folder and wiggling it in illustration. Maggie nodded and offered him a smile. "That was fast."

"Lucky for you, it's a slow day." Dr. Jenkins wheeled the stool over to her bedside and sat, then glanced at Thorne. "Do you mind if we talk in front of your friend? I'm afraid someone is going to need to take care of you for the next few days, so it'll be good for him to hear the instructions firsthand."

Great. Just wonderful. Before Maggie could clarify that Thorne would definitely *not* be her caretaker, the man in question sat on her bed and pulled out his phone. "Do you mind if I record this so I don't miss anything?"

Dr. Jenkins nodded. "Be my guest." Then he turned to look at her. "Okay, so here's the deal. The CT scan revealed you have a minor concussion and a few cracked ribs. There's not much we can do about either of those things—you need rest and time to heal. And I do mean rest." He tilted his head down so he could level a serious look at her over the top of his glasses. "Your brain has been bruised. It is imperative you give it time to heal. That means no reading, no watching TV, nothing that would cause any kind of physical or mental strain. How is your head now?"

"It hurts," she admitted.

He nodded, as if he'd expected that response. "You can take Tylenol for the pain. Stay away from ibuprofen or aspirin, as they may cause bleeding."

"What about her ribs?" Thorne asked, leaning forward as if he was hanging on the doctor's every word.

Dr. Jenkins shrugged. "Again, rest is what she needs." He turned back to Maggie. "We can't really do anything except make you aware of the problem so you don't exacerbate it. I want you to do some breathing exercises a few times a day—I'll have a respiratory therapist come show you what to do before you're discharged."

Maggie nodded. "That doesn't sound so bad. Why do I need help?"

"Because I'm serious about you needing to rest. You basically need to stay in bed for the next few days—no fixing yourself food, or doing any household chores, or anything like that. The only time I want you up and about is when you're walking to and from the bathroom."

"But—" she began, but the doctor shook his head.

"No buts. Besides, I'm pretty sure the OB will tell you the same thing."

Maggie frowned. "What are you talking about? Why would an obstetrician have anything to say about my recovery?"

Dr. Jenkins stared at her for a moment, as if reassessing her mental status. Then realization dawned on his face, along with a flicker of horror. "Oh, dear," he said, under his breath. "You didn't know."

"Know what?" Maggie's stomach started to churn threateningly and her heart pounded hard against her breastbone, causing the monitor beside her bed to beep in protest. Dr. Jenkins glanced at it and pressed a button, silencing the electronic noise.

"Ah, take a deep breath for me and try to relax," he said. He pushed his glasses up on the bridge of his nose and ran a hand through his graying hair, clearly uncomfortable.

"Doctor," Maggie replied, careful to keep her gaze

locked on him and away from Thorne. "Why am I going to see an obstetrician today?"

The older man let out a breath and met Maggie's eyes, and the sympathetic look on his face set her world spinning.

"Because you're pregnant."

Chapter 4

Because you're pregnant.

Thorne heard the doctor's statement, but his brain refused to comprehend what was going on. He examined the words, looking at each one individually, trying to put them together in some new combination that didn't translate into an earthshaking announcement. But no matter how hard he tried to search for an alternate translation, he kept arriving at the same conclusion.

Maggie was going to have a baby.

As he came to terms with the news, a question formed in his mind: Was the baby his?

He glanced over at Maggie. Her skin was white as chalk and her eyes were wide with disbelief. Either she was one hell of an actress, or she truly hadn't known she was pregnant. He saw her mouth move and shook his head to clear it of the buzzing in his ears.

"Are you sure?" she was asking.

Dr. Jenkins nodded and placed his hand over Maggie's in a kindly gesture. "Quite sure. The fetus was clearly visible on the CT scan."

Maggie shook her head, as if denying the truth of the doctor's words. "But I can't get pregnant!"

The older man smiled ruefully. "If I had a nickel for every time I've heard that…"

"No, you don't understand," Maggie said forcefully. "I have endometriosis. I've had it since puberty. It's so bad I had a surgical ablation six months ago to help relieve my symptoms. My gynecologist told me I probably wouldn't be able to have children due to all the scar tissue that's developed over the years."

Dr. Jenkins nodded. "I hear what you're saying. But the scan clearly showed you're pregnant. As for the how of it, I think the obstetrician will be better suited to answer your questions. That's not my area of expertise."

Thorne finally found his voice. "How far along is she?" He held his breath, feeling like he was standing on the edge of a cliff. What the doctor said next would determine whether he plunged into a free fall or stepped back to the safety of his normal life.

Dr. Jenkins cast him a glance. "I can't say for sure—" he began, but Maggie cut him off.

"Three months," she said evenly. She met Thorne's gaze; her blue eyes glinted with challenge, as if she was daring him to question the paternity of the baby.

The doctor nodded. "I'd say that's consistent with fetal measurements and development. The obstetrician will likely be able to narrow it down further."

"I see," Thorne said weakly. He tried to take a deep breath, but there wasn't enough oxygen in the room. He gasped, his chest tightening with effort. His fingertips began to tingle and he leaned forward, trying to stand.

A hand shot out and grabbed his upper arm, holding him steady. Thorne looked up and Dr. Jenkins's concerned face filled his vision. "Are you okay?"

Thorne nodded. "I just need some air." He managed to get his feet under him and staggered out of the room, feeling like his body weighed a thousand pounds.

A baby. He was going to be a father.

He found a chair in the hall and collapsed into it, grateful for the support. How was this even possible?

Well, he knew *how* it had happened. He remembered every second of that night—every touch, every kiss, every sigh. He'd been living off the memories for the last three months, knowing it was all he'd ever have.

But even though he'd finally indulged in his attraction to Maggie, he'd made sure to use protection. He wasn't ready to be a father, and he hadn't wanted to saddle her with a child, either.

Especially not his child.

A cold chill gripped his heart as he thought of his brother Knox and his nephew, Cody. A few months ago, one of Livia's old cronies, Earl Hefferman, had kidnapped Cody in a bid to get back at Livia for cheating him out of some money. Fortunately, Knox had found his son safe and sound, but the aftershocks of that terrifying ordeal still affected them all.

What would happen if Livia or, God forbid, her enemies found out about this baby? He harbored no illusions about how his mother would react; she would see this child as another pawn to be moved around in her sick game of chess. And her accomplices would feel the same way. His stomach cramped at the thought of an innocent baby being exposed to such wicked people. Maggie wasn't safe, either. As long as she carried his child, she was a target.

And it seemed like someone was already trying to hurt her.

He shuddered, imagining the giant fireball that had consumed her car. A few more minutes, and Maggie would have been inside the car when it exploded. She was definitely a target, but who would want to do her harm? And more importantly, why?

Given the look of shock on her face, she hadn't known about the pregnancy, which meant no one else did, either. But it was possible Livia or one of her goons had figured out that Maggie held a special place in his heart. Livia wasn't above hurting an innocent person to get what she wanted, and if she had her sights set on punishing Thorne for his lack of support during her trial it made sense she would target the one woman he'd shown an interest in, even if he had walked away after their night together.

He wouldn't put it past Livia to have hired people to keep tabs on her children, reporting back any developments that she could use against them. And his night with Maggie would not have gone unnoticed. It had been years since he'd dated anyone, and he didn't enjoy one-night stands. A woman staying the night in his apartment certainly would have been news, and he could picture all too well Livia's gleeful reaction at the discovery of a new button she could push.

Thorne shook his head, cursing under his breath. He'd wasted so much time worrying about Maggie's reputation should anyone find out about their connection.

He should have realized the true threat came from Livia, especially after her escape from prison months ago.

"There you are."

Thorne glanced up to find his brother Knox walking toward him. A wave of relief washed over him; next to Mac, Knox was the glue that held their family together. He'd always looked up to his older half brother and just seeing him now made Thorne feel like everything was going to be okay.

"What are you doing here?" Thorne stood and met his brother halfway down the hall. "It's good to see you, but what's going on?" A terrible thought occurred to him, and Thorne's stomach dropped. "Are Cody and Allison okay?" God, had someone targeted them, as well?

Knox clapped a hand on his shoulder, steadying him. "They're fine, everyone's okay," he said. "I'm here for you. Mac called me," he explained. "Said there'd been an explosion at the ranch and you were here with Maggie."

Thorne nodded, glad to know no one else had been hurt today. "She's in with the doctor now. She has a concussion and some bruised ribs." He paused, wondering if he should tell Knox the rest of the news. Maggie might not want anyone to know about the baby yet.

Knox picked up on his hesitation. "And?" he prompted.

Ah, to hell with it. Her pregnancy affected his life, too, and Knox wasn't the kind of man to spread gossip. Still, Thorne glanced around to make sure no one was nearby to overhear his next words. "And she's, uh, she's pregnant," he said, keeping his voice low.

Knox's eyebrows shot up. "By the way you're acting, can I assume the baby is yours?"

Thorne nodded. "I think so."

"You think so? You mean you don't know for sure?"

Thorne looked down, resisting the temptation to scuff the toe of his boot on the shiny linoleum floor. "We haven't had a chance to talk yet."

Knox leaned back against the wall, blowing out his breath in a sigh. "Well. That will be some conversation."

Thorne fell into place beside his brother with a small laugh. "Yeah."

Knox was silent a moment. Then he leaned over and bumped Thorne's shoulder with his own. "Don't you know how birth control works?"

"We used a condom." Thorne felt his face heat and knew he was blushing. "I still have that box you bought me."

"You've got to be kidding me!" Knox turned to face him, incredulity shining in his bright blue eyes. "I gave you that box when you were still in high school! Do you mean to tell me you haven't used them all yet?"

"No." Thorne's shoulders hunched and he looked down again, searching for an escape from this conversation. "Wendy Smithson broke up with me a few weeks after your little sex ed lesson, and I haven't really dated a lot of women since then."

"Yeah, but..."

"There were a hundred condoms in the box," Thorne pointed out dryly. "I'm glad you think so highly of me, but I haven't had a lot of success with women. I understand horses a lot better."

"Who doesn't?" Knox muttered. He ran a hand through his hair, ruffling the short light brown strands. "You know they have a shelf life, right? They're not as reliable after the expiration date. The latex starts to break down."

Thorne leveled an arch stare at his brother. "Do tell."

Knox chuckled and clapped a hand on his shoulder. "Fair enough. I suppose congratulations are in order, then?"

"I…" Thorne trailed off, wondering how he should respond. In truth, he wasn't quite sure how he felt about the news. He'd gone from an initial sense of shock to fear over what Livia might do to Maggie or the baby. He hadn't really considered what having a baby actually meant, and all the ways in which his life was going to change. Having children was something he'd thought was years down the line. To be faced with the prospect now was a bit unsettling, and to be honest, it was still too soon for him to know what to think.

Knox lifted one eyebrow, taking in his reaction. "Still in shock?"

Thorne nodded. It was easier than explaining everything, and it was close to the truth.

"I can relate," his brother said, offering a sympathetic smile.

Several months ago, Knox had reunited with his old high school love, Allison, and learned that her son, Cody, was his. At the time, Thorne hadn't wanted to pry into his brother's personal life, especially after the boy was kidnapped. But now, faced with his own paternity surprise, Thorne needed some advice.

"How did it work for you?" he asked bluntly. "I mean, how did you come to terms with learning about Cody?"

Knox scratched the side of his jaw, his expression turning thoughtful. "It was different for me," he said.

"I already knew about Cody, I just didn't know I was his father. I realized it as soon as I saw him, though. Everything just kind of clicked into place."

"Yeah, but didn't you worry about how your life was going to change? How different things would be now that you have a child?"

"Of course I did. And let me tell you, everything does change once you have a kid. There's really no way to prepare for that—it's just something you have to accept. It's kind of like trying to swim against the current. You can struggle and fight to stay where you are and burn up all your energy for nothing. Or you can relax and let yourself be carried into your new life." He shook his head with a rueful laugh. "I'm terrible at metaphors, but hopefully you get the idea."

"I don't know if I can be that Zen about it," Thorne said. He was a planner by nature and he liked routine. Some might call his life boring, but it served him well with the horses—his methodical, careful actions engendered their trust, which was a gift he never took for granted.

Knox tilted his head to the side, his gaze bright with understanding. "It'll come," he said quietly. "Besides, you have months to adjust to the idea of being a father."

"That's true," Thorne allowed. Hopefully it was enough time to figure things out.

"For what it's worth, I think you're going to make a great dad."

Thorne closed his eyes, absorbing Knox's words. It meant a lot to know that the brother he looked up to thought he could do this job. Maybe he could borrow his confidence until he found his own.

"I hope you're right," he whispered.

"I am. Now, let's go check on your girl."

Thorne opened his mouth to correct Knox, but thought better of it. Maggie wasn't his girl, not anymore. His actions had seen to that. But now that she and his unborn child were in danger, would she let him back into her life?

One of the overhead lights was about to burn out.

It flickered randomly, alternately dimming and flaring bright, humming faintly in the otherwise quiet room. Maggie hadn't noticed it before, but now that Dr. Jenkins had left and she was alone—

No, she thought. *I'm not alone. Not really.*

She placed her palm flat on her abdomen, right between her hip bones. Over her baby.

Baby. She marveled at the word, hardly daring to believe it. Was it really true?

Of course it was, she thought. Dr. Jenkins wouldn't lie. Not about something like that. She closed her eyes, picturing the older man's face as he'd told her the news. *You're pregnant.* He'd said the words so casually, as if he spoke them every day. Perhaps he did. But to Maggie, those two little words did more than just explain her recent fatigue and nausea. They signified a miracle had taken place, marking a transformation she'd never thought she would experience.

She hadn't really given the idea of children much thought, until her doctor had told her that due to her endometriosis she likely wouldn't be able to get pregnant. The painful condition that had plagued her since the onset of puberty had damaged her body, leaving swaths of scar tissue in its wake.

"Your fallopian tubes are almost completely

blocked," Dr. Owens had said, her voice calm and kind as she broke the news. She pointed to two thin lines on the diagram she held, the tip of her pen leaving little blue dots against the pink of the illustration. "It's a delicate area to begin with, and because of the chronic inflammation, I'm afraid it's been damaged beyond repair. I'm so sorry."

It had taken a while for the news to sink in. Maggie had been nineteen at the time, still at a stage in her life where the idea of children was more scary than appealing. But as the years had ticked by, a sadness tinged with anger had filled her. It was one thing to not want children; it was quite another to have that choice taken away before she'd even had a chance to decide for herself.

For a while, she'd stopped dating. Most men wanted a family, and since she wasn't capable of having a baby, she didn't want to fall in love with someone who would eventually leave her or grow to resent her for the things she couldn't provide. Better to be alone than experience the pain of unmet expectations.

Except…she'd grown tired of being single. There had to be a few men out there who didn't want kids, or who would be happy to adopt. She just had to find them.

Her girlfriends Sonia and Amber had celebrated her return to the dating scene. They'd been after her for a while to take a chance. And while Maggie had never been one to act rashly, their words had clearly influenced her because she hadn't hesitated to hop into bed with Thorne as soon as the opportunity presented itself.

Now she had one hell of a souvenir to remember him by.

She closed her eyes, trying to imagine what the baby might look like. Thorne's light brown eyes and her blond hair? Or her blue eyes and his brown hair? How would her pale skin blend with his darker shade? Whatever the result, she knew their child was going to be beautiful.

"I'll take care of you," she promised softly, a sense of determination settling over her like a second skin. And she would. Better to be a single mother than to deal with a man who might not be interested in being a father. This baby was a new life, a blank slate. Maggie was determined to do right by her child, even if that meant her own life would be more difficult than she'd wanted.

A soft knock interrupted her thoughts. "Come in," she called. Anticipation made her stomach flutter— was the obstetrician here to tell her more about the pregnancy?

The door opened, and Thorne poked his head around the edge. "Hello," he said, sounding a little shy. "Do you mind if we come in?"

We? Who was he talking about? Curiosity had her nodding her head.

Thorne pushed into the room, followed by his older brother, Knox. Maggie didn't know Knox all that well, but Mac often spoke well of him, so that was enough for her.

Thorne resumed his seat next to her bed while Knox stood at her side. He offered her a kind smile. "I heard you had quite a scare today. How are you?"

Maggie cut a glance over to Thorne. Had he told his brother about the baby? He met her eyes, his expression unreadable. "I'm okay," she said carefully. "A little shaken up."

Knox nodded. "That's to be expected."

"Are you here as part of an investigation?" She knew he'd retired from the Texas Rangers, but perhaps Knox was consulting with the police because the explosion had taken place on Mac's ranch.

He shook his head. "Not exactly. Mac called me and told me what had happened. I was in the area, so I figured I'd stop by and see how you and Thorne were holding up."

Maggie leaned back against the too-small pillow with a sigh. She hadn't really given the explosion much thought after learning about her pregnancy—funny how her priorities had already shifted. Now the memory of her new car going up in flames invaded her thoughts, and the heavy weight of worry dropped onto her shoulders.

"I'll be doing much better when the police figure out why my car blew up."

Knox shifted, cocking one hip and hooking his thumb through a belt loop. "See, that's the thing," he said, his tone friendly. "In my experience, cars just don't explode for no reason. This was the result of a deliberate act."

A chill skittered down Maggie's spine, and goose bumps broke out on her arms. "There's no chance this was some kind of mechanical flaw? A frayed wire, maybe?"

Knox gave her a pitying look. "I don't think so."

Maggie suddenly felt very small and vulnerable. She drew her knees up to her chest and hugged them, then practically jumped out of her skin when a hand fell on her shoulder. She looked over to find Thorne standing next to her, his expression apologetic.

"I'm sorry," he murmured. "I didn't mean to scare you."

"It's okay," she said, surprised to find that she meant it. She hadn't expected Thorne to touch her, but she hadn't minded it, either. It seemed her body was willing to draw comfort from any source, no matter what her heart had to say about it.

Dismissing the moment, she returned her focus to Knox and the issue at hand. "Why would someone want to blow up my car? I'm nobody important. What could possibly be the motive here?"

Knox opened his mouth to respond, but a voice from the door beat him to it.

"Excellent questions, Ms. Lowell. Fortunately, I think I have the answers."

Chapter 5

Sheriff Bud Jeffries strolled into Maggie's hospital room, acting like he owned the place. He stopped at the end of her bed and eyed her like a cat sizing up a trapped mouse. Then his gaze shifted to Knox and Thorne, and his brown eyes hardened.

Thorne felt an answering disgust rise in his chest. There was no love lost between the sheriff and his family. The man's incompetence had been on full display after Cody's abduction—if Knox hadn't gotten involved, they'd probably still be looking for the boy.

Bud returned his focus to Maggie. "I have a few questions for you, Ms. Lowell. Gentlemen," he said, not bothering to look at Thorne or Knox again, "I'm going to need you to leave."

Maggie cast a quick glance at Thorne, her eyes wide. Her distress ignited his protective instincts, and he placed a hand on her shoulder in a show of solidarity. "I'm not going anywhere," he said, quietly but firmly. He didn't want to pick a fight with the sheriff, but he wasn't going to let the man run roughshod over Maggie just because of her connection to the Coltons.

Bud didn't bother to hide his disdain as he glared at Thorne. "That wasn't a request."

Thorne's blood began to boil, but he clenched his jaw and held his tongue. Jeffries smirked, knowing the barb had hit home.

"I want them to stay," Maggie said.

Bud glanced at her dismissively. "I'm afraid you don't have much to say about it."

Finally, Knox stepped forward. "Sheriff Jeffries, are you here to make an arrest?"

The man's expression turned sour, as if he'd just bit into a lemon. "No," he said grudgingly.

"Then, as I'm sure you know, Ms. Lowell's visitors are not required to leave the room for this conversation."

"I'll take her down to the station if I have to." Bud's chest puffed out in belligerence, the buttons of his shirt straining to contain his indignation over Knox's challenge to his authority. Thorne eyed the one right above his belly button and smothered a smile as he imagined the button popping off. The sheriff was already a joke; losing a few buttons would only enhance his resemblance to a clown.

Knox nodded. "That's one option," he said agreeably. "But she hasn't been cleared medically yet, so you'll probably be waiting awhile. Why don't you just ask your questions now?"

Bud narrowed his eyes and his voice dripped venom

as he spoke. "You're not a Texas Ranger anymore, Colton. Keep this up, and I'll arrest you for interfering in an active investigation."

Knox didn't respond, but his level stare made it clear he wasn't impressed by the threat.

Maggie found her voice again. "You said you have some answers." It was an obvious attempt to change the subject and get things back on track. Thorne gave her shoulder a gentle squeeze in appreciation. Bud Jeffries had felt threatened by Knox ever since Cody's kidnapping, and the man couldn't resist baiting Knox into a pissing contest every time the two of them crossed paths. His brother generally refused to engage, but Bud took any response as a challenge.

Better him than me, Thorne thought. Knox's tolerance for the sheriff was several orders of magnitude greater than Thorne's. If the shoe was on the other foot and Bud Jeffries was going after him, Thorne didn't think he would handle it nearly as well as Knox.

After a moment's silence, Jeffries turned back to Maggie. "Do you have any enemies, Ms. Lowell?"

She frowned and shook her head. "I don't think so, no."

"No professional rivals, anyone who views you as competition and wants to see you fail?"

"Not that I know of."

"What about personally? Anyone angry with you, or want to see you come to harm?"

"No."

Bud flicked a glance at Thorne. "You sure about that? Because if this is the company you keep…" he trailed off, the implication clear.

Thorne narrowed his eyes at the man, but didn't

speak. He refused to give Jeffries the satisfaction of a response.

"No." Maggie's voice was sharp and cold, and Thorne blinked, touched by her unspoken defense of him. It was far more than he deserved, given his recent actions toward her. Further proof that Maggie was far too good for the likes of him.

The sheriff ignored her tone. "All right then," he said. "That's all I needed to hear." He turned and headed for the door.

"Wait," Maggie called out. "Do you have any suspects?"

Bud paused by the door and nodded. "I sure do."

"Can you tell me who it is?" Maggie pressed. Thorne's exasperation grew with every passing second—it was clear Jeffries was dragging out the process, enjoying the drama of the moment. He was a disgrace to the office of sheriff, and not for the first time, Thorne wished Knox would run for the position.

Bud tilted his head to the side, his brown eyes glittering with satisfaction.

"You, Ms. Lowell."

The man hunkered down at the edge of the tree line bordering Mac's farm, careful not to make any sudden moves that might give away his presence. The barn and main buildings were about fifty yards away, so realistically there was little chance anyone would see him, especially with everyone focused on the smoldering remains of the car in the dooryard. Still, best to be careful.

He lifted binoculars to his eyes and peered through the lenses, surveying the aftermath of the explosion.

The car was nothing more than a steaming pile of twisted metal, a broken skeleton lying naked in the dirt. Firemen still moved around it, searching for any residual flames among the smoke, but he didn't linger on the sight.

He was interested in other things.

He turned his gaze to the surrounding buildings, searching for signs of damage amid the breaks in the thick gray smoke polluting the area. The stables were directly in front of the car, but from this angle he couldn't tell if the explosion had had the desired effect. The supply building to the right of the stables showed gaping black holes where the glass of the windows had shattered. The structure to the left hadn't fared much better—the wood paneling was scorched and several patches of shingles had blown right off the roof. He felt a small measure of satisfaction as he surveyed the area. It wasn't quite the Armageddon he'd hoped for, but it wasn't bad for a first effort.

Unfortunately, his enjoyment was short-lived.

As he watched, Mac emerged from the barn. His clothes were streaked with soot and his face gleamed with sweat, but otherwise he looked fine. Damn him.

He thought he'd timed things perfectly; he'd been watching Mac for weeks, learning the man's daily routine. Mac was a creature of habit, and he should have been crossing the dooryard from the stables to the supply shed at the exact moment the car detonated.

Instead, he'd still been inside the stables, safe from the brunt of the explosion.

It hadn't been a total loss, though. A woman had been hurt. He hadn't recognized her, and she didn't look like an employee—her blue skirt and wedge sandals were far too impractical for ranch work. For a brief second, he'd thought she might be Mac's lover. Why else would she have noticed the fire in Mac's trunk? But then he'd seen the way Thorne had come flying out of the stable after her and realized he was the one who cared about her.

He'd filed that tidbit of information away, knowing it might come in handy later.

As he watched, Mac gave the car a wide berth and walked over to one of the men standing next to the gleaming red fire truck. He pulled a green bandana out of his back pocket and mopped his brow, his lips moving as he spoke to the fireman. The pair of them stood in place for a moment, talking and gesturing to the remains of the car and the buildings. Finally, Mac held out his hand and the two men shook, both of them blissfully unaware of his surveillance.

He couldn't read lips, especially not at this distance, but it was easy enough to guess that Mac was thanking the men for saving his property. Their timely arrival had spared the nearby buildings further damage and probably saved lives. Mac and that son of his likely thought they had dodged a bullet today, and in truth, they had.

Too bad they didn't realize what was coming next.

The man smiled as he slipped the binoculars back into their black leather case. He pushed himself off the hard dirt and headed down the gentle slope of the hill, back toward the car he'd parked on the side of one of La Bonne Vie's abandoned service roads. Today had been a practice run of sorts. He'd discovered the explosives weren't as reliable as he'd hoped; the initial fire in Mac's trunk had tipped that woman off and in the future, he didn't want there to be any warning before he struck. Time to try a different tack for his next move.

He unlocked his car and climbed inside, tossing the binoculars into the passenger seat next to the birding book. The thick tome was his excuse if anyone stopped him and wanted to know why he'd been roaming around the area in the wake of the explosion. He hadn't seen a large police presence at the ranch, but that didn't mean they weren't in the area. Better to be prepared for any eventuality, no matter how unlikely it may be. He had to stay out of trouble, at least until he'd taken care of Mac.

He pointed the car north and headed back into town. Thanks to today's events, Mac would be on edge for a while. And as much as it pained him, he was going to have to wait to strike again. He needed Mac to let his guard down so he could catch him unawares—it was the best way to ensure he was successful.

"Enjoy your time," he muttered, glancing in the rearview mirror at the smoky haze rising from the ranch. "You don't have much more of it."

Chapter 6

Bud Jeffries did his best to slam the door as he left, no doubt hoping to make a dramatic exit. Under any other circumstances, Thorne would have laughed at the man's pathetically obvious attempt to seem important. But one glance at Maggie's pale, worried face and his animosity toward the incompetent sheriff melted away.

"I don't understand," she said softly, her voice small and scared. "How could he think I would blow up my own car?"

Thorne sat on the edge of her bed and reached for her hand. Even though he had no right to touch her and he knew she might well pull away from him, he wanted—no, *needed*—to connect with her.

"Bud Jeffries is just being an ass," he said. She glanced over at him, her expression uncertain. But she left her hand in his, a gesture he didn't take for granted.

"He's trying to scare you," Knox added. "He's a man on a power trip, that's all."

"I'm not so sure," she said, her tone doubtful. "He seemed pretty serious to me. But why am I his chief suspect? It was my car that was destroyed!"

Knox lifted one shoulder in a dismissive shrug. "It's not unheard of for people to ruin their own property in the hopes of filing a fraudulent insurance claim. When people need money, they can get pretty desperate."

Maggie frowned and shook her head. "But surely if he did any actual investigating he'd know I'm not in financial trouble. There's no reason for me to try something like that."

Thorne snorted. "You're assuming the man is capable of doing his job properly." Jeffries had displayed nothing but incompetence during the search for Cody, and Thorne wasn't about to give him the benefit of the doubt now. A small kernel of fear formed in his belly. If the sheriff was so shortsighted as to really believe Maggie was responsible for the explosion, he would probably dismiss any evidence to the contrary. That meant the true culprit was free to strike again.

And next time Maggie and the baby might not be so fortunate.

"I don't want you to worry about this," Knox said. "I still have some friends on the Shadow Creek police force. I'll put out a few feelers, see where the investigation stands. It's going to be okay." He offered her a reassuring smile. "I'll go make some calls and check in when I know anything."

"Thank you," she said. Thorne saw her body relax into the mattress and felt a flash of gratitude toward Knox for his offer. If anyone could point the police in the right direction, it was his brother. All the more reason for him to run for the sheriff's office...

"It's my pleasure," Knox replied. "I'm happy to help." He turned to go and Thorne stood up. "Let me walk you out," he offered. He gave Maggie's hand a gentle squeeze and let it go. "I'll be back in a few minutes, okay?"

She nodded, and for a brief second he wondered if she would miss him while he was gone. *Probably not.* He shook off the thought and walked to the door to join his brother.

Knox turned to him once they were in the hall, the door safely closed behind them. "What's on your mind?"

"The investigation," Thorne said shortly. "I'm worried the sheriff is going to let his hatred for our family blind him to the evidence. You and I both know Maggie didn't do this."

Knox nodded thoughtfully. "I wouldn't worry too much about it," he said. "The guys on the force are pretty sharp. It won't take long to clear her from the suspect list."

"That's not all I'm worried about." Thorne briefly described his concerns regarding Livia and her goons, and his fears for Maggie's and the baby's safety.

His brother stilled, no doubt reliving the horror of his own son's kidnapping. "Do you think I'm overreacting?" Thorne asked, feeling a little paranoid. After all, Livia hadn't been seen or heard from in weeks. She was a smart woman; she likely had no desire to get arrested again, so she'd probably gone to ground after sticking her neck out to kill Cody's kidnapper and Leonor's assailant.

"No," Knox said flatly. "I don't think we should discount the possibility that Livia is somehow involved. It would be a mistake to underestimate her."

"What can we do?" He'd feel better if there was some concrete action he could take to protect Maggie and his unborn baby. But short of wrapping Maggie in Kevlar and locking her in a windowless room, there was no surefire way to keep her safe.

"Stay close," Knox said. He glanced back at the closed door. "As close as she'll let you, anyway. I got the impression things aren't totally smooth between you two?"

Thorne shook his head, reluctant to go into the details. He felt bad enough as it was; he didn't want his brother knowing just how much of a fool he'd been. "I'm working on it," he said.

"You want my advice?" Knox continued before Thorne had a chance to respond. "Grovel. A lot. Flowers, chocolates, you name it. But get back into her good graces, and the sooner the better. Both of you are going to experience a life-changing event soon. It'll be a lot easier if you can face it as a team."

Thorne nodded, knowing his brother was right. He didn't think a bouquet of roses would earn Maggie's forgiveness, but it might help soften the ground. "Thanks."

"Anytime." Knox set off down the hall. "I'll call you," he said over his shoulder.

Thorne stood by the door to Maggie's room for a moment, considering his options. They clearly needed to talk. He owed her an apology—had owed her one for quite a while, in fact. Now might be the best time to offer it, while she was stuck in the hospital bed. It was a little cowardly of him to use her situation to his advantage, but he did have things to say and he wanted to make sure she heard them. Since she was essentially a captive audience until the doctor released her, he might as well bite the bullet and plunge ahead, despite the fact that he wasn't used to trying to explain his actions to someone else. Still, he had to try. He might not get another opportunity like this again.

Nerves jangled in his stomach, making him feel like he'd just jumped off a galloping horse. He took a deep breath and decided to take a page from Knox's book. Flowers might not be the answer to every problem, but they certainly wouldn't hurt. And the walk to the hospital gift shop would give him a little time to compose his thoughts.

He glanced around, checking to see if there was a doctor nearby who might be going to see Maggie. He definitely didn't want to miss the obstetrician's visit, provided Maggie was okay with him staying in the room. Fortunately, there were no white coats in sight.

He set off down the hall in search of a peace offering. He couldn't think of the right words to say, but hopefully the flowers would help make up for that.

He'd find out soon enough.

Maggie sighed and rubbed her eyes, trying to massage away the dull throb of her headache. Now that she knew she was pregnant, she didn't want to take anything stronger than Tylenol for fear of hurting the little life inside her. She mentally reviewed her actions over the last few months, trying to recall if she'd done anything that may have harmed the baby. Nothing came to mind; she hadn't so much as had a drink since the beginning of the year. That was good news for the pregnancy, but a rather sad commentary on her social life.

Or lack thereof.

What would her friends say about this news? The last time they'd had a girl's night had been New Year's Eve, five long months ago. They stayed in touch with regular texts and a few phone calls, but everyone was so busy it was hard to find time to get together. They all worked too much, and on top of that, Sonia and Amber had families of their own keeping them occupied.

And soon I will, too.

She smiled at the thought. Her life was going to irrevocably change in a few months. Was she ready?

Was Thorne?

He had seemed different somehow when he'd returned to the room with Knox. Still quiet, but she'd sensed a determination there, as if he'd made up his mind about something. And then when Sheriff Jeffries had stopped by to make his nasty allegations, Thorne had practically vibrated with silent indignation on her behalf.

She wasn't quite sure what to make of this apparent shift in his behavior. Had he experienced a true change of heart, or was this simply a reaction to the explosion and the news of the baby? Would he go back to ignoring her after the shock wore off and life returned back to normal?

Only time would tell. She was going to have to be patient.

A wave of dissatisfaction swelled in her chest. She wanted answers now, not in a few months! But pushing Thorne for a response might actually drive him further away. And while she was going to protect her baby no matter what, she didn't want to deny her child a father.

An upbeat jingle interrupted her thoughts, and she grabbed her cell phone off the rolling lap desk next to her bed. It was a wonder the thing still worked, but she supposed her body had absorbed the brunt of the impact when she'd been blown across the yard.

"Hello?"

"Hi, sweetie." Her mom practically sang the words. "Your father and I are taking the RV to Big Bend to do some camping, and we thought we'd stop by on our way out so we could all have dinner together. We should be there in about a half hour."

Maggie's stomach dropped. She loved her parents, but her mom had a tendency to overreact. The last thing she needed was for them to find out she was in the hospital—she'd never hear the end of it.

"Oh, this is a surprise," she said, stalling for time. How could she convince them to skip the visit without raising suspicions?

"Well, it's not too hot yet, and we've been wanting to go for a while. And we haven't seen you in ages, so I thought it would be a nice chance to catch up."

"Sure," Maggie said, trying to sound enthusiastic about the possibility. "Um, but the thing is I'm pretty swamped at work and I don't know if I'll be able to get a break for dinner—"

"Oh, honey," her mom said, disappointment and disapproval warring for dominance in her tone. "You have to eat. And I know you've been working a lot lately. You need to take a break. You know what they say about all work and no play."

"I do. But this is such short notice, I don't think I can

get away tonight." Inspiration struck, and she nearly cried out in relief. "Why don't you swing through town on your way home? I'll make sure to take the afternoon off and we can spend a few hours together. How does that sound?"

"Well…" her mother said, a bit grudgingly. "That might be okay."

"Paging Dr. Thompson. Dr. Thompson, please report to the ER." The disembodied voice blasted into her room without warning, and Maggie scrambled to cover the phone with her hand.

Please don't ask…

"Maggie? What was that?"

She cursed silently. Brenda Lowell had ears like a bat. Of course she had heard the loudspeaker announcement.

"I don't know what you mean," Maggie said, striving for nonchalance. "Maybe it was the radio."

"Margaret Helen Lowell." Her mother's voice was sharp now, all business. Were all women born with a "mom voice," or was it something that manifested during pregnancy thanks to the effect of hormones on vocal cords? One more thing she would find out soon enough… "Don't lie to me. Where are you?"

Maggie sighed, knowing she'd been caught. "There was a small accident. I'm in the hospital."

"Oh my God! What happened? Steve—she's in the hospital. No, don't slow down—drive faster! We have to get there! Where are you? No, take the next right. The next *right*. Hold on, honey, we're almost there."

Maggie could hear the rumble of her father's voice in the background and couldn't help but smile. After thirty years of marriage, he was used to her mother's knee-jerk reactions.

"Fine, just wait a minute, will you?" Her mother sighed. "Maggie, your father wants to talk to you. Do you feel up to it?"

"Of course. I really am okay, Mom."

"If that were true, you wouldn't be in the hospital." Her mother sniffed and Maggie could tell she was trying to hold back tears. She felt a pang of guilt for making her mom cry, but she had tried to protect the woman from the news...

There was a muffled sound as the phone was passed, and then her father came on the line, his voice calm and measured. "Sweetie, what's going on? Are you hurt?"

A rush of love filled Maggie's chest and tears sprang to her eyes. She really was fortunate to have two parents who still worried about her, even though she was a fully functioning adult. Sometimes she felt smothered by their concerns, but she knew they only wanted the best for her.

"I had a car accident, and I got a little banged up. But I'm doing okay. Just waiting for the doctor to clear me so I can go home."

"That's good. How's your car?"

"Well..." Maggie hedged. "It's going to need some work."

"I'm sorry to hear that, honey. I know it was new. Hopefully your insurance won't give you a hard time about it." She heard the phone shift, and then her father spoke again. "She's okay, Brenda. Here's a tissue—you don't have to cry, honey."

"I'll deal with the insurance company later. I'm

sorry to have worried you," Maggie said. "I hope this doesn't ruin your vacation."

"It won't," her mom said. Maggie realized her dad had put her on speakerphone. "We're canceling it and coming to see you."

"Mom, I don't think that's really necess—"

"Don't bother trying to talk her out of it, Mags," her father advised. "Your mother won't breathe easy until she sees you with her own eyes. We'll just pop in and make sure you're really okay, then we can continue on our way."

He sounded so reasonable, and Maggie knew she was beaten. Better to just agree and not waste any more time or energy arguing with the immovable objects that were her parents. "That's fine," she said with a sigh. "I should be home in a couple of hours. Why don't you just let yourselves in and wait for me?"

"Oh, no," her mom replied. "We're coming to the hospital."

"I'd rather you didn't," Maggie said, putting a bit of an edge on the words. Parental concern was one thing, but she was an adult and it wasn't unreasonable to exercise some autonomy when it came to her health care decisions.

"How are you planning to get home?" her mother challenged. "A taxi?"

Maggie was silent a moment, considering. In truth, she hadn't thought that far ahead. But a taxi was a perfectly reasonable option, and she might as well get used to taking one now, since she didn't have any other options until she got a new car.

Just then, a quiet knock sounded at the door and Thorne slipped in. Maggie's eyes widened when she saw the large bouquet of flowers he carried, and he blushed a little at her reaction. "I have a friend here with me," she said, thinking fast. "He's already offered to give me a ride home."

"Well you can tell him not to worry about it, because we'll be there in about thirty minutes."

"Mom—"

"We have to hang up now so your father can drive," her mom said, talking over Maggie's objection. "Just hold on, sweetie—I'll take care of everything once I get there!"

Maggie set the phone on the table and offered Thorne a weak smile.

"Everything okay?" he said. "You look exhausted."

She huffed out a laugh. "I made the mistake of answering my phone. My parents are on their way to the hospital now."

Thorne lifted one eyebrow. "That happened fast."

"You have no idea." She glanced at the flowers he held, the blooms hanging upside down by his leg as if he'd forgotten what he was carrying. "Those are pretty," she remarked, grateful for the distraction.

"I'm glad you like them," Thorne said, sounding a little shy. "I thought it might be a nice addition to the room."

"Thanks." He handed over the fragrant cone and she brought the flowers to her nose, inhaling appreciatively. "That was sweet of you. But you should probably leave soon. Hurricane Brenda is about to make landfall, and you don't want to get caught up in the chaos."

"I'm not leaving you," he said solemnly. "I'll take my chances with your mother."

His declaration was unexpected and Maggie wasn't

sure how to respond. She'd thought he would welcome an excuse to leave, but he clearly had other intentions. "Are you sure?" she asked, trying to give him one more chance to back out.

He nodded. "I'm staying. The doctor said you're going to need someone to take care of you. And besides, we need to talk."

Her stomach dropped. He was right, of course. They did have things to say to each other. She just didn't feel like having that conversation now, while she was lying in a hospital bed and wearing a scratchy gown.

A light knock on the door saved her from having to respond. A tall, brunette woman in a white coat walked in, dragging a cart behind her. She maneuvered the equipment to the side of the bed, then turned to face Maggie.

"I'm Dr. Walsh," she said. Her smile was quick but genuine, and Maggie immediately liked her. "Dr. Jenkins asked me to stop by for a consult. I understand you've had a bit of a day."

"That's one way to put it," Maggie said. She sketched out the details of the accident, and her concerns for the baby. "I didn't know I was pregnant," she finished. "My regular gynecologist didn't think it was possible. And we—" she glanced over to Thorne, feeling suddenly embarrassed. "We used protection," she said.

Dr. Walsh nodded, her expression sympathetic. "I see. Let's take a look at things, and then we can talk about your options." She tilted her head, nodding ever so slightly to indicate Thorne. "Are you ready for me to proceed?"

"Yes." If Thorne wanted to stay for the ultrasound,

she wasn't going to stop him. This was his baby, too, and he deserved to know if everything was fine.

She shifted a little as the doctor applied gel to her lower belly; the slick liquid was cool and triggered a rash of goose bumps on her arms and legs. Then the doctor applied the wand and turned on the sound, and Maggie forgot her discomfort as a steady "whoosh whoosh" sound filled the room.

"Is that the heartbeat?" Thorne's voice was low, as if he was afraid of interrupting.

"Yes, indeed," Dr. Walsh confirmed. She moved the wand around, pressing here and there in her search. "And this is the baby."

She rotated the monitor and Maggie gasped softly. There on the screen was her baby. It was small, but instantly recognizable, with a large head, rounded belly, and two thin arms and legs that shifted and stretched as she watched, as if the little one was exploring its boundaries.

"Why can't I feel it move?" she said, her eyes glued to the screen.

"The baby is still pretty small," Dr. Walsh replied. "Right now, it's about the size of a lime, so even though it's pretty active in there, it still has plenty of room and isn't bumping into the walls of your uterus yet. Give it a few weeks."

"Is that…" Thorne's voice was husky and Maggie realized he was now standing next to the bed. She'd been so focused on the screen she hadn't even noticed his approach. "Is that the nose?"

Maggie's gaze traveled back to the head, which was shown in profile. She ran her eyes along the line of the baby's face, from forehead to chin. How could something so small already look so perfect?

"Yes. And here are the lips." Dr. Walsh moved an arrow along the image, pointing out features in a running commentary. "Here is the heart, and this is the stomach and kidneys." She moved the wand lower on Maggie's belly. "Here you can see the long bones of the legs forming. And this is the placenta."

Maggie hung on her every word, hardly daring to breathe for fear of missing anything she might say. She glanced over and found Thorne leaning forward, his expression rapt as he took everything in. He must have felt her gaze because he turned to look at her, and in that moment, all of Maggie's hurt feelings and disappointment were buried in an avalanche of joy over the shared experience of seeing their baby for the first time. No matter what might happen between them, they had created this miracle together. They were no longer just Maggie and Thorne; they had new roles to play now. Mother and father.

"Congratulations," he whispered, his brown eyes shining with emotion.

"Congratulations," she whispered back. Her heart was so full she could barely speak, but words weren't needed right now.

Thorne took her hand in his own, his warm, calloused fingers wrapping around hers. In silent agreement, they turned back to the monitor to watch their baby squirm and kick, safe inside her body and blissfully unaware of today's dangerous encounter.

I will keep you safe, Maggie vowed silently. *Always.*

Chapter 7

Thorne eyed the staircase that led to his apartment, his mind whirring as he considered his options. It wasn't an especially dangerous structure, as far as stairs went. He ran up and down the things on a regular basis, never giving it a second thought. But now that the mother of his unborn child was involved, he saw them in a new light. They were steep, strewed with bits of hay that might cause her to trip and not terribly well lit. He was going to have to install a light overhead, he mused, and maybe put down some traction strips to keep her from slipping…

Not that she would be using them anytime soon. Maggie's doctors had been very clear with their discharge instructions: she was to spend at least three days in bed, doing nothing more strenuous than walking from the bed to the bathroom and back again. He'd seen the mutinous glint in her blue eyes, but it had quickly faded once the obstetrician had stressed how important it was for her to rest and recover completely, lest she risk complicating the pregnancy.

He heard her sigh and glanced over in time to catch a look of frustration flit across her face. She caught his gaze. "I don't suppose you're going to let me walk upstairs by myself?" she asked, sounding a bit hopeful at the prospect.

Thorne shook his head. "That's definitely against your doctor's orders. Besides, I think you've been through enough already today—no need to put any more stress on your body."

"I suppose you're right." She paused, and they both looked at the stairs. Was she thinking of the last time she'd walked up to his apartment, on that fateful night that felt like a lifetime ago? "How am I supposed to get up there? I'm guessing there's not an elevator tucked away in an unused corner of the building."

"Well...no, there isn't." Truth be told, Thorne hadn't really thought this far ahead when he'd suggested Maggie come stay with him for a few days. He'd been so focused on keeping her close he hadn't considered the logistics of everything. But he wasn't about to let a little thing like a flight of stairs prevent him from taking care of her. Not only was he worried about her health and that of their baby, but he wanted to make sure Livia and her goons didn't get another chance to hurt Maggie.

"I'll carry you up," he declared. "If you'll let me," he added quickly, seeing her eyes widen at his suggestion.

"I don't think so," she stated flatly. "I'm way too heavy for that."

"Oh, please." Thorne rolled his eyes. "Don't worry

about your weight—you're perfect just as you are. Now come here."

He stepped close and handed her his keys, then bent to get an arm under her knees. Maggie gasped as he lifted her up, snugging her against his chest. He started up the stairs, trying hard not to register the warm weight of her body in his arms or the feel of her breath on his neck. She smelled like smoke and hospital, but as she shifted against him he detected notes of vanilla and coconut, that same tropical scent he remembered from their night together.

His body relished the contact of hers, and his soul purred in contentment. It felt so good, so right to be holding Maggie again! It was almost enough to make him forget about the rift between them, a gulf he had caused and had yet to apologize for. Her parents' visit to the hospital had prevented him from saying his piece. But he would. Now that she was staying in his apartment, he could wait for the right moment to explain everything.

Thorne paused at the door, and Maggie fumbled it open. Then he stepped across the threshold, his skin prickling with awareness of the symbolism inherent in the gesture. If he hadn't made such a mess of things, perhaps they would have shared this moment in a happier time, with her in a white dress and him in a tux, bits of rice falling from their hair...

He ruthlessly stomped on the image, knowing it would do no good to dwell on what might have been. Moving down the hall, he carried her to his bedroom and placed her gently on the bed. He stepped back immediately, needing to put some distance between them as images from that night battered him from all sides.

The bedside lamp let out a quiet "snick" as he turned it on, and the resulting flood of light chased his memories back into the shadows where they belonged. "The sheets are clean," he said, sounding a little gruff even to his own ears. He cleared his throat and tried again. "You know where the bathroom is, and I'll set out some fresh towels for you. Are you hungry?"

"Thorne, I can't take your bed." Maggie stared up at him, her expression shuttered. "It isn't right. I'll sleep on the couch." She made to get up, but he shook his head.

"Absolutely not. If you honestly believe I'm going to let the woman carrying my child stay on the couch, I'm taking you back to the hospital for another brain scan."

"Thorne—" she began, but he cut her off.

"Are you hungry?" he asked again.

She sighed, apparently recognizing he wasn't going to budge on this issue. "A little."

He nodded. "I'll go make some sandwiches. And after that, I'll run out and get you some toiletries and clothes."

"You don't have to do that," she said quietly. "You can just pick up some of my things from my apartment."

"Do you have a key? I thought your bag was destroyed in the explosion."

She frowned, her mouth pulling down at one corner as if she'd just tasted something bitter. "It was. But I have a key hidden in the flowerpot on the porch."

Now it was his turn to frown. "That doesn't sound very safe. Anyone could find it and let themselves in."

"Can you save the lecture for another time? I don't really feel up to it right now." Maggie closed her eyes, and he noted the slump of her shoulders and the lines of fatigue on her face. Contrition slammed down on him, making him feel two inches tall. She was clearly exhausted and in pain, and he should be supporting her, not questioning her approach to home security.

"You're right," he said. "I'm sorry. I'll go work on those sandwiches."

He made it to the door, but the sound of his name made him pause. He looked back at Maggie, so small in his big bed. She looked fragile, but he knew her bruised and battered body housed a will of iron. "Yes?"

"Thank you," she said softly. She gestured to the bed, the room and him. "For everything."

He smiled, unable to put into words how relieved he was that she was alive. Seeing her lying unconscious on the ground had taken years off his life, and it was an image that would haunt his nightmares, especially now that he knew she was pregnant. He'd made a lot of mistakes where Maggie was concerned, but starting now he was going to do his best to make things right between them.

"Of course," he whispered. "It's the least I can do." He swallowed hard and turned away before she could see the glint of tears in his eyes.

Thorne finished slicing a tomato just as his phone rang. He wiped his hands on a dish towel and dug the phone out of his pocket, not bothering to check the display before answering.

"I've got good news," Knox said.

His words lightened Thorne's mood considerably. He hadn't spent much time thinking about the sheriff's visit—seeing the baby and then dealing with Maggie's parents had been more than enough distraction. But the idea that Jeffries would mismanage the investigation due to his hatred of Thorne's family had been a nagging worry in the back of his mind.

"That was fast," he remarked, tossing the towel to the counter. "What did you find?"

"They found explosives in Maggie's trunk."

Thorne frowned and smeared mustard on a slice of bread. "Well, yeah. Isn't that kind of expected, since her car blew up?"

"Not necessarily," Knox informed him. "The explosion could have been due to a spark hitting the gas tank, or something along those lines. The fact that they found an actual incendiary device makes it clear this wasn't an accident."

Fear wrapped cold fingers around Thorne's heart and for a second, he struggled to draw breath. It was just as he'd suspected; someone was targeting Maggie.

"I thought you said you have good news," he managed. Maybe Knox or the police already had a suspect, and it was just a matter of time before Maggie would be safe again.

"That is the good news," his brother insisted. "Look, these were professional grade explosives, not something an amateur whipped up from a recipe in *The Anarchist Cookbook*. That means the focus of the investigation is shifting away from Maggie as the perpetrator to Maggie as the victim. They still have a few loose ends to wrap up, but the guys I talked to don't consider her to be a serious suspect anymore."

"I'm glad to hear it," Thorne replied. "But what about Jeffries? Do you think he might try to interfere just to make our lives more difficult?"

"He might." Knox's tone was thoughtful. "I hope not, though. He has to know there's nothing for him to gain if he tries anything. And besides, the officers on this case seem very focused and professional. I don't think they'd let Jeffries bully them into doing something that wasn't beneficial to their investigation."

Thorne digested his brother's words, hoping he was right. Knox usually had a pretty good read on people, thanks to his skills as a former Texas Ranger. Thorne would just have to trust the man's instincts on this one. He'd never been wrong before. Hopefully this wasn't going to be the first time.

"Do they have any suspects?" Unfortunately, Thorne had no idea who among his mother's associates would have the connections and know-how to plant explosives like that, but Knox might. And while he hated the thought of his family being dragged through the mud again, newspaper and internet exposés were a small price to pay for the safety of Maggie and his unborn child.

"Not yet," Knox replied. "Or if they do, they're keeping things close to the vest."

"Did you mention Livia?"

"I didn't have to. They're already considering her, thanks to Cody's case. The only problem is that they recently received some security footage from a Las Vegas hotel. It looks like Livia has been spending some time in Sin City, and given the time and date stamps on the footage, she can't be the one who planted the explosives."

Thorne wandered over to the windows in the kitchen, which had been damaged by the explosion. He peered through the cracked glass and looked down into the dooryard. The security lights attached to the barn cast the yard in a yellow glow, washing out most of the burn marks on the grass. The twisted wreckage of Maggie's car had been removed, but he could still see the crater that had formed as a result of the blast. It was a stark reminder of how close she'd come to dying today, and he swallowed hard, anger building in his chest.

"Her fingerprints might not be on those explosives, but you and I both know Livia is involved somehow," he said, his voice tight. "No one is safe as long as she's free."

"Believe me, I know," Knox said. "And they're working to find her. Her escape was quite an embarrassment for all involved."

"I don't give a damn about anyone's reputation," Thorne replied. "I just want to keep Maggie safe."

"Where is she now?"

"At my place. Her doctors said she needed complete rest, and I volunteered to take care of her."

"Wow." Knox sounded impressed. "And she agreed? Just like that?"

"Not exactly." Thorne thought back to their conversation in her hospital room. It had taken a lot of time and effort on his part to get Maggie to even entertain the idea of staying with him, and despite that, if her parents hadn't shown up and insisted Maggie come home to Houston with them, he wasn't sure she would have agreed to his plan.

He smiled a little at the memory, able to find the humor in it now that he was removed from the situation. Maggie's mother, Brenda, had come storming into the small room, her eyes wild and her hair an untamed tangle of curls around her face. She'd taken one look at Maggie and raced to her daughter's bedside, talking a mile a minute. About thirty seconds later, a tall, slender man with salt-and-pepper hair had walked in. Maggie's father had been more outwardly composed, but Thorne had seen the lines of strain on the man's face and knew he shared his wife's worry. He'd quickly taken up position on the other side of Maggie's bed, but while her mother kept up a steady stream of chatter, her father had been content to sit silently, holding one of her hands between his own.

Thorne had stood in the corner of the room, quietly watching the domestic scene unfold. Part of him had felt like a voyeur, like he was intruding on a private moment. But he hadn't been able to leave. He'd been fascinated by Maggie's parents, and the way they genuinely seemed to care about their daughter. Having grown up with Livia for a mother, he'd never experienced true maternal concern. Mac had always been there, of course, but somehow his father's love had only made Livia's lack of affection even more apparent.

So this is how families are supposed to act, he'd mused, filing the scene away. At least his child would have one grandmother who actually cared…

"You still there?" Knox's voice broke through his reverie, and Thorne shook free of the memory.

"Yeah, I'm here." He turned back to the counter and the half-assembled sandwiches and resumed his task. Maggie needed to eat, and he did, too.

"So how'd you talk her into staying with you?" Knox sounded curious and a little bit amused.

"Her choices were either me or her mother."

"Is the woman that bad?"

"Hardly," Thorne said. "I think she can be a little overbearing, but it's clear that she and Maggie have a good relationship." He flashed back to the look on Maggie's face when her mother had insisted on either taking her back to Houston or staying with her. Maggie had stared at the woman, annoyance and affection warring for equal dominance of her expression. But underneath her exasperation, Thorne had detected a fierce love and knew this was a family that supported each other, no matter what.

"I wonder what it's like to have a mother who actually acts like one," Knox mused, apparently reading Thorne's mind.

"Your guess is as good as mine."

They were silent a moment, each lost in his own thoughts. Then Knox cleared his throat. "I don't really know Maggie all that well, but for what it's worth, I think she'll be a good mom."

"I do, too," Thorne said. Even though he didn't doubt Maggie's maternal abilities, it was nice to know his brother had the same opinion.

"Get some rest," Knox said. "You've both had a crazy day."

"Thanks for everything," Thorne said. "I appreciate you following up on the investigation."

"No problem. I'll let you know if I hear anything new. In the meantime, just keep your eyes and ears open. Livia might be in Vegas now, but she won't stay there forever. She has too much unfinished business here in Shadow Creek."

Thorne said goodbye to Knox and hung up the phone, trying to ignore the sense of dread his brother's parting words had triggered. Would he be able to keep Maggie and the baby safe? Would she even let him try?

He shook his head, trying to cast off the pessimistic thoughts that were sprouting like mushrooms after a rain. He was exhausted, drained emotionally and physically from the day's events. Maggie had to be feeling the same way. A little food and some sleep, and things would look better in the morning.

For both of them.

Chapter 8

Four days later...

Maggie sank into the warm water with a sigh of pleasure, leaning back to immerse her shoulders in the hot suds. For the past few days, she'd been careful to adhere to her doctor's orders to rest; she'd stayed either in bed or on the couch, whiling away the hours with copious naps. Under any other circumstances, she would have welcomed an excuse to relax and do nothing. But between her mother calling to check on her every five minutes and Thorne tiptoeing around the place like a nervous horse, the time had not been as peaceful as she had hoped.

At first it had felt a little strange to be staying in his apartment, but over the past few days the place had started to feel like home. Thorne's decorating style was minimalist, to say the least, but the furniture he did have was both practical and comfortable. Her favorite feature in the place was a faded, worn quilt hanging on the wall of the den. It was the only embellishment in the apartment, and she was sure there was a story behind it. Maybe tonight she'd ask him about it.

Even though Thorne hadn't had much to say over the past few days, she felt more connected to him simply by virtue of living in his space. In truth, a small part of her was thrilled that he had insisted on taking her home with him. Even though he'd given her the cold shoulder after their night together, her heart still held out hope that he had feelings for her. She was trying to keep her expectations in check, but it was hard not to think he might have brought her here because he still wanted her.

The idea was appealing, especially since there was now a baby involved. But Maggie didn't want Thorne as a partner if he was only there because of their child. She deserved someone who wanted her for her own sake. She'd spent a good chunk of the last few days lying in bed, trying to figure out if Thorne was that man.

She had to admit the forced inactivity had been good for her brain, but her muscles now ached from lack of use. Since she didn't want to risk taking anything that might harm the baby, the heat of the bath was a welcome relief, easing the tension in her back and hips and shoulders.

Aside from that minor physical annoyance, she was feeling much better. Her bruises had faded to a sickly yellow, and looked worse than they felt. Her headache was gone, and her ribs only pained her when she took an especially deep breath. Overall, she was quite happy with the pace of her physical recovery.

Now it was time to do something about her mental state. There was only so many naps a person could take before going insane from boredom.

Maggie figured she had reached that limit about two days ago.

She wanted to go home, but the obstetrician had nixed that idea at her follow-up appointment yesterday. "I'm concerned about your blood pressure," Dr. Owens had said. "And given your recent trauma, I want you to stay on modified bed rest a little bit longer."

"How much longer?" Maggie had asked, her stomach dropping with the news.

"At least until your next appointment" had been the doctor's reply.

So she was stuck here, at least for the next two weeks. And since her laptop had been destroyed in the explosion, she couldn't get any work done. Although maybe Mac would let her use the computer in his office... It was on the older side, but all her client files were stored in the cloud so she should be able to access them. She made a mental note to ask Mac about it the next time she saw him. It was time for her to get back to work—not only would it help combat the boredom of forced rest, but she couldn't really afford to take more time off. Not only did she need a new car, but she had to start saving for the baby.

Maggie let her mind wander as she soaked in the tub, tallying up bottles and blankets and onesies. *Just how many diapers does a baby go through in one week?* she wondered. *And what's the best kind?* She'd seen all the different boxes in the grocery store, their pastel packaging making a rainbow on the shelves as she walked past the aisle. She'd never really paid attention to the details before, but that was going to change soon. Hopefully Sonia and Amber could give her some tips.

She still hadn't told her friends about the accident or her pregnancy. Not that she wouldn't, soon. But for now, she liked keeping the information to herself. It made it seem even more special somehow, this secret knowledge of the miracle inside her.

She stayed in the bath until the water turned cold, determined to wring every drop of enjoyment out of the experience. Moving carefully, she stood up and closed her eyes as a wave of dizziness hit. Maybe she wasn't quite as recovered as she thought…

The towel rack on the wall was just the right height for her to grab, and she used it as support while she climbed out of the tub. She moved like an invalid, but it was better than going too fast and falling down for her efforts. If Thorne found her lying in a heap on the bathroom floor, she'd never hear the end of it.

There was a knock on the door just as she pulled her T-shirt over her head. That was interesting—Thorne didn't bother to knock, and he hadn't had any visitors since she'd arrived. Either he'd asked people to stay away so as not to bother her, or he lived as quiet a life as she did.

Maggie walked over to the door, her curiosity peaking. Given the apartment's location above the supply building, it was unlikely her caller was a solicitor of some kind. That meant whoever was here knew her or Thorne and specifically wanted to see one of them.

A prickle of unease made her pause before answering the door. Had Sheriff Jeffries come back to ask more questions? Knox had said she was no longer a suspect in the investigation, but perhaps the sheriff was determined to give her grief because of her connection to Thorne and his family.

Let him try, she thought, squaring her shoulders. She'd been shocked and in pain when she'd seen him in the hospital. She wouldn't be so easy to push around now.

The doorknob was cool in her hand and she took a deep breath before twisting it to open the door. If the sheriff was on the other side, she didn't want to give him the satisfaction of appearing flustered or upset by his presence.

She needn't have worried. Mac stood on the stoop, his hat in one hand and a brown paper bag in the other. "Hi, there," he said, smiling down at her. "Thorne got held up out in the back pasture, so he asked me to stop by and check on you and make sure you had something decent for lunch." He lifted the bag and jiggled it a little in illustration. "Hope you like turkey."

"That sounds wonderful," Maggie said, stepping to the side to welcome him into the apartment. "Thanks for thinking of me."

"My pleasure," Mac said as he brushed past her. "But like I said, Thorne was the one who mentioned it." He seemed intent on making sure his son got the credit for this act of kindness, and Maggie nodded her understanding. In truth, she was a little touched that Thorne had thought about her. He could have simply called, but he'd chosen to go above and beyond and instead had sent Mac to check on her in person. It was a sweet gesture, the kind of thing a man did for the woman he cared about.

Or the mother of his child.

Just accept it, she told herself, determined not to read too much into his actions.

She smiled at Mac. "I'll make sure to thank him when I see him later tonight."

Mac nodded and set the bag on the round Formica table just off the kitchen. He pulled out one of the chairs and gestured for her to sit, then bustled about the kitchen retrieving plates, napkins and a couple of bottles of water. Maggie squirmed a bit in the chair, feeling a little uncomfortable being waited on by Thorne's father in Thorne's apartment. It was one thing to stay here out of necessity. Quite another to let the men of the family treat her like some kind of delicate porcelain doll. But true to form, Mac waved away her offer of help. "Just rest," he said, patting her shoulder absently as he walked by. Coming from anyone else, it would have sounded patronizing. But Maggie knew Mac was genuinely concerned for her health, so she leaned back and tried to accept the attention with good grace.

After getting everything together, Mac sat across from her and reached into the bag, withdrawing two large, paper-wrapped sandwiches and two bags of chips. Maggie felt her eyes widen at the sight of all that food. Her nausea had improved somewhat, but her appetite had yet to return to normal. Mac apparently read her mind and chuckled softly. "Just do the best you can," he said. "You can save the rest for later."

"It looks wonderful," she said, hoping her enthusiasm would make up for her lack of hunger.

"It is," he said, taking a healthy bite. He took a moment to chew and swallow, then said, "A Rye for a Rye is the best deli in Shadow Creek. Don't tell me you've never eaten there before?"

Maggie shook her head and took a bite of her own sandwich. It *was* good; even her apathetic taste buds approved. She moaned involuntarily, and Mac nodded knowingly. "Glad you like it," he said.

They ate in silence for a few moments. Maggie was cautious at first, uncertain how her stomach would react to the influx of food. But the sandwich went down easily and, by some strange alchemy, it settled well in her system. As the threat of vomiting grew more unlikely she relaxed, and she began to actually enjoy eating.

Mac took a sip of water and eyed her appraisingly. "So how have you been? Settling in okay?"

Maggie shrugged. "I suppose. It's kind of Thorne to let me stay here, but I have to say I'm ready for things to go back to normal." She'd be able to think better once she was back in her own apartment, no longer sleeping in a bed that smelled of Thorne and seeing the man every day.

Mac nodded. "Don't blame you. Your life got turned upside down in short order. It's only natural to resent the changes."

"I don't know if *resentment* is the right word for it." Maggie frowned slightly, trying to articulate her feelings. "I certainly don't resent the baby. But I do wish I still had my car and that I wasn't stuck in bed all day."

"I might be able to help with that," Mac said. He took another bite, keeping her guessing for a few seconds as he chewed. "Not with the car," he said, a little apologetically. "But I could use some help in the office. Filing, organizing paperwork, that kind of thing. Nothing too strenuous. What do you think?"

Maggie's mind raced as she chewed her food. Mac's offer was right up her alley—it was as if the man had read her mind. But would a filing project really fill the hours until she could go home?

Mac mistook her silence for rejection. "I'd pay you, of course," he said. "I'm not trying to use you for free labor."

Maggie shook her head. "I didn't think you were," she assured him. "And I'd be happy to work on your project. But I want to take it a step further."

"What do you mean?" A note of wariness entered his voice, as if he was bracing for an unpleasant request. Maggie couldn't help but smile.

"I want to update your system so everything is digitized."

Mac's eyes went wide. "Wait a minute—"

"I know it's a big change, but this will be good for you in the long run. It will make it easier for you to find invoices and files—"

"I don't have any trouble finding them now," he grumbled.

"And it will free up room in your office—"

"I like it the way it is."

"And once we digitize everything, I'll be able to complete your books online, rather than driving out here once a quarter."

"Maybe I like the company."

Maggie merely tilted her head to the side and looked at him, and after a moment, Mac's expression softened. "Okay, fine. But remember, I'm not a computer guy.

So you're going to have to make sure this new system is simple enough that I can use it."

"That won't be a problem," she promised.

"If I let you do this, I have a condition of my own."

"Let's hear it."

Mac leaned forward. "I don't want you to be a stranger. I always liked you, Maggie. And now I have an even greater reason to enjoy your company." He nodded ever so slightly at her belly, his meaning clear.

Tears pricked the back of her eyelids, and she blinked them away, touched by his words. She knew without a doubt that Mac was going to be a wonderful grandfather, and she'd known he would want to spend time with the baby. But it was nice to hear he wanted her around, too.

"I'm not going anywhere," she said. "I want this baby to know its family."

He nodded, his expression serious. "I'm glad to hear you say that. Thorne's family isn't perfect, by any stretch. His mother—" Mac stopped abruptly and shook his head. "Well, the less said about her, the better. I did the best I could while he was growing up, but a mother's presence is so important in a child's life." His dark brown eyes took on a faraway look, as if he was reliving moments from long ago.

Maggie remained still, not wanting to disturb him. This was the first time she'd heard anything about Thorne's childhood, and her curiosity was piqued. She'd read the newspaper articles and blog posts about Livia and her crimes, and she'd driven past the woman's abandoned compound. But she hadn't asked Thorne about growing up with Livia as a mother. If the look on Mac's face was any indication, she hadn't exactly been a candidate for mother of the year.

Maggie's heart clenched as she imagined Thorne as a boy: a tall, slender kid with long, lanky legs and big brown eyes. Anyone could see his resemblance to Mac, and not just because of his skin color. He had Mac's nose and the same slope to his jaw, and even though Thorne's eyes were a lighter brown, they had Mac's shape. There was no doubt he was unique among his siblings, and Maggie had to wonder if Livia had treated him any differently than the rest of her children. The thought made her blood heat, and she felt a pang of sympathy for Thorne.

After a few seconds, Mac shook himself free of his memories. "The things I could tell you…" he trailed off with a sad smile. "But that's not my place. Those are Thorne's stories. You should ask him about them."

"Do you really think he'd talk to me?" Maggie had her doubts, and just the thought of asking him such a personal question was enough to make her stomach quaver. But they were going to be parents in a few months. They needed to work through their differences, to at least become friends again, if not something more. They owed their baby that much.

Mac nodded thoughtfully. "I do. He's a tough nut to crack, but if you give him a little time, I think you'll be surprised."

I hope you're right. Maggie glanced down at the table and ran her finger along a fold of the sandwich wrapper. Truth be told, she missed Thorne. She'd gotten a glimpse of the man underneath that quiet exterior and she'd felt a true connection to him. That's why she'd been so upset at his about-face in the days after their encounter. Even though they hadn't spent that much time together, when he'd pulled away she'd felt like she'd lost a good friend.

Would she be able to find him again? Or was he lost to her forever, locked away behind a door that had no key?

One thing was certain—they couldn't keep dancing around each other. She was going to be living with him for the next two weeks, and beyond that, he would always be a part of her life. It was time to smooth things over between them.

"On a happier note, when do you want to get started?" Mac asked. He crumpled the sandwich wrapper and tossed it back into the bag, then reached for his chips.

"Right away," Maggie replied. "But first, I need to ask you a favor..."

Thorne opened the door and was hit by the delicious scent of hot food. His mouth watered and his stomach began to rumble as he sniffed appreciatively at the air. Was that...oh, yes, it was. Roast. His favorite.

A note of concern rang in his mind even as he inhaled deeply, closing his eyes in pleasure. Maggie was supposed to be on bed rest—she shouldn't be cooking. But how could he tell her that without sounding like a controlling ass?

He paused for a second to shrug out of his work shirt and hang it on the hook by the door. Then he headed for the kitchen, the source of the wonderful aroma that had made his apartment smell like a home.

Maggie sat at the round table, sipping a glass of

water and leafing through a magazine. He relaxed a bit at the sight—at least she was off her feet.

It was strange to see her there. Even though she'd been living with him for the past few days, he still hadn't gotten used to her presence in his apartment. He didn't mind, though. On the contrary, it was nice to have her there. She softened the place, made it feel more welcoming rather than simply the space he used to sleep and shower. It was definitely something he could get used to, if he wasn't careful.

He stepped into the kitchen, his boot heels clopping on the tile floor. Maggie looked up, clearly startled by his appearance. "Oh! I didn't hear you come in."

"Must be a good story." He nodded at her magazine, the glossy pages shining in the gleam of the overhead lights.

"I don't know about good, but it's entertaining at least. Now I know that the 'it' colors this spring are buttercup, fiesta and limpet shell."

Thorne frowned. The words sounded like English, but she might as well be speaking a foreign language. "If you say so," he said doubtfully.

Maggie giggled at his confusion. "Yellow, red and blue," she clarified.

"Okay. Why not just say that?"

She flipped the magazine closed and picked up her glass. "Someone probably got paid a lot of money to come up with such poetic descriptions. Which is proof that I went into the wrong business." She stood, and Thorne reflexively reached out to steady her. "I'm fine," she said, waving him off. "I just need to check on dinner."

"It smells amazing," he said. "But why don't you

relax and let me finish up? You're supposed to be resting." He was trying to sound concerned, but instead it came out as mildly scolding. He mentally winced— he wasn't trying to pick a fight with her, but he really didn't want her to overdo it.

Fortunately, Maggie didn't seem to take offense. "I know. And I have been. Mac is the one who went to the store for me and unloaded all the groceries. I simply put the ingredients together and popped it into the oven." She leaned down and pressed a button, turning on the oven light. Apparently satisfied by what she saw, she nodded and reached for the pot holders lying on the counter next to the stove.

Thorne intercepted them and shooed her out of the way. "Let me." He opened the oven and pulled out a gleaming roast surrounded by potatoes and carrots that looked almost as good as it smelled. "I'm glad you had Mac go to the store for you," he said, placing the pan on the counter. "You could have asked me to do it—I would have been happy to get you what you need." A small part of him was stung at the fact she'd gone to his father and not him for help. But he quickly dismissed the feeling. The important thing was that she had stayed home and rested.

Maggie shrugged and retrieved two plates from the cupboard. "He came by for lunch, so I figured I'd just ask him. Thank you for that, by the way. It was sweet of you to send him to check on me."

He nodded, the acknowledgment making him feel warm inside. "I thought you might like the company. I know it must be hard for you to be cooped up in here all day." He glanced around the room, trying to imagine how he would feel if his world suddenly shrank to the size of his apartment. Restless didn't even begin to describe it. But Maggie had handled it well, which was a testament to her inner strength. She hadn't complained once, at least not to him.

She finished setting the table, and he carried the roast over and carved it into slices. "I hope it turned out okay," she said, sounding a little worried. "I haven't fixed a roast in a while. I'm a little out of practice."

Thorne took a bite and nearly groaned. "It's perfect," he assured her. "But you don't have to cook for me."

"I know I don't have to, but I wanted to. It's the least I can do to thank you for letting me stay here."

He speared a carrot with his fork. It was tender and sweet, a perfect complement to the savory meat. "You're not beholden to me, Maggie. I brought you here so you could rest and recover." *And to keep you safe*, he added silently. Knox hadn't called with any updates on the investigation, but Thorne hoped it was just a matter of time before the police discovered who had planted the explosives in Maggie's trunk.

"And because of the baby. I know." She let out a soft sigh, and a flicker of what might have been sadness passed across her face. Thorne leaned forward, concern making his heart beat a little faster.

"Is everything okay?" In all the turmoil of the past few days, he hadn't thought to ask her how she felt about the baby. She'd seemed excited in the hospital, but now that she'd had a little time to process the news, maybe she was having second thoughts about becoming a mother.

A cold spike of fear drove into his chest, and in that moment he realized just how much of his heart was already involved. There were months to go before he would get to meet this baby, but just seeing him or her on that computer screen in the hospital had filled him with a sense of wonder and awe unlike anything he'd ever felt before.

He didn't know what kind of father he was going to be, but he wanted the chance to find out.

But how did Maggie feel? She was the one who had to carry the baby for all those months and then undergo labor. And that was just in the short-term. What if she didn't want the lifelong commitment of a child?

Thorne bit his lip and pushed the food around on his plate with his fork. "Can I ask you a personal question?" For better or worse, he had to know what Maggie planned to do about the baby.

She took a sip of water and met his eyes, her expression a little guarded. "Sure. What's on your mind?"

He hesitated a second, but there was really no good way to ask the question. If she didn't want the child, maybe she'd sign over custody to him. Being a single father would be tough, but based on his experiences growing up he wagered it was a damn sight better than having a disinterested mother.

"Are you going to keep the baby?"

Chapter 9

Maggie leaned back in her chair, feeling a little blind-sided by Thorne's question. He seemed to mistake her silence for uncertainty, because he forged ahead before she had a chance to gather her thoughts.

"If you don't want the baby, I'll understand. I'm willing to raise it by myself. If you can just give me these next few months, you can walk away after the little one is born and I won't ask anything of you ever again. Just please, don't do anything…permanent."

Her temper flared in her chest, making her face heat and her blood boil. How dare he try to dictate what she did with her own body? Even though she hadn't considered an abortion, she didn't appreciate Thorne's presumptuous declaration, like she was some kind of impulsive woman whose actions needed to be policed. Furthermore, did he really think she was just going to hand him the baby and walk away without a second look?

She opened her mouth, ready to tear into him for his offensive assumptions. But just as she was about to give voice to her anger, Thorne met her eyes and she saw a glimmer of fear in his light brown gaze.

In that instant, she realized he wasn't trying to control her or dictate her actions. He was asking her about her plans because he was afraid of losing the baby. A rush of relief quenched the fires of her anger. He might be a man of few words, but Thorne's questions revealed he wanted this child just as much as she did.

"I'm going to keep the baby," she said. He nodded, as if he'd expected that answer. But she saw the way his shoulders relaxed and knew he hadn't been certain of her intentions.

"What makes you ask?" she said, curious why he was just now wondering about their child's future.

He lifted one shoulder in a shrug. "A minute ago, when you mentioned the baby, you looked a little sad. It got me thinking about how you're feeling. I know the pregnancy came as a shock to you, and now that you've had time to process everything, I didn't know where you stood."

Fair enough. It was a legitimate question. But she didn't want to talk about the flash of dismay she'd felt at hearing Thorne's confirmation he was only worried about the baby, not her. So she changed the subject. "I was definitely surprised," she admitted. "But I'm also excited. For years, I didn't think I'd be able to have children."

"Because of your condition?" he interrupted, frowning slightly.

"Yes. My doctor had told me I probably wouldn't be able to get pregnant. So I had kind of resigned myself to that reality. But now that I am pregnant..." She trailed off and placed a hand over her lower belly, unable to contain her smile. "Well, I wouldn't trade this for the world."

Thorne was quiet for a moment, studying her carefully. Then he nodded thoughtfully. "I'm glad to hear you say that." His voice was quiet in the otherwise still room. "A baby needs its mother."

Maggie's heart leaped into her throat at the echo of Mac's earlier words. Would Thorne tell her about his childhood? In that moment she felt she was close to gaining his trust, but one false move and he'd bolt.

"Mac said that same thing earlier today," she said, careful to keep her voice soft. If she pressed him or sounded too eager to pry he'd likely shut down. And while she wanted to know about his past for the sake of their baby, she couldn't deny her curiosity had roots in her attraction to Thorne. Despite her aching heart, she still felt drawn to him and wanted to be close to him.

Even though he didn't feel the same way about her.

"Did he?" Thorne sounded slightly amused, an impression that was confirmed by his wry smile. "Well, he would know. He had a front-row seat for Livia's antics."

"I take it she wasn't terribly maternal?"

Thorne laughed, but there was no humor in the sound. "Hardly. Except for Leonor, she treated us like accessories, to be trotted out on social occasions, or whenever she had to give the appearance of being a model mother. The rest of the time she barely spoke to us."

"That must have been hard." Maggie tried to imagine her own mother acting that way, and couldn't. Brenda Lowell wasn't a perfect woman, but she took her job as "Mom" seriously and would never ignore her children.

"The silent treatment wasn't so bad," Thorne said. "The worst was when she would drag me into the fights she had with her husband, Wes. My brother, River, is Wes's child. But it's pretty obvious I'm not."

"And he held that against you?"

"Oh, yes. I was a constant reminder of Livia's infidelity. He would get so angry whenever he saw me—there was always such hatred in his eyes when he looked at me. I knew he wanted to hurt me, but he was afraid of what Livia might do in response if he did. Even so, I tried to stay out of his way and spent a lot of time at the stables with Mac. But there were times when Livia would force me to join them, and I knew she was doing it to deliberately provoke Wes. She enjoyed his anger, and she didn't care how I felt about the situation."

"That's terrible," Maggie murmured. "What about your brother? Did River take after his father?"

Thorne shook his head. "No. None of my siblings have ever treated me badly. If anything, I think they might have been a little jealous of me sometimes."

"Why's that?" It didn't sound like Thorne had had a happy childhood. Why would anyone be jealous of his situation?

"We all loved Mac," he said simply. "Mac has been there for every one of us, oftentimes acting as a surrogate father while Livia hopped from bed to bed without a second thought. He was the one stable presence in our lives, and he treated us all the same. Not like Livia, who often played favorites depending on her mood." He shrugged and popped the last bite of roast into his mouth, chewing thoughtfully. "The one thing I had going for me was that Mac was my actual father. I got to see him all the time, whereas my other siblings didn't have the advantage of seeing their fathers very often, either because they had died or Livia had divorced them and cut off all contact."

"I don't understand how she could do that to her kids," Maggie said. She pushed her plate away, no longer hungry. The thought of Livia's actions was enough to spoil her already fragile appetite. At least Thorne had had Mac. How much worse would his life have been without the older man's presence?

"Don't waste your time thinking about her," Thorne advised. "I certainly don't."

His voice was flat and emotionless, but Maggie's heart clenched with sadness for him. "She doesn't deserve you. Or any of your siblings, for that matter."

"We don't send her any Mother's Day cards, trust me." He pushed his plate aside and leaned forward, a sudden glint of determination in his eyes. "Listen to me," he said, the words underlined by a note of urgency in his voice. "It's important you know that I'm not my mother. I'm not going to treat this baby the way she treated me. I want to be a father to my child, the same way Mac was and still is a father to me."

Maggie nodded in agreement. "I'd like that. I want the baby to know you. I grew up with both parents in my life, and it's important to me that my child experience the same thing, if possible."

He stared at her for a moment, a growing sense of

disbelief stealing over his features. "You are too good," he murmured, shaking his head slightly.

She tilted her head to the side, trying to make sense of his words. "What does that mean?"

"I'm amazed that you're so willing to let me be a part of all this after the way I treated you."

"Oh." Maggie sat back, a little surprised at the shift in conversation. She hadn't expected Thorne to acknowledge the awkwardness between them, but it was nice to know he recognized his actions had hurt her.

"I owe you an apology, and I'm sorry it's taken me so long to say this." He took a deep breath, as if bracing himself. "I'm sorry for the way I acted toward you after we…" He trailed off, twin spots of pink appearing on his cheeks. "After our night together," he finished. "I was worried that with Livia back in the news and the whole town talking about her, people would shun you if they knew you were with me. So I pulled away, thinking it was the best way to protect you."

Maggie didn't say anything at first. She was too busy digesting his words, trying to figure out the best way to respond. It was nice to finally have an explanation for his sudden change of personality. But part of her was angry that he had unilaterally decided what was best for her, without stopping to ask her opinion on the matter. She wasn't some shrinking violet who was afraid of what people said behind her back. And even if the town had talked about her, that was the kind of thing she and Thorne could have faced together.

But they hadn't had that chance. And perhaps now they wouldn't.

Thorne sat across from her, patiently waiting for her to react. There was no sense of expectation about him, no indication of what he was hoping she might say. He was still and quiet, and she got the sense that he would take whatever abuse she wanted to dish out, if that was what she needed to do to feel better.

But it wasn't.

Yelling at Thorne would give her a moment's satisfaction, but after the moment passed she would be left feeling hollow and sad. So she settled for a sigh. "I wish you had said something to me before."

He looked down, his lips pressed together in what might have been regret. "I know," he said softly. "I should have. But I was scared."

It was such an honest admission that for a second, she felt bad for him. She couldn't be angry with him anymore—she simply didn't have the energy for it. He'd made a mistake, but he'd done it with good intentions. It was time for her to let go of the hurt he'd caused. Besides, if she held on to her sense of being wronged, she'd never be able to forge a working friendship with him, which was something they needed in order to coparent their child.

"I understand why you acted the way you did," she said finally. "And in a way, I appreciate that you were trying to protect me. I want us to put this behind us so we can move forward."

Thorne's eyes shone with gratitude and he let out his breath in a gust. "I'd like that, too," he said. "I want us to be friends."

Friends. Nothing more. Her heart thumped painfully at the confirmation that Thorne was only interested in the baby, but she ignored the sting. "I have a condition." Maggie leaned forward, one eyebrow arched as she met Thorne's gaze. "If we're going to be friends, you have to talk to me. You can't just decide what you think is best and act accordingly. I deserve a say in anything that affects my life or the baby. Deal?"

"Yes." He responded without hesitation. "I can do that."

Maggie nodded and leaned back in her chair. For a moment, they were quiet as they stared at each other across the table, the remains of their dinner growing cold in the silence. Finally, she offered him a small smile. "I'm glad we got that straightened out."

Thorne's answering smile was full of relief. "Me, too. It's a real load off my mind. Thanks for being so understanding." He shoved back from the table and stood, then began gathering up the dishes. "Let me clean this up. It's the least I can do after you went to all the trouble of cooking."

Maggie stayed in her chair, content to let Thorne do the dishes. There was a spring in his step she hadn't seen over the past few days, and he hummed softly to himself as he stood at the sink. She was glad to see he was feeling better after they'd cleared the air.

Her own spirit felt lighter, as well, but she wasn't ready to celebrate this new turn in their relationship just yet. As much as she wanted to be positive, Maggie couldn't help but wonder: If it wasn't for the baby, would Thorne have bothered to apologize for the way he'd treated her?

The dooryard was empty, but he stuck close to the wall of the stable, darting from shadow to shadow as he made his way toward Mac's office. Fortunately, the moon was just a sliver of light in the sky, a thin crescent that barely pierced the blue-black darkness of the night. He heard a muffled sigh from within the stables, the gentle whuff of a horse as it shifted and settled again. Did they sense him? Perhaps. But if they registered his presence, they didn't seem alarmed.

A light gust of wind stirred the air of the yard, carrying the scent of stale smoke. He glanced over to the dark crater in the center and shook his head, kicking himself for his mistake. If things had gone according to plan, he could be sitting at home right now, toasting his success with a snifter of brandy. Instead, he was out here in the dark, creeping around with a sack full of trouble.

The sack in question moved in his hand, its occupants shifting as they tested the boundaries of their fabric prison. He shuddered involuntarily and kept moving. The sooner he was free of this particular burden, the better.

Moving carefully, he gently set the bag on the ground, making sure to keep it well away from his feet. He reached into his pocket and retrieved a few tools, then set to work picking the lock of the office door.

It took a few minutes, as his skills were rusty. But the lock was a simple, older model, and it eventually yielded to his efforts. The door opened with a high-pitched whine of the hinges, and he froze, his heart in his throat. A few of the horses stomped and nickered softly, but seemed to lose interest after a moment of silence.

He waited until the animals had returned to their rest and his heart had slowed to its normal rhythm. Pocketing the tools, he bent and picked up the bag, making sure to hold it at arm's length as he slipped inside the office.

It was as dark as a tomb, nearly impossible for him

to see anything. He squinted, trying to make out the shapes of the furniture in the gloom. He really didn't want to chance turning on a light, but he needed to put the cargo in the correct place...

He risked a step forward, and his foot connecting with something solid. Pain shot up his leg and he bit back a curse, nearly dropping the bag. It shifted wildly in response and revulsion crawled up his arm. Caution be damned—he wanted to get this over with.

He used his free hand to dig out his cell phone and touched the screen to make it glow. In the soft electronic light, he surveyed the office, debating on the best place to leave his little gift. Not by the door; they might escape before morning. And not on the desk; he didn't want their presence to be immediately obvious. No, he needed someplace protected but also accessible. Someplace where they would be found, but not before the damage had been done.

The desk sat in the middle of the room, a big wooden construction that looked solid enough to withstand any number of onslaughts. The surface was scarred by years of use and covered in neat piles of paper. A computer monitor sat in one corner like an afterthought, the screen turned at an angle that suggested the machine didn't see a lot of use. But the light on the bottom right corner blinked green, which indicated the thing was on.

He traced the cords down and found the tower on the floor, tucked away under the desk. The fan whirred softly, but he put his hand on the shell just to be sure. It was warm, but not hot. Perfect.

He set the bag on the floor, in the corner opposite the computer tower. It snugged against the side and front supports of the desk, making it all but invisible to anyone in the office. A person would have to get down on their hands and knees to see it, and given the bits of hay and small clumps of dirt on the carpet, he was willing to bet no one spent a lot of time thinking about the floor.

The knife hissed quietly as he pulled it free from its sheath. He lifted the top of the bag up as far as he could, then made a quick cut in the fabric to create an exit. His instincts screamed at him to run, but he was careful to control his actions. If he hurried now, it would only provoke the beasts within.

He gently placed the fabric back onto the squirming bundle, then scooted out from under the desk as quickly as possible. Once on his feet, he wasted no time getting back to the exit and stepping outside. Just before he shut the door, he reached inside to twist the lock back into place on the handle. The last thing he wanted was to arouse suspicion in the morning. Everything needed to appear normal, with no signs of the danger within.

The wood of the building was cool against his back and he leaned against it, the adrenaline draining from his muscles with every beat of his heart. A sense of relief stole over him, along with a giddy anticipation of what was to come. He allowed himself a smile, then pushed off the wall of the stables and melted into the shadows of the night.

Chapter 10

Maggie woke the next morning and stretched in bed, enjoying the pull of her muscles as she moved. She slid her hands down her stomach, resting them on her lower belly.

"Good morning," she whispered with a smile.

It was still too early for the pregnancy to be obvious, but her body was already changing. Her breasts felt fuller and often ached during the day. A dull soreness had settled into her hips—not enough to cause her trouble, but definitely noticeable. And her lower belly had taken on a subtle curve as the baby continued to grow. Her pants were getting a little tight, and soon she'd have to buy maternity clothes.

The thought filled her with happiness, and she spent a few pleasant moments imagining how she would look in the coming months, when the pregnancy would be advanced enough for everyone to see. She couldn't wait to grow big and round. But more than that, she wanted to feel the baby move. The doctor had said it would probably be a while yet, and she hoped the time passed quickly.

Working on Mac's books would be just the distraction she needed to keep her mind occupied.

Eager to get to work, she showered and dressed as quickly as she was able. Breakfast didn't sound especially appealing, but she knew it was important to eat, even if it was just a piece of toast. The prenatal vitamins she took every morning ensured the baby was getting what it needed to be healthy, but she still required food. With that in mind, she walked into the kitchen and drew up short as she caught sight of Thorne standing at the sink. He was usually gone by the time she woke up in the morning—the days started early on the ranch.

He saluted her with his coffee cup. "Howdy."

"Hey," she said, heading for the fridge. "Everything okay? I'm not used to seeing you in the morning."

He nodded. "There was a little trouble with a few head of cattle out on the west pasture last night. Mac left early to deal with it, and he asked me to stay behind and get you set up in his office. Says you're going to be working on a project for him?"

Maggie grabbed the juice and turned to find Thorne holding out a glass for her. She took it with a smile of thanks. "Yes," she confirmed. "I'm going to bring your father's records into the digital age."

Thorne whistled long and low. "I've been trying to get him to join the twenty-first century for years. How'd you manage to convince him?"

Maggie shrugged and took a sip of cranberry juice. "I'm not sure. Maybe he just likes me better," she said, unable to resist teasing him a little.

He nodded thoughtfully. "Probably." Then his voice dropped, coming out as no more than a whisper. "Can't say I blame him." His eyes ran up and down her body, appreciation flaring in the depths of his gaze. Maggie's stomach fluttered at the attention and she felt her face heat. She turned away, focusing on the toaster to hide her reaction. Not knowing how to respond to his compliment, she decided to ignore it. "I don't think it will take me long to get started. I'm sure you have things to do today." She gestured to the bread, silently asking if he wanted some toast. He nodded and stepped closer, gently nudging her out of the way so he could take over.

"I've got this," he said, tilting his head at the kitchen table and surrounding chairs. "Why don't you have a seat?"

She picked up her glass of juice and crossed the room, sliding into one of the chairs with a silent sigh. It did feel good to sit down, even though she hadn't been on her feet for very long. But she wasn't going to admit that to Thorne. Unless she missed her guess, he'd seize upon any excuse to insist she stay in bed.

"So…" he said, his tone oh-so-perfectly casual. "Are you sure you feel up to working in Mac's office today?"

Maggie whipped her head around to look at him, certain he'd read her mind. She expected to see him watching her, a knowing expression on his face. But he stood at the counter, head bent as he spread butter on the toast.

"I should be fine," she said. "Why do you ask?"

He was quiet a moment as he finished making their

breakfast. He walked over and slid a plate in front of her, then took the seat across from her with his own in hand. "I'm just worried," he said finally. "The doctor ordered you to stay on bed rest—"

"Modified bed rest," she interrupted. "There is a difference."

He acknowledged the point with a nod. "Okay. But I don't want you to overdo it. If it were up to me, I'd drape you in Bubble Wrap and have you stay in bed all the time, at least until the baby is born. But I'm trying not to be overbearing, and I know you're responsible enough not to take any unnecessary risks."

Maggie's jaw dropped and she quickly closed it, hoping he hadn't noticed her reaction. It seemed Thorne had really taken their conversation to heart last night, and part of her was gratified to know he was making an effort to respect her wishes.

It was a good start, and she owed him a similar response.

"I'll be sitting the whole time," she said. "Which is in line with my doctor's recommendations. I think I'll be fine, but if I start to feel tired I'll come upstairs and lay down to rest."

"Call me if that happens. I'll carry you up."

It was a tempting offer, especially since she knew exactly how it felt to be cradled in Thorne's strong arms and to feel the play of his muscles as he moved. When he'd brought her home from the hospital, he'd lifted her as if she weighed nothing, and his hold had been gentle but firm as he'd carried her smoothly up the stairs. For a moment, she'd allowed herself to imagine that he was holding her close because he loved her, but given his words last night, she now knew he'd simply been worried about the baby.

Nothing had changed in that respect, and she needed to remember it. No matter how nicely Thorne treated her, no matter how many times he did the dishes, fixed her breakfast, or sent Mac to check on her, all his actions were motivated out of concern for their baby.

Maggie finished her toast and juice and took the dishes to the sink. She turned around and stifled a gasp as she nearly ran into Thorne. He'd sneaked up behind her, and his wide chest filled her vision.

"Whoa," he said, reaching up to place his hands on her upper arms. His touch was warm against her skin as he steadied her in place. "I didn't mean to startle you, but I do wish you'd let me take care of these things."

Maggie took a deep breath and immediately wished she hadn't. The clean scent of Thorne's soap filled her sinuses, and his breath smelled appealingly of fresh coffee and toast. For a split second, she wanted to lean forward and press her body against his chest, to feel his solid frame against hers. The intensity of her desire sent her reeling, and she shook her head to clear it. *Must be the pregnancy hormones*, she decided.

"I insist," Thorne said, clearly mistaking her attempt to regain control of her emotions for argument. He gently steered her away from the sink and made quick work of their dishes. Maggie stood there watching, mesmerized by the leashed strength in his movements as he carefully washed and dried the plates and glasses. There was something very appealing about the contrast of his strong, capable hands and the fragility of the white glass he held.

He hung the towel to dry and turned to her. "Ready to go?"

Maggie nodded, glad to have something else to focus on. Thinking about Thorne would only drive her crazy; she had to remember he was nothing more than a friend now, even though her body might wish otherwise.

They descended the stairs together and walked the short distance to Mac's office. The horses in the stable were stomping and huffing, eager for attention after their night alone. Maggie was tempted to linger and pet the velvety soft noses poking over stall doors, but she knew Thorne had work to do and that he wouldn't leave until she was settled.

His keys jingled musically as he pulled them from his pocket, and he held the door open for her, indicating she should precede him into the office. She stepped inside and glanced around, taking note of the desk covered in piles of papers and the filing cabinets that were no doubt filled to bursting. All of a sudden, the enormity of the task hit her, and a wave of fatigue slammed down onto her shoulders. Mac had been using this system for twenty-five years at least—did she really think she could digitize everything in a matter of weeks?

"You appear to have your work cut out for you," Thorne said, his voice laced with equal parts amusement and sympathy. "It's not too late to back out, you know."

She very nearly nodded, but caught herself just in time. This would be a big job, but it was far preferable to sitting upstairs with nothing to do. And besides, she wasn't going to break her back trying to do everything in one day. She'd focus on one thing at a time, finishing one task before moving on to another. It was the only way to finish a job of this size.

Now she had to decide where to start.

She walked over to the desk chair and sat, surveying the sea of papers before her. "Do you know anything about your father's filing system?" she asked. "I don't want to keep you, but if you could point me in the right direction, that would be great. He usually has the relevant documents pulled for me when I come to do his books, so I don't have a sense of how he organizes things overall."

Thorne blinked, looking like a deer caught in the headlights of an approaching car. "I— uh. I think the invoices are arranged by date, with the earlier stuff starting in that drawer." He pointed to one of the filing cabinets, and she swiveled to see which one he indicated.

"Do you know if he alphabetizes things, or arranges them by merchandise?"

Thorne shook his head. "I don't. I'm sorry."

"That's okay." She swiveled back to the desk and reached for the pile of papers nearest to her elbow. "I'll just take a look and see—"

A strange rattling sound started up, catching her off guard. It sounded a bit like someone was shaking rice in a jar, but that didn't make any sense...

"Maggie." Thorne's voice held a note of command she'd never heard before. "Don't move."

She froze, the intensity of his words making her heart trip. The dry buzzing continued, and after a second, she finally put a name to the noise.

"Oh my God," she whispered, feeling the blood drain from her head. "Is that a rattlesnake?"

* * *

Thorne had never been so scared in his life.

Unless he was hearing things, there was a pissed-off rattlesnake under Mac's desk.

Right by Maggie's legs.

If she moved, if she startled it in any way, it would strike. Rattlers were not known for their patience.

"Stay still, Maggie," he said, trying to sound calm. He could tell by the look on her face she understood the danger she was in, and he didn't want her to panic while she was still within range of those fangs. Based on the intensity of the sound, he guessed they were dealing with a rather large snake. A shudder of revulsion ran through him, and he fought the urge to run away. How was he supposed to deal with this creature when his instincts screamed at him to make tracks?

Just then, a second buzz started up and Thorne's heart dropped into his boots. A *second* snake? How was that even possible?

He dismissed the question immediately—now was not the time to worry about the source of these creatures. He had to get Maggie away from them, and fast.

She heard the new addition and let out a soft whimper. "Thorne," she whispered, her voice tight with fear. "I don't know what to do."

That made two of them. "Just don't move," he said, sounding more confident than he felt. "They're warning you because they're scared. If you don't move, they should calm down." *Right?* Wasn't that what all the nature shows said? His thoughts tumbled in one after another as he called up everything he knew about rattlesnakes. It was a pathetically short list of facts, dominated by one word: *run*.

"I don't know how long I can sit here," she said, trembling slightly. The rattling intensified, and she closed her eyes, a tear sliding down her cheek.

He couldn't wait much longer. Despite his assurances to Maggie, there was no guarantee the snakes would relax enough to let her move away to safety. And the longer she stayed there, the madder they were likely to become. It was only a matter of time before they struck, and he didn't want to imagine the effects of rattlesnake venom on her pregnancy.

But how could he save her without provoking the snakes? If he walked up behind her to pull her back, the animals would likely see him coming and feel the vibrations of his approach, making them even more agitated.

He eyed the desk, an idea forming as his mind raced. It was crazy, but it just might work. Besides, he didn't exactly have a ton of workable options…

Moving carefully, Thorne toed off his boots and set them aside. Then he began to creep closer to the desk, walking as softly as he could.

Maggie's eyes went wide. "What are you doing?" she whispered.

Thorne put a finger to his lips and stopped in front of the desk. This part was going to be tricky. If he jarred the desk at all, the snakes would strike.

He held his breath as he climbed on top of the desk, wobbling a bit as he gained his balance on the slick wooden surface. He crouched in front of Maggie and met her gaze, the panic in her blue eyes hitting him like a blow to the chest. "I need you to lift your arms," he said softly.

"What?"

"Lift your arms," he repeated. "Slowly."

"I—I don't think I can move," she stammered.

"It's okay. Just take a breath and try to relax. You can do this."

"What are you going to do?"

"I think it's better if I just show you," he said. The rattling hadn't stopped—the hidden snakes were clearly unhappy with the situation. If something didn't change soon, there would be trouble.

"Please, Maggie," he said, injecting some of the urgency he felt into his voice. "Trust me."

She stared up at him, her fear so intense he could practically feel it hanging between them like a thick, greasy fog. After an endless moment she raised her arms, reaching up to him. Her face was lined with uncertainty but her movements were determined. He felt a rush of gratitude for her faith in him—even though she didn't know exactly what he had planned, she was willing to give him the benefit of the doubt.

"I'm going to count to three," he said. She nodded, her eyes never leaving his.

Thorne took a deep breath, tensing his muscles in preparation. "One… Two…" On three, he grabbed her under the arms and stood, pulling her out of the chair in one smooth motion. Maggie gasped and grabbed on to his shoulders, her hold desperate. He pivoted to the side to set her feet on the desktop, sliding his hands to her lower back to anchor her in place.

They turned and looked down in time to see a flash of brown as one of the snakes lunged forward. It retreated just as quickly, sliding back under the relative security of the desk. The dry, rattling hum continued though, a visceral reminder that they were still in danger.

Maggie shivered against him. "Are you hurt?" he asked. "Were you bitten?"

She shook her head. "No. At least I don't think so."

Thorne frowned. Given all the adrenaline in their systems, it was possible she'd been hit and just didn't know it yet. He'd feel better once they were out of here, with the snakes safely contained on the other side of Mac's heavy office door.

He slid down, landing on the front side of the desk. A shiver ran through him at the thought of the snakes lying coiled behind the wood front piece. He knew it was a solid barrier, but it was still too close for comfort.

Thorne reached up and lifted Maggie down from the desk, and the pair of them wasted no time rushing from the office. He shut the door behind them with a heavy thunk, and didn't stop moving until he and Maggie were back at the stairs that led up to his apartment.

He guided her down and knelt in front of her, his hands tugging up the ankles of her pants so he could see her legs. He had to see for himself that she was whole and unharmed. Without saying a word, he stripped her shoes and socks off and pushed the hems of her pant legs to her knees, his eyes scanning for bite marks and his hands running over her feet, her ankles and up her calves as he felt for any wetness that might indicate blood from a bite.

"Thorne," she said, squirming a bit under his examination. "Thorne, I'm fine!"

He heard her voice, but the words didn't register. He couldn't stop until he'd examined every inch of her legs and knew for certain she was fine. If she'd been hurt, he'd never forgive himself... And the baby—oh,

God, what if he'd hurt the baby when he'd yanked her out of the chair?

Maggie's hands landed on his, stilling him. "Thorne," she said firmly. He looked up into her blue eyes, which were now full of determination and showed no hint of her earlier fear. The wild feeling in his chest calmed to see her so poised, and he nodded.

"I'm fine," she repeated. Her hand fluttered to her belly. "We both are."

He rocked back on his heels and sucked in a deep breath, trying to expel the remainder of his tension on the exhale. He lowered his head, focusing on the ground. His socked feet looked absurd against the dark floor, and he belatedly remembered his boots, waiting patiently in Mac's office. *They'll have to wait a bit longer*, he thought wryly, unwilling to go back inside while the snakes were still loose.

Something touched the back of his head, a gentle, almost inquisitive brush. A second later, Maggie's hand cupped the curve of his skull, her skin soft and cool. Without stopping to think, Thorne leaned forward until his forehead rested on her knees. Her fingers stroked him gently, each touch a reminder that she was safe and the baby was fine. Gradually, his heart calmed and the tight band of fear around his chest relaxed enough that he could breathe without struggling.

As his system returned to normal, Thorne's awareness of Maggie grew. The muscles of her calves were solid and strong under his hands, her skin smooth and soft against his work-roughened palms. He breathed in her scent, the warm perfume of her vanilla-coconut soap mingling with the sweet smell of hay and horses.

It was an intoxicating combination and he tightened his grip on her legs before he could think better of it.

Maggie let out a soft "oof" in response, and her hand tightened on the back of his neck, holding him in place. Her fingernails scraped lightly against his skin, sending a shiver down his spine. His heart began to pound again, but this time, he wasn't looking for an escape.

Thorne released her legs and reached up to thread his arms around her hips. Before he could think twice, he kissed her, pouring all his anguish and relief into the connection between them. His blood raced at the feel of her lips, and he surrendered to the moment, slipping free from the leash he'd put on his desire for her.

He'd spent many a moment reliving their night together, remembering the exquisite pressure of her mouth against his own. But the reality was far more impressive, and his awareness of his surroundings faded as he and Maggie shared a breath.

She hummed softly, and her gentle sound of contentment made his heart soar. He could have stayed like this forever, but the rumble of an engine in the door yard reminded him they were not alone.

Maggie probably wouldn't appreciate being caught in a kiss with him, so he leaned back, breaking their connection. Then he pulled her forward, rearranging their bodies until he could rest his head against her lower belly. He might not be able to keep kissing her, but that didn't mean he had to completely disconnect from her. She was warm and soft, blessedly whole and unharmed. If he could, he would stretch out to cover her and the baby, intercepting any threats before they had a chance to do harm.

Maggie cradled his head in her lap, her hand moving

from his neck to between his shoulders with smooth, steady strokes. Part of him marveled that she was allowing him to touch her—after the way he'd treated her, he hadn't expected her to let him get this close ever again. She must have truly forgiven him, and the realization both humbled and thrilled him.

Time seemed to stop as he held Maggie close and was embraced by her in return. But he couldn't ignore the dangerous reality she faced for much longer. Someone had planted those snakes in Mac's office—he was sure of it. Rattlesnakes did not simply appear out of thin air. They were surprisingly shy animals who would never deliberately seek out the busy environs of the stables. They had been left there to wreak havoc on an unsuspecting victim, the unwitting agents of a treacherous assault.

It was almost the perfect crime, a devious act that was exactly the kind of thing Livia would enjoy. Even though the police thought she was in Las Vegas right now, Thorne didn't doubt her reach extended all the way back to Shadow Creek.

"Thorne? Maggie?" Mac's voice cut into his thoughts, and Thorne released his grip on Maggie, easing back onto his heels as he slid away from her. Mac walked over to them, frowning in concern. "What's going on? Is everything okay? Maggie, are you feeling all right?" He reached out to her and she offered him a reassuring smile.

"I'm fine," she said. "Thanks to Thorne."

Mac cut him a questioning look. "What happened?" His gaze slid down, landing on Thorne's feet. "And where are your boots?"

Chapter 11

Maggie sat on a bench in the stables, her eyes glued to the closed door of Mac's office. About ten minutes ago, a man from Animal Control had arrived, toting heavy burlap bags and a long pole. After slipping on a pair of thick rubber knee-high boots, he'd ducked into the office with his implements.

"I hope those snakes didn't slither into my boots." Thorne sat down next to her and shivered slightly. "I'd never be able to look at them the same way again."

Maggie smiled at the thought of strong, capable Thorne being affected by the knowledge that snakes had once curled up in his shoes. "I'm sure they're still under the desk. The smell alone was probably enough to stun them."

"Are you saying my boots stink?" He sounded surprised, as if the idea had never occurred to him.

In fact, she hadn't ever been close enough to identify an odor, but she couldn't resist teasing him a little. "You do work around animals all day," she pointed out. "And it gets hot here in the summers. That's a potent combination."

"I guess. Probably time for a new pair anyway."

"That might be for the best. That way you can guarantee they've always been snake-free."

"Not a bad idea," he said thoughtfully. "That's really an underutilized selling point, if you think about it. I for one appreciate knowing my footwear has never been used as a hiding place for venomous creatures."

"They don't leave behind a residue," she pointed out logically.

Thorne shook his head. "Doesn't matter. It still makes me queasy."

"Then I suppose I should be extra grateful for your assistance in there. I had no idea you were so affected by snakes."

"You don't have to thank me," Thorne said. "I'm just glad you and the baby are okay."

"All thanks to you," she said.

He shifted slightly, and she could tell by the look on his face her praise made him uncomfortable. So she changed the subject. "I hope he finished up in there soon. I need to get started on Mac's files."

Thorne turned to look at her, his expression incredulous. "You can't possibly be serious."

"Why not? Once the snakes are gone, I see no reason why I can't get started on the project." She had to do something, or else she'd spend the rest of the day analyzing Thorne's kiss, searching for meaning that probably wasn't there.

Her lips still tingled and she resisted the temptation to rub her fingers over her mouth to dispel the sensation. It was tempting to imagine Thorne had kissed her because he wanted her, but she'd seen the wild look of panic in his eyes and knew he'd acted on impulse, thanks to an abundance of adrenaline. He'd been relieved that the baby was safe, but the only way he could express that was by embracing her. It was a sweet gesture, but she couldn't let herself read too much into it.

He reached out and took her hand, his light brown eyes full of an emotion she couldn't identify. "Maggie, someone put those snakes in Mac's office—they didn't just wander in looking for a place to stay. This was a deliberate attempt to hurt you."

She frowned. "But that doesn't make any sense. This was going to be my first day working in his office. No one else knows about our arrangement. So how can you be so sure someone is trying to hurt me? Maybe they were trying to injure Mac."

"Maybe." He tilted his head to the side. "I'll talk to Mac, see if he's noticed anything suspicious lately. But even if he's the true target of this attempt, you came awfully close to being collateral damage today."

"But I didn't," she pointed out. "Why should I let something that didn't happen control my life?"

Thorne paused for a moment, appearing to gather his thoughts. "Let's assume the snakes were supposed to bite Mac. Since they didn't, whoever put them in his office is going to come back, looking for another way to hurt him. What if you get in the way again? I might not be there next time."

There was something about his tone that made Maggie think he wasn't telling her the whole story. "What's really going on here?"

He sighed, and for a second she thought he wasn't going to respond. When he did speak, his voice was low, almost as if he was reluctant to talk. "You know my mother's reputation," he began, glancing at her for confirmation. She nodded, and he continued, "She's not the type of woman to let bygones be bygones. Given the way things ended for her in this town, I'm worried she might be lashing out at people close to me, as a way to punish me for not supporting her during her trial."

"You think she's the one who put explosives in my trunk?"

He nodded, looking miserable. "It's possible. And putting snakes in Mac's office is exactly the type of calculated strike she favors."

"But why would she target me in the first place? I'm nothing to her—we've never met before."

"You're connected to me," he said simply. He opened his mouth to say more, but seemed to think better of it.

Maggie wasn't satisfied with his response. "I wasn't until my car exploded," she pointed out archly.

He ducked his head and ran a hand over his close-cropped hair. "She probably found out about our night together and figured you're important to me. That's why she went after you." He shook his head. "I'm so sorry."

"I see." And all of a sudden, she did. "That's why you wanted me to stay with you, isn't it? You feel bad about what happened to my car." Her heart sank as she waited for him to reply. She'd thought Thorne had insisted on bringing her back to his apartment because he cared about her. It stung to find out he didn't want her company—he was only acting out of a sense of guilt, because he thought his mother had tried to harm her.

"Well, yes," he confirmed. "But there's more to it than that. I'm scared you're still a target, since you survived her first attempt. I figured if you stayed with me, I could keep an eye on things and make sure you and the baby are safe."

Maggie clenched her jaw, feeling like a fool. How could she have ever thought Thorne was interested in her romantically? It was clear the only reason she was here was due to the baby. If she hadn't turned up pregnant, he likely would have left her in the hospital and she'd be home now, sleeping in her own bed.

Tears sprang to her eyes, but she blinked them away. She would not cry in front of Thorne; her pride wouldn't allow it. Besides, if he saw her tears he would want to know why she was upset, and she didn't want to explain the disappointment and hurt she felt after finding out he didn't have feelings for her. *I'm sad because you don't want me—talk about pathetic!* Definitely a conversation she would never let happen.

Just then, Mac's office door opened and the Animal Control officer stepped out carrying two wriggling sacks. Maggie instinctively leaned back, and she felt Thorne brush her shoulder as he did the same. The bags were tied securely, but she didn't relax until the man had placed them both in a locker in his truck and shut the door behind them.

She rose and started walking toward Mac's office, Thorne a half step behind her. She knew he was going to try to talk her out of starting on Mac's files, but she wasn't in the mood to listen. Now more than ever, she needed to focus on something else as a distraction from her thoughts and her aching heart.

Fortunately, the Animal Control officer stopped Thorne and held out a clipboard, clearly needing a signature or acknowledgment of some kind. Maggie used the opportunity to duck into the office alone. She was surprised to find it looked the same as before—apparently, capturing the snakes hadn't involved much of a struggle. Thorne's boots lay sprawled on the floor, and in that instant, she hoped the snakes *had* been hiding in them.

She picked them up and deposited them in the hall just outside the office door. Hopefully he would take the hint.

If only her heart had done the same.

"What's wrong?"

Thorne jerked, startled by the unexpected sound of Mac's voice. They'd been grooming horses for the past hour, the brush of the currycombs and the chirps of birds the only sounds in the otherwise quiet pen.

Earlier that morning, he and Knox had questioned Mac about possible enemies who might want to harm him. But his father hadn't been able to come up with any names. Knox had left them to return to work, and Thorne and Mac had gone back to the horses. Given Mac's natural reticence, Thorne had figured his father had already used up his quota of words for the day, so it was a bit of a shock to hear him speak now.

"Nothing's wrong. Why do you ask?"

Mac lifted one eyebrow and shook his head. "I know you, son. I can tell when something is bothering you.

If you don't want to talk, that's fine. But could you at least quit sighing like a moody teenager?"

Thorne couldn't help but smile at the description. "That bad, huh?"

Mac nodded, turning back to the blue roan mare he was brushing. He smoothed a callused hand over her silvery-gray coat and she nosed him affectionately, huffing a breath as she searched his pockets for a treat. "Fine, fine," he said, laughing as he pushed her questing head away. He reached into his pocket and pulled out a small apple, which he offered to her. "Here you go." The mare's lips moved delicately as she plucked the treat from his palm, and he resumed brushing her while she chomped happily.

"So what's it going to be then?" he asked, his eyes on the horse. "Want to share? Or would you rather pretend everything is fine?"

Thorne considered the question for a moment as he brushed the horse in front of him. He normally didn't like to talk about his feelings, but if he was going to share, Mac was the person he'd choose to listen to him. His father had been a great sounding board throughout the years and it would be nice to get his take on things. It certainly wouldn't hurt to have another opinion on the subject.

"I'm worried about Maggie," Thorne said finally. "I think something is bothering her."

"Have you asked her?" Mac said reasonably.

If only it was that simple! "I have. She says nothing is wrong."

"Maybe you should take her word for it."

Ordinarily, Thorne would agree with him. But this

was Maggie—he couldn't simply ignore the situation when his gut was telling him something was wrong.

He shook his head, trying to find the words to articulate his feeling. Maggie acted like she was fine, but ever since he'd impulsively kissed her there was a sadness about her he hadn't seen before, a melancholy air that seemed to cling to her, dulling the normal shine of her blue eyes.

He wished she would confide in him, but she probably didn't trust him enough for that yet. She said she had forgiven him for his actions, but he knew it would take time to rebuild their relationship.

In the meantime, how could he help her?

"Haven't you noticed how quiet she's been lately?" he asked, trying a different tack. Mac was an observant man—surely he had noticed the signs as well! "In the two days since we found the snakes in your office, she seems to have withdrawn into herself, like she's trying to shut out the world."

"Maybe she is," Mac offered. "A lot has happened to her recently. Her car exploded, she finds out she's pregnant, then she's nearly bitten by an angry rattler. That's enough to make anyone want to pull the covers over their head and hide."

"I suppose," Thorne said. He set down the curry-comb and picked up the hard brush, then set about removing the dirt and loose hair from the horse. She shifted a bit as he moved down her neck, but he didn't see any troubling marks or bites. He lightened his stroke and she stilled again, relaxing once more under his hands.

"You don't sound convinced," his father observed.

"I just feel like there's something more going on," he said finally.

Mac was quiet for a few moments, and Thorne figured he had moved on. He relaxed back into the rhythm of the work again, the sun warm on his shoulders. At least the weather was nice today…

"What are your intentions?" Mac's voice floated softly above the birdsong, calm and soothing.

Thorne frowned. "What do you mean?"

"I mean," his father replied, a slight edge on the words, "what are your intentions toward Maggie?"

"Oh." For a second, Thorne was dumbstruck, unsure of how to answer the question. "I care about her, of course," he said. "After all, she's carrying my child."

"Is that all there is to it?" There was a note of disappointment in Mac's voice, as if Thorne had failed an important test.

"What do you mean, Dad?"

Mac sighed and dropped his arm. "I thought I raised you better than that," he muttered.

Thorne reeled back, bewildered. "What the hell?"

"Watch your mouth," Mac said automatically. He shook his head and turned to face Thorne. "So that's it, then? You only care about her because she's pregnant with your baby? She's just some kind of vessel to you?"

"Well, no," Thorne stammered.

"Then stop treating her like one."

Thorne was incredulous. "When have I ever acted like she's just a-a-an incubator?" he finished.

"Every time I've heard you talk to her, you only ask her about the baby. You don't seem to care about how she's actually doing—just how her health is affecting the pregnancy. It's no wonder she's pulling away.

You're making her feel like she's nothing more than a walking uterus!"

Thorne opened his mouth to refute his father's words, but as he thought over the last few conversations he'd had with Maggie, he realized Mac was right. He had emphasized the baby, but not out of any desire to erase Maggie's identity. It just seemed like a safe topic of conversation, something they both shared and could discuss without any hurt feelings.

"You may have a point," he said grudgingly.

Mac accepted his acknowledgment with a nod. "Now back to my original question," he said, returning to the horse. "What are your intentions regarding Maggie? Do you simply want to maintain the status quo, or do you want to have a real relationship with her?"

"I want—" Thorne began, but then he stopped. How could he put into words his hopes for his relationship with Maggie? How could he explain their complicated past to his father? He was still embarrassed by the way he'd treated her, and Thorne knew Mac would have several choice words if he found out about it.

Mac gave him a moment, then spoke again. "I'm going to assume you had feelings for her at one point, given her current state."

"Yes."

"And I'm going to further assume that given the awkwardness between you two now, something unfortunate happened?"

Thorne swallowed. "Yes. I—"

Mac held up his hand, stopping him from saying anything more. "Son, I think it's best if I don't know the details. That's for you and Maggie to work out."

"I thought we had," Thorne said, feeling miserable. "But now I'm not so sure."

"You want my advice?" It was a rhetorical question, and they both knew it. "You need to focus on Maggie for a while, let her know you care about her not just because of the baby, but because of who she is."

Thorne gave the horse's hindquarters a wide berth as he walked around to her other side and began brushing down her neck, working his way to her shoulder. His father's words were an echo of Knox's earlier advice, a coincidence he would have found amusing under different circumstances. As it was, maybe the universe was trying to tell him something. He was certainly willing to listen—he'd always felt more comfortable around horses than people, so he didn't always say the right thing.

But hopefully he could learn before it was too late.

"You're awfully quiet," Mac observed.

"Just thinking," Thorne said.

"Don't hurt yourself."

"Thanks, Dad," he said dryly.

"You know I love you," Mac said. "Things might be tough right now, but you'll get through this. You and Maggie both."

The horse in front of him grew blurry, and Thorne blinked to clear his eyes. "Thanks, Dad," he said again, his voice husky this time. His father's faith in him meant more than he could express and renewed his confidence that he could patch things up with Maggie.

And he knew just how to start.

Chapter 12

Maggie leaned back in Mac's desk chair and lifted her arms above her head, stretching out the knots in her shoulders. She'd been working steadily for the last couple of days and, bit by bit, the piles of paper that were stacked here, there and everywhere were beginning to shrink. There was still a lot of work left to be done, but she felt a flare of satisfaction as she glanced at the plastic recycling bin, which was now overflowing with the shredded scraps of invoices she'd scanned and entered into the digital system. If she continued working at her current pace, she could probably have all of Mac's records digitized and organized in about a week.

Which would hopefully coincide with her return home.

She had a doctor's appointment in eight days, and she was hoping to get the all clear to return to her normal life. There was nothing wrong with Thorne's apartment, but now that Maggie knew he cared about her only because of the baby, it was too hard to live with him. Every day brought new reminders that she had no real place in his life, and never would.

She'd tried to put on a brave face, but she could tell by the way Thorne looked at her that he thought something was wrong. He'd asked her several times if she was okay, and each time she'd smiled and said yes, lying through her teeth in the hopes that he would leave her alone.

After all, what could she say? *I'm sad because I had hoped we might get back together, but I realize now that's not a possibility.* Definitely not—she had some pride left.

Maggie couldn't hold Thorne's feelings, or lack thereof, against him. He'd been honest with her and he hadn't tried to lead her on or make her think his attentions were anything more than a man worried about his unborn child. It was her own heart that had leaped to conclusions and looked for meaning that wasn't there. She'd let her expectations get the better of her, and now she had to deal with the reality of her situation. It hurt, but she'd get over it.

Eventually.

Working on Mac's books had helped. Keeping her mind engaged had prevented her from wallowing in self-pity and had given her something to look forward to every day. And Mac had been kindness itself, aside from some good-natured grumbling about teaching an old dog new tricks. He was only teasing her, though; despite his protestations, he was already well on his way to mastering the new system.

"Wow" came a voice from the doorway. "You've made a lot of progress already."

Thorne's voice washed over her, making her heart kick and her stomach flutter with awareness. It was the same reaction his presence always triggered, but she refused to let it show. Maggie took a deep, bracing breath and turned to greet Thorne. "Thanks," she said simply. "I'm enjoying the work, and so far it's going well."

He nodded and pushed off the doorjamb, taking a few steps into the room. "It's going to look like a whole new office when you're done. I wonder what Mac's going to do with all the free space?"

"Probably expand his collection of photographs," she said, eyeing the already large group of pictures crammed into every available space. Most of them were photos of Cody, but there were a few of Thorne and his siblings interspersed throughout, along with a couple featuring horses that must have been especially important to him. It was an interesting mix, and soon he'd have one more family member to add to the assembled images.

Boy or girl? she wondered, not for the first time. Maggie didn't have a preference either way, as long as the baby was healthy. But she *was* curious. She glanced at Thorne to find him examining the pictures, a half smile on his face as he took in the moments his father deemed important enough to display in his office. She tried not to enjoy his unguarded expression and the sexy curve of his lip as he moved from one picture to the next. But she found herself wondering about his thoughts all the same. Did he want to know the sex as well, or would he rather be surprised? She hadn't thought to ask him before. But regardless of his preferences regarding the big reveal, they would have to start thinking about names soon; she definitely didn't want to leave that decision until the last minute.

"Can you take a break?" His question interrupted her musings, and she jerked back to attention.

"Ah, a break for what?" she asked, curiosity sparking to life. Did he have something planned? Or was he just worried she was overexerting herself and possibly harming the baby?

"I need new boots," he began. Maggie laughed, cutting him off.

"Do you need them, or are you just too chicken to wear your old ones because of possible snake cooties?"

He adopted a wounded look. "Do you think I'm that much of a coward?"

Maggie held her tongue but raised one eyebrow as she regarded him. After a second, he sighed. "Okay, yes. I want a new pair because of the snakes. Happy now?"

She giggled and nodded. "Yes. Are you asking me to help you pick some out?" Looking at work boots wasn't exactly her idea of fun, but it would be nice to get off the ranch and see some new faces. And maybe the shoe store would have something in her size as well—or rather, her new size. Her feet were already expanding, another one of those unexpected joys of pregnancy.

"Well, no, not exactly." Maggie's stomach sank and the smile slid off her face. It seemed she had once again misread his intentions. When would she learn?

"Oh." She didn't try to hide her disappointment, and Thorne's face took on an alarmed expression.

"Ah, the thing is, the boot store is just down the street from my sister Claudia's boutique. She's having her grand opening in a few days, but I know she wouldn't mind if we stopped in and looked around. I thought you might like to visit with her while I did my shopping."

The invitation was so unexpected that for a few seconds she simply stared at him, not at all sure she'd heard him correctly. Was he really going to take her into town? Since the explosion, the only time she'd been off the ranch was when she'd gone to her followup OB appointment a couple of days after her trip to the ER. It would be good to go shopping for a bit, to do something normal again.

"That sounds nice," she said, her excitement building as she thought more about the opportunity. She'd never met Thorne's sister Claudia. She did the books for his sister Jade, and she considered her to be a friend, although they weren't terribly close. A new face would be a welcome change of scenery. "When can we leave?"

He smiled, his light brown eyes warming as he looked at her. "Whenever you want."

Thorne cut the engine and glanced over at Maggie, who was practically vibrating with excitement in the passenger seat. It was good to see her so lively again; her cheeks had taken on a rosy hue, and her eyes had regained their usual sparkle. She seemed happy for the first time in days, and Thorne felt a burst of pleasure at the knowledge he had contributed to her change in mood.

"Ready?" he asked with a smile.

She nodded and took a deep breath, a flicker of unease marring her eager expression.

"What's wrong?"

Maggie blinked, apparently taken aback by the question. "Why would you ask that?"

He shrugged. "For a second there, it seemed like you were uncertain about something. Maybe I'm just seeing things."

"No," she admitted, glancing down into her lap and her folded hands. "You're not. I'm a little nervous about meeting your sister."

"You don't need to be," he said. "Claudia is a sweetheart, and I know she'll love you. I think the two of you will get along great."

A glimmer of hope shone in her eyes. "I hope so. It would be nice to make a new friend in town. My two best girlfriends stay pretty busy with their families, so we don't get to spend a lot of time together."

"I'm sure Claudia would enjoy hanging out with you," he said. "Jade would too, come to think of that. And I know they'll be thrilled to find out she's going to be an aunt."

"You haven't told them yet?" Maggie eyed him curiously, and he knew she was wondering why he'd kept such big news to himself. Truth be told, he'd wanted to shout it from the rooftops, but aside from Knox and Mac, no one else in his family knew about the baby yet. It wasn't that he didn't trust his siblings—he just didn't want the news to get out. The less Livia and her goons could find out about the baby, the better.

"I haven't had a chance to talk to either of them yet," he said, feeling a little guilty at glossing over his true reasons for keeping things a secret. But he didn't want to scare Maggie with talk of Livia; she was in such a good mood, he hated to spoil it and ruin her enjoyment of this shopping trip.

"Then this will be quite the surprise for Claudia," Maggie remarked, reaching for the door handle. Thorne slid from his seat and rounded the hood of the truck in time to offer his arm as Maggie climbed down. She landed on her feet with a quiet "oof," squeezing his biceps as she balanced herself. Even though there was nothing remotely sexual about her touch, the feel of her hand on his arm sent a thrill of sensation through his limbs, as if he'd grabbed hold of a live wire.

He ignored his body's reaction and took a step back, putting some distance between them. It was enough to clear his head again, and he locked the truck and gestured for her to walk before him as they stepped over the curb and onto the sidewalk that ran in front of the buildings. Claudia's boutique was almost at the end of the block on Main Street, wedged between Marie's Salon and Spa and The Secret Garden, a flower shop.

Thorne had to admit the building looked good, its cream paint and brown trim making it stand out from its neighbors. When Claudia had first announced the location of her boutique, he'd been skeptical. The building she'd chosen had been abandoned for a while and had fallen into a state of disrepair. But where he had seen problems, Claudia had seen opportunities. And thanks to Rafferty Construction, run by Knox's new wife, Allison, the space had been renovated and now looked better than ever.

A bright red sign hung over the door, the words *Honeysuckle Road Boutique* scripted in a whimsical font that somehow perfectly captured Claudia's free spirit. The windows of the store were papered over, but there was a square cut out of the paper covering the glass panels of the double doors. Thorne rapped on the door and a moment later was rewarded with the sight of Claudia's face framed by the brown paper.

She unlocked the door and pulled it open, grabbing his arm to practically drag him inside. "Thorne! Come in, come in! It's so good to see you!" As soon as he was fully inside she threw her arms around him, squeezing hard enough to make his ribs groan in protest.

He returned the hug but was careful not to use his full strength. "Hey there, Little Bit," he said, using his old nickname for her. "Long time, no see." Claudia had come back to Shadow Creek a little over a month ago, but between one thing and another, Thorne hadn't spent as much time with her as he would have liked. He was happy to see she looked well—her long blond hair was pulled back from her face, and she had a pencil stuck behind her ear. He glanced down at her hands and saw the telltale smudge of ink on the sides of her palms. She'd been drawing again, probably working on more sketches for her clothes or the shop.

"Are we interrupting you?" he asked.

"No, it's fine," Claudia replied. "I'm just messing around a bit with some ideas. Nothing that can't wait until later." She turned and gave Maggie a warm smile. "Forgive my manners," she said, sticking out her hand. "I'm Claudia."

"Nice to meet you. I'm Maggie."

"How do you know Thorne?" Claudia asked, eyeing them both curiously. Thorne could practically see the wheels turning in his sister's head, and realized with a sudden jolt of panic he didn't know how to describe his relationship with Maggie. She was the mother of his child, but they weren't together. There wasn't a word to adequately describe their situation; "friend" was too casual, but "partner" seemed to presume too much.

Maggie saved him. "I'm an accountant, and I do Mac's books. That's how we met."

Claudia nodded, and Thorne shot Maggie a grateful look.

"I see. What brings you into town, Thorne? Not that I don't love seeing you, but I usually have to come out to the ranch if I want to spend time with you."

"I need some new boots," he said, deciding not to tell her about the snakes. "I figured we'd drop in for a visit, and I thought Maggie could do a little shopping." He glanced around the boutique, a little disappointed to see there wasn't any merchandise yet. "I thought you might have some clothes in stock, but it looks like I was wrong."

Claudia laughed, a light, lilting sound that seemed to float in the air. "Sorry about that. I'm still several weeks away from opening, so nothing's here yet. I'm putting the finishing touches on the interior, and then I'll be ready for the goods." She gestured them over to a large wooden table a few feet away, strewed with papers and colored pencils in every shade of the rainbow. "I'd be happy to show you some of my designs, though, if you're interested."

"I am," Maggie said quickly. She followed Claudia over to the table, but Thorne hung back a bit, taking the opportunity to look around the store. It was surprisingly large inside, and the clopping of his boot heels echoed in the space as he walked across the wooden floor. There were a few shelves and racks in place already, and he could envision how traffic would flow through the store, winding from one area to another as shoppers searched for that special something. The walls were painted a fresh spring green, and the place had a warm, muted glow thanks to the papered windows blocking the harshness of the sun.

"What's with the camouflage?" he asked, fingering a corner of the paper. "Are you hiding from someone?"

He'd meant it as a joke, but Claudia didn't answer right away. He turned just in time to see a flicker of fear cross her face, but she pasted on a smile and shook her head. "Of course not," she said, laughing awkwardly. "But people are curious, and I got tired of seeing noses pressed to the glass. I want people to see the interior for the first time when the boutique opens, rather than seeing all the behind-the-scenes stuff that goes into setting the place up."

"I don't blame you," Maggie said. "I'd feel really self-conscious working in a fishbowl like that."

The women both turned back to Claudia's sketches before Thorne had a chance to respond, but he made a mental note to ask Claudia about her reaction. She'd spent the past several years in New York, and while he thought her time there had been good, maybe he was mistaken…

The women talked softly, their voices a low murmur as they bent over Claudia's pages. Thorne watched them a moment, enjoying the sight of his sister and the woman he loved—

Whoa. He mentally reared back, shying away from the word like a horse on the edge of a cliff. He had feelings for Maggie, of course, but did he really want to call them love? He wasn't even sure he knew what the word meant, at least in the romantic sense. Livia and her husband-hopping hadn't exactly set a stellar example while he was growing up, and his own relationship track record wasn't exactly impressive. Until Maggie, he'd never met a woman who made him want to risk his heart. And thanks to his stupid mistakes, he might not get another chance with her.

The easiest thing would be to maintain the status quo. He and Maggie were on stable ground, and if they weren't emotionally close, at least they didn't dislike each other. If he tried to win back her heart, there was a very real chance it would irreparably damage the truce they had formed. They were about to bring a child into the world—could he risk disturbing the peace at this delicate junction?

Yes. The answer came to him immediately, along with a sense of urgency he couldn't ignore. He knew what it was like to grow up with parents who couldn't stand each other. It wasn't the kind of life he wanted for his child. Maybe he was being old-fashioned, but he'd always figured he would get married before having a baby. He wanted to give his children the domestic stability he had never experienced, and in order to do that, he was going to have to win Maggie over.

But more than that, he wanted Maggie for herself. He'd been drawn to her from the beginning, and now that he knew her better, his attraction to her had only grown. She was an amazing woman—cool under pressure, smart, generous and kind. She was everything he'd ever wanted in a partner, and he couldn't afford to let her think she didn't matter to him.

He'd done a poor job of communicating his feelings, but that was going to change.

Starting now.

"Uh, ladies?"

Maggie and Claudia were so engrossed in her designs they didn't hear him. So he walked over and touched Maggie on the elbow. She jumped, then smiled sheepishly. "Sorry to scare you," he said. "I was thinking I could run down the street and look at boots, if you don't mind?"

Maggie shook her head. "Go on. We'll be here."

He nodded, then looked at Claudia. It was time to tell his sister the news. Ignoring the butterflies in his stomach, he said, "Take good care of them for me, will you?"

Claudia began to nod, then stopped, her eyes widening. "Wait, 'them'? Are you saying what I think you're saying?"

He smiled and winked at his sister, then leaned down and kissed Maggie's cheek. She sucked in a breath and her pupils dilated, but he couldn't tell if she welcomed the gesture or was simply shocked at his presumption. "I'm just down the block if you need me," he whispered. "I'll be back soon."

"Good luck," she said. He noted the sparkle in her eyes and his worry eased; she wasn't upset with him for the kiss. "I hope you find a nice pair."

"I will," he said. He started for the door, wanting to race through this errand so he could be back in Maggie's presence. He felt a small twinge of worry as he left the store, but he knew she would be safe with Claudia. Besides, Livia was a wanted woman—she wouldn't dare try to harm Maggie in broad daylight with witnesses around. Livia was brazen, but she wasn't stupid.

Despite the logic of his conclusion, Thorne didn't waste any time walking down the street. The sooner he was with Maggie again, the better.

Chapter 13

"Are you pregnant?" Claudia's voice was full of barely suppressed excitement and her eyes shone as she grabbed Maggie's hand. She dropped it a second later and took a half step back. "I'm sorry, that's very rude of me. I know we've only just met. But given what Thorne said…"

Maggie smiled. "It's okay. Your brother did drop a pretty big bombshell on his way out the door. In answer to your question, yes, I am pregnant."

Claudia let out a little squeal and pulled Maggie in for a quick hug. "I'm so happy for you both! When are you due?"

"November 19. But my doctor told me babies rarely come on their due date."

Claudia held her at arm's length and eyed her up and down. Even though there was no hint of judgment in her gaze, Maggie couldn't help but feel a little self-conscious at the scrutiny.

"You look amazing," Claudia decreed. "You're glowing."

Maggie felt her face heat. "I don't know about that," she protested, but Claudia held up her hand.

"No, you are," she said firmly. "You're beautiful. Thorne is a lucky man."

Her words were kind, even if they were incorrect. But Maggie didn't bother to set the record straight. Besides, she couldn't very well tell Claudia her brother was only interested in her because she was carrying his child.

"Are you in need of maternity clothes yet?" Claudia asked.

Maggie smoothed a hand over her belly, feeling the small bulge that seemed to grow bigger by the day. "Soon, I think."

Claudia looked appraisingly at Maggie's waistline and hummed thoughtfully. "You know, you have the perfect body for my clothes. I think I could easily modify some of my designs to accommodate your baby bump."

"Really? You'd do that for me?" A sense of delight filled Maggie, and her imagination took flight as she pictured herself wearing some of the beautiful clothes in Claudia's sketches. The fabrics and silhouettes in the sketches looked so glamorous and lovely—the exact opposite of the frumpy tunics she'd thought would be her only options. Maggie wasn't a clothes snob, but she did like to feel pretty. And Claudia's creations were so feminine and beautiful that Maggie knew she'd look amazing in whatever Claudia made for her.

"Of course! It would be my pleasure. You and I have the same body type—curves everywhere. I've always wanted to design clothes for women like us, since we deserve to feel pretty, too."

Maggie laughed and nodded. "That's very generous of you."

Claudia shook her head. "More like selfish. I'm getting paid to design clothes I want to wear. But I've been thinking about branching out, and designing a maternity line might be just the way to stretch my creative muscles. You'd make a great model for my prototypes."

"I'd love that," Maggie said, already looking forward to the experience.

"I do have one request, though," said Claudia, tilting her head to the side.

"Name it," Maggie said, expecting Claudia to ask for help with her books. It would be a nice way to repay Claudia for her kindness, and she would enjoy having the other woman as a client.

"I want to make your wedding dress."

Claudia's response was so unexpected it took Maggie a moment to fully process her words. "I'm sorry," she said, certain she had misunderstood. "You want to what?"

"Make your wedding dress," Claudia repeated.

"That's what I thought you said," Maggie murmured, stalling for time. How could she explain to Thorne's sister that her brother had no intention of marrying her? She didn't necessarily want to air their dirty laundry, even to Claudia, but she couldn't let the other woman labor under the misapprehension that she and Thorne were engaged.

"Are you engaged yet?" Claudia asked. "I didn't notice a ring, but that's not always a sign nowadays."

"Uh, no, we're not," Maggie said. *And we'll probably never be*, she added silently. The thought triggered a mild pang in her heart, but her acceptance of Thorne's feelings for her, or lack thereof, was growing by the day. She looked forward to a time when she could see Thorne and not feel a sense of longing for what they might have shared. Maybe she'd even get to a point where she wouldn't care if he found someone else, someone he wanted to share his life with. Anything was possible...

"Ah." Claudia nodded, as if she had expected this response. "Well, I'm sure Thorne will pop the question soon."

Maggie's first instinct was to deny the possibility, but her curiosity prevented her from contradicting Claudia. "What makes you say that?" she asked, wondering if Thorne's sister had some kind of special insight into his behavior. They had grown up together, which meant Claudia knew him better than almost anyone else. Maybe he had said something to his little sister before they came to the boutique?

"It's the way he looks at you," Claudia confided. "Thorne's always been a very private person. Even when we were kids, he was the quiet one. It was always hard to figure out what he was thinking or feeling because he kept things so close to the chest. But he's never been able to control the look in his eyes when he's around something or someone he loves. When he's working with his horses or talking to Mac, you can practically *see* the love shining in his eyes. And he had that same glow a few minutes ago, when he walked over to say goodbye to you."

"Really?" Maggie whispered. She wanted so badly to believe what Claudia was saying. But she couldn't ignore the nagging doubt in the back of her mind. Claudia may have seen the glimmer of love in her brother's eyes, but perhaps she had misinterpreted the object of his affections. It was clear Thorne was already in love with their baby. That was probably what Claudia had detected.

Maggie brushed aside her disappointment, determined not to let Claudia see her reaction. Fortunately, the other woman seemed oblivious to the dip in Maggie's mood.

"And he kissed you," Claudia continued. "He's never done that in front of family before!"

Maggie's cheek tingled with the memory of Thorne's lips on her skin. He had given her a quick peck goodbye, but she'd figured he was simply trying to keep up appearances so Claudia wouldn't ask too many questions about their relationship. If that was his plan, it had backfired spectacularly.

Not that he was here to know it.

For the first time, Maggie regretted not going with Thorne on his hunt for new boots. Claudia was a nice person, but everything she said made Maggie second-guess her interpretations of Thorne's actions. And though she appreciated the other woman's take on things, Maggie was just too tired to keep searching for signs that *might* indicate Thorne had feelings for her. Better to take him at his word and accept that their relationship was never going to go beyond friendship.

Claudia kept talking, going on about Thorne and

his previous relationships with other women. Maggie listened with half an ear, growing more uncomfortable by the minute. Under normal circumstances, she would have appreciated this glimpse into Thorne's personal life. But hearing this information from his sister felt wrong somehow, like an invasion of privacy.

Her discomfort must have shown on her face, because Claudia suddenly stopped talking. "Oh, I didn't mean to make you feel bad," she said, sounding concerned. "I just wanted you to know how special you are to him. And I can't tell you how happy I am to know he's found someone. He's been alone for so long." Claudia shook her head, a sad smile crossing her face. "I worried about him. We all did, you know." She reached out and grabbed Maggie's hand, her touch friendly and warm. "But we don't need to worry any longer!"

Maggie wasn't sure how to respond. Words piled up in her throat, forming a logjam of sentiment she didn't know how to navigate. She settled for nodding her head, which seemed to satisfy Claudia.

"Now let's talk about colors," Claudia said, turning back to her pile of sketches. "I'd love to see you in this dress. My original design has it in red, but if that's too bright for you, we can tone down the shade..."

Maggie seized on the change of subject, happy to have a reason to stop thinking about Thorne. But as much as she enjoyed talking about clothes with Claudia, she knew the woman's comments about her brother would stay in her mind.

I just wanted you to know how special you are to him...

At that moment, the door opened and the man in question strode inside. Maggie felt a brush against her elbow as Claudia jumped in surprise at his sudden entrance, but she couldn't spare the other woman a glance. Her gaze was locked on Thorne, and the half smile that appeared on his face when he saw her made her stomach flutter. She met his eyes and felt a jolt of shock as she registered the emotion shining in those dark depths.

Maybe Claudia was right after all. But if Thorne really did have feelings for her, how could she trust he cared about her for her own sake, not just because she was the mother of his child?

"You're very quiet."

"Am I?" Maggie said absently. "Sorry. I don't mean to ignore you. I just got lost in thought, I guess."

"You don't have to apologize," Thorne assured her. "Did you have a nice visit with Claudia?"

"Yes." Her tone was heavy with some kind of implication, but before he could dissect it further, she went on, "Your sister is great. Her sketches are amazing— I can't wait to see her clothes in person. And did she tell you what she's going to do for me?"

Thorne smiled to hear the excitement in Maggie's voice. "No, she didn't. But to hear you talk it must be something good."

"She's going to make me some maternity clothes! She said she wants me to serve as the model for some maternity pieces she's thinking about adding to her collection."

"That's wonderful! I'm sure you'll look beautiful in whatever she makes for you."

"You think so?" Maggie sounded doubtful.

Thorne reached over and found her hand, giving it a

squeeze. "I know so. You're already a beautiful woman. Claudia's clothes will only enhance your loveliness."

"Thank you," she said, sounding a bit choked up. "I don't mean to fish for compliments. It's just hard to feel pretty sometimes, with all the changes going on in my body right now."

"I can imagine," he said, feeling a pang of sympathy for her. He wished there was something he could do to make this time easier on her, but it was something she had to experience alone.

"I know my belly isn't very big right now, but for the past few days I've felt huge," she went on. "I might need to borrow some of your sweatpants, if you have any."

"You're welcome to anything I own. But wouldn't you rather get something that fits you properly?" He pictured her in his pants, the fabric of the legs hanging past her feet. That was a tripping hazard if he'd ever seen one...

"Well, yes, I would. Do you have time to make a quick stop? There's a band I can buy to hold my pants up until Claudia has time to make some of the clothes for me."

"That's no problem," he said, changing course to take her to the local baby store.

An hour later, they climbed back into the truck. Thorne felt overwhelmed, and he could tell by Maggie's wide eyes and thousand-yard stare that she did, as well.

"Babies sure do need a lot of things," she said quietly.

"I had no idea," he replied. He'd known about the diapers, of course, but he hadn't thought there was much more to it than that. After all, babies were tiny. How much stuff could they actually require?

A lot, if the store was anything to go by.

Where was it all going to fit? His apartment had never felt small before, but as he considered all the paraphernalia they were apparently going to need, he began to worry there might not be enough room at his place.

"Do you think all that stuff is really required?" she asked, sounding a little hopeful. "I mean, people have been having babies for centuries without all that gear. Surely most of it is just crap that we're made to think is indispensable. Right?"

"It's got to be," Thorne agreed, feeling a wave of relief at her words. "We can definitely get by with just the basics. The baby won't know if the diapers are coming out of a decorative cloth hamper or the cardboard box we bought them in. It would be silly for us to waste money on stuff like that when we'll need it for other things."

Maggie let out a sigh. "That's exactly what I was thinking. I'm glad you agree."

A warm glow started in Thorne's chest. They hadn't exactly made a huge parenting decision just now, but it was nice to know they were starting out on the same page. The quiet that settled over the cab of his truck as he drove home was calm and peaceful, a nice change from the charged silences from a few days ago. This subtle change in their interactions gave him hope he could convince Maggie of his feelings for her. Not today, of course. But soon.

He pulled into the drive and killed the engine, but didn't open the door right away. He didn't want to break this moment between them. Even though they hadn't talked much after the baby store, he felt connected to Maggie in a new way. He wanted to strengthen that tie between them before it snapped.

"I want to show you something," he said softly.

She glanced over, her expression curious. "What is it?"

"You'll see." He climbed out of the truck and walked around the hood to open her door and help her down. Taking a chance, Thorne tucked her hand in the crook of his elbow. She didn't pull away.

Mindful of her shorter stride, he led her into the barn and down the main aisle until they reached the far end. He stopped in front of the stall tucked into the back corner, away from the other horses and the noise of the dooryard.

"How's my girl?" he crooned into the shadowed depths.

There was a soft rustling, then the horse approached and stuck her golden head over the low boards of the stall door. Maggie gasped softly, but he saw she wasn't afraid.

"She's beautiful," she breathed.

"Yes, she is," Thorne agreed. He reached forward to stroke the mare's velvety-soft ears. "Her name is Yellow Rose, but we just call her Rose."

"Can I touch her?"

"Sure. Just present your hand so she can sniff you first." He took her hand and curled her fingers into a loose fist, then extended it toward Rose. "Like this," he said. "You always want to keep your fingers tucked under, in case the horse you're meeting decides to get snappy."

Maggie held her fist still as Rose snuffled her skin. She glanced over and he gave her a nod. Moving slowly, she raised her arm and placed her palm on the flat expanse of Rose's cheek. "Hello," she said quietly, stroking her gently.

Rose blinked her dark brown eyes and nuzzled against Maggie's shirt. "Oh!" Maggie said, letting out a little giggle at the horse's actions. "Does she think I have food for her?"

"She's an eternal optimist," he explained, smiling at the pair of them. "She gets a treat once a day, but that doesn't stop her from investigating every visitor in the hopes they might have a spare morsel."

"Is it time for her treat?"

Thorne checked his watch. "She's probably already had it for the day, but I suppose we can make an exception." He walked over to a bin of apples a few feet away and retrieved one, which he offered to Maggie. "Want to give it to her?"

"Oh, yes! I want her to like me."

He smiled at that, taking in Rose's relaxed stance and Maggie's obvious enjoyment of the horse's presence. "I don't think you need to bribe her with a treat for that, but here you go." He took Maggie's hand and placed the apple on her flat palm. "Hold it like this, so she doesn't accidentally nip your fingers."

Maggie offered the fruit to Rose and grinned widely as the horse lipped it up. After a few quick chomps, Rose swallowed her treat and nuzzled Maggie again.

"You're so friendly," Maggie observed. She stroked along Rose's neck, murmuring softly in her ear. Thorne leaned against the stall and watched them, a warm feeling of contentment spreading in his chest. He was happy to see the pair of them getting along so well. Yellow Rose was his favorite horse; she was a sweet, gentle soul, a true joy to be around. It meant a lot to him that Maggie liked her.

"Why are you here all by yourself?" she asked the horse. "You're so pretty and good-natured. Don't you want to play with the other horses?" She glanced quizzically at Thorne.

"Normally, she stays in a stall farther down," he said, nodding toward the front of the barn. "But I've got her back here because I don't want her to get too stressed."

"Is she sick?" Maggie stood on tiptoe and craned her neck, peering inside the dimly lit stall in an apparent search for signs of injury or ailment.

Thorne smiled at her concern. "No. But she is expecting."

"Oh," Maggie said. "When is she due?"

"Within the next ten days or so," he replied. "It's her first time foaling, so I'm keeping a close eye on her."

"You're just surrounded by pregnant females," she observed dryly.

"Yeah, but at least I know how to help the horse." He spoke without thinking, and immediately wished he could take the words back. But it was too late. *Might as well go all in*, he thought with a silent sigh. "I'm worried I won't be able to help you, when the time comes."

Maggie was silent a moment. She was facing the horse so he couldn't see her expression, but her hand continued to stroke Rose's neck with slow, sure movements. "I'm scared, too," she said, her voice small in this quiet corner of the barn. "Not that you won't help, but that I won't know what to do."

He wanted to reach out to her, to offer her the comfort of his touch. He hesitated, but decided to take a chance. He needed to show her with his actions that he truly cared.

She didn't move when he placed his hand on her shoulder. Thorne decided to take that as a good sign; she might not be jumping into his arms, but she wasn't pulling away, either. It was a start.

"I don't know much about human births, but I've seen my fair share of foalings. If people are anything like horses, your body will know what to do."

Maggie laughed softly. "I'm not actually scared of giving birth. Not yet, at least." She turned to face him, her face half-hidden by the shadows. "I like my doctor, and I know she'll do her best to help me through the delivery. It's the stuff that comes after I worry about."

"The diapers and 3:00 a.m. feedings?" he asked lightly.

She gave him a wan smile that didn't reach her eyes. "Not exactly." She paused, apparently weighing her next words. "For the longest time, I thought I wasn't going to ever be a mother. Now I can't help but wonder if I'm going to be able to handle it."

"Of course you will," he said, a little more forcefully than he'd intended. "Maggie, you're one of the strongest women I know. And you have so much love in you—it's one of the things that first drew me to you. You will make an outstanding mother. In fact, I don't think you could be a bad mother even if you tried." He squeezed her shoulder gently for emphasis.

She laughed and shook her head. "I think that's a bit of an exaggeration."

"I'm serious," he said. "I'm kind of an expert in bad

mothers. Please believe me when I tell you that you have nothing to worry about in that regard."

She turned back to Rose and began to thread her fingers through the horse's mane. "Thank you for that," she said softly. "It means a lot to know that you believe in me."

Thorne trailed his hand down her arm, his fingertips grazing her skin as he dropped his hand back down to his side. "I do," he confirmed. "You're one of the only people I do believe in. And I know my faith in you is not misplaced."

Maggie looked down, her forehead nearly touching Rose's nose. The horse sniffed inquisitively at her hair, but Maggie didn't appear to notice. He saw her throat move as she swallowed hard, and she closed her eyes. For a second, he thought he heard her whisper, "I wish you wouldn't say things like that." But her words were lost in the shuffle of Rose's feet as the horse adjusted her stance on the shavings covering the floor of her stall.

Thorne's hands itched to gather Maggie into his arms and hold her close, but he sensed she didn't want to be touched right now. So he tried to change the subject, hoping it would help lighten her mood.

"You know, I think Rose gets lonely back here during the day. I take her out for exercise, but since she's so close to foaling I've been keeping her away from the other horses. I think she might like some company, if you've a mind to visit."

Maggie sniffed quietly and visibly pulled herself together. "I'd like that," she said, blinking the sheen from her eyes. "Can I give her a treat when I come?"

Rose's ears pricked forward at the word, and the two

females regarded him with such hopeful expressions he couldn't help but smile. "That's fine," he said. "But not too many, okay?"

Maggie nodded and dropped a kiss on Rose's long nose. "I'll see you tomorrow, sweet girl."

Rose whuffed agreeably and nudged Maggie's shoulder, as if to pat her new friend goodbye.

Thorne made a mental note to set out a stool for Maggie in the morning. If she was going to spend time with Rose, he wanted to give her the option of sitting down while she visited.

They headed back to the front of the barn. Maggie smothered a yawn as they walked, and Thorne glanced at his watch, surprised to find it was later than he'd thought. No wonder she was tired—he'd kept her out for most of the day. He'd help her upstairs, get her settled on the couch with a glass of water, and then he'd head to the kitchen and whip up a quick dinner. He searched his brain, trying to come up with a mental inventory of the contents of his fridge and pantry. There had to be something he could make that would appeal to her delicate stomach...

He was so caught up in his musings that when he felt the soft touch on his upper arm he dismissed it, thinking it was simply the shifting of his shirt fabric as he moved. But then he registered the feel of Maggie's fingers as they curled around his biceps, and he realized she had reached for him as they walked.

His breath stalled in his chest and his stomach fluttered with sudden awareness. This was the first time Maggie had initiated any kind of physical contact since her car had exploded. He wanted to shout in triumph at this development, but he settled for a small, private smile. Right now, Maggie reminded him of a skittish horse showing the first signs of trust. He knew from experience it was best not to make a big fuss, lest he frighten her back into her shell. But he couldn't ignore the gesture, either. This small step forward was too important for him to pretend otherwise.

Thorne placed his hand over Maggie's in silent acknowledgment. They climbed the stairs to his apartment together, his heart glowing with renewed hope.

Chapter 14

He stared through the windshield of his car, hatred narrowing his field of vision until the only thing he could see clearly was the large red barn, standing tall and proud among the surrounding buildings.

He still couldn't believe his earlier attempts had failed. To survive a car explosion was one thing, but he'd thought for sure that being trapped in a room with angry rattlesnakes would have done the job. The man must have been born under a lucky star to still be alive.

Bastard.

Memories assaulted him, visions of Livia pelting him one after the other until he wanted to scream. He gripped the steering wheel, the solid feel of the plastic under his palms anchoring him to the here and now.

In a way, he should thank the bitch. Her escape from prison had given him the perfect cover for his revenge.

As soon as the job was done, he'd make sure the blame was placed squarely on her shoulders. No one would question it—her reputation as a vicious psychopath was well established, and no one would think twice about adding another death to her tally.

The man just had to die first.

But how? It was a question he normally didn't mind pondering. In fact, it gave him great pleasure to imagine his nemesis suffering, writhing in pain and crying out for a relief that would never come.

In hindsight, perhaps it was a good thing the explosion had failed. He would have died too quickly. The snakes would have maximized his suffering, but then again, the bites might not have proved fatal. As disappointing as it was to know the man was still alive, he relished the new opportunity to inflict pain on this most deserving target.

He focused on the barn once more, a fresh plan forming in his mind. He would need a distraction, something serious. Something that might kill his target outright. The other man's luck had to run out eventually.

But if it didn't? If his nemesis somehow survived once more?

He'd be waiting for the opportunity to strike. The man wasn't going to walk away again. He was going to end this, once and for all.

"Soon," he whispered in the silence of his car. "This will all be over soon."

The next morning, Maggie walked softly down the main aisle of the barn, eager to see Rose but not wanting to startle her by making a noisy arrival. She reached the stall door and was just about to call out when she hesitated, uncertain if the horse would remember her from yesterday. Would her sudden appearance frighten the animal? Thorne had said she was a little on edge as she approached her foaling time. What if her visit upset the horse so much she went into early labor, or otherwise hurt herself in a bid to get away from a stranger? Maggie had seen the look on Thorne's face when he'd brought her to see Rose—she could tell how special the horse was to him. She'd never forgive herself if something happened because she had made a mistake around the animal.

She took a step back, intending to sneak away without bothering Rose. The horse shifted in the stall and let out a curious-sounding whicker. Then she stuck her head over the stall and let out a welcoming whinny.

"Hello," Maggie said, stepping forward with a smile. She held her hand out for Rose to sniff, careful to make a loose fist the way Thorne had shown her yesterday. Rose nuzzled her skin with her soft nose, her whiskers a rough contrast to the velvety feel of her muzzle.

"I wasn't sure you'd remember me," she said. Rose's ears flicked forward and she tilted her head to the side as if to say, *Whyever not?* Apparently, horses were much smarter than Maggie had thought.

"How are you feeling today?" Maggie felt a little self-conscious talking to the horse as if she could really understand her words. But there was a sweet intelligence in Rose's dark brown eyes, and something told Maggie the animal comprehended quite a bit.

Rose shook her head lightly and pressed her nose to Maggie's belly. "Oh, it's like that, is it?" Maggie said with a laugh. She reached into her pocket and withdrew the apple Thorne had left on the table this morning, along with a note that read simply: *your bribe for the day.*

She presented the treat to Rose, marveling at the delicate, precise movements of such a large animal. While the horse enjoyed her treat, Maggie stepped over to the stool someone—*Probably Thorne*, she thought—had left next to the barn wall. She pulled it closer to the stall door and climbed on, settling into a comfortable position as Rose finished the fruit. A narrow window high on the wall next to the stall was open, letting in fresh air and bathing this end of the barn in a soft golden light that made Rose's pale tan coat glimmer. She looked almost too pretty to be real, and in that instant, Maggie understood why people were so passionate about these animals.

"Did you like that?"

Rose nodded once. It was probably just a coincidence, but it made Maggie smile to think the horse had actually answered her question. She expected Rose to retreat back into the quiet sanctuary of her stall now that there was no more food on offer, but she stayed put, taking the opportunity to sniff Maggie's shirt, hair, hands and face. Maggie held still during these explorations, trying not to laugh as Rose's nose grazed a ticklish spot on her neck.

Apparently satisfied, Rose pulled back to study Maggie, her soulful brown eyes aware.

Something about the horse's quiet, patient demeanor put Maggie at ease and she started talking to Rose. At first, she made meaningless small talk, offering simple platitudes as she stroked Rose's neck, cheek and mane. But as she sat there, the world seemed to shrink to the pair of them. And Maggie found herself telling the horse everything—about her long-standing crush on Thorne, their ill-advised encounter, the months of silent treatment. The destruction of her car and the surprise of her pregnancy. Her worries about taking on this new role of mother. And her naive hope that Thorne might still have feelings for her, despite all evidence to the contrary.

The words came pouring out of her, as if they'd been bottled up under pressure for so long they could no longer be contained. Fortunately, Rose was the perfect listener; she stood there, her head pressed to Maggie's chest as she talked, her eyes kind and her demeanor relaxed and nonjudgmental. It was as if the horse understood the extent of Maggie's turmoil and instinctively knew how to help.

Maggie came to the end of her story and sat in silence a moment, feeling simultaneously drained and effervescent. She was surprised at how much talking had helped loosen the tight knot of emotion she'd been carrying in the center of her chest ever since she'd slept with Thorne. Even though Rose hadn't offered any advice or suggestions, her quiet presence had been enough. Just the act of sharing her thoughts and feelings with a witness had brought Maggie a sense of relief, and she inhaled deeply, feeling like she could breathe freely for the first time in months.

"She's a good listener, don't you think?"

Maggie's heart leaped into her throat, and she whipped around in the direction of the voice. Startled by her sudden movement, Rose jerked her head back and neighed apprehensively.

"Jade! You scared me." Maggie's alarm faded rapidly, replaced by a growing sense of happiness at the sight of Thorne's sister. She considered her a friend, even though she wasn't as close to her as she was to Amber and Sonia. She reached for Rose, stroking her nose and murmuring softly in an attempt to soothe her. Rose calmed under her touch, and Maggie felt honored that the animal already seemed to trust her.

"I'm sorry, I didn't mean to startle you. Either of you." The young woman approached slowly, her hand extended for Rose to sniff. "How are you doing, pretty girl?" she said softly. "Ready to have that baby yet?"

Maggie watched Jade interact with Rose and had to smother a laugh as the horse sniffed at Jade's pockets, clearly on the hunt for another treat.

"I don't think so, mama," Jade said. "I have it on good authority you've already had your apple for the day."

Rose nickered in response, and Jade reached up to stroke her ears. "Have you enjoyed your visitor?"

To Maggie's great surprise, the horse nodded her head. She turned to glance at Jade, expecting her friend to find the coincidence amusing, but Jade wasn't laughing.

"I'm glad to hear it," she said, her tone indicating she took Rose's gesture seriously. And maybe she did. Maggie knew Jade had a way with horses, the same as Thorne. It was a trait that seemed to run in their blood, thanks to Livia's penchant for bedding ranching men— Thorne's father, Mac, was also good with animals, and Jade's father had been a horse breeder. It was quite possible the pair of them were simply more attuned to the creatures than the rest of the world, which would certainly explain why the horses appeared to love them so.

"And how are you?" Jade asked, turning her attention to Maggie. "It's good to see you."

"You, too," Maggie responded, stepping from the stool so she could give her friend a hug. Jade always made her feel like an Amazon—she was about four inches shorter and considerably smaller, her petite frame compact compared to Maggie's generous curves. Now that she had a baby on board, Maggie felt positively Godzilla-like next to her friend.

"I heard about your car," Jade said, shaking her head. "I'm so sorry."

Maggie shrugged. Truth be told, her car was the last thing on her mind these days, what with everything else going on. She knew she'd have to address the issue soon, but it paled in importance to her thoughts of the baby and her musings about Thorne. "Thanks. It was quite a shock, to say the least."

Jade nodded sympathetically. "I can imagine. Not exactly the kind of thing that happens every day. I'm just glad you weren't hurt."

"Not much, anyway."

"So I hear you're staying with Thorne," Jade said, her tone deceptively casual.

Maggie rolled her eyes. She'd known news traveled fast in Shadow Creek, but Thorne's siblings seemed to take gossip to new levels. "Is that right? Did you hear anything else?"

Jade blinked her brown eyes, the very picture of innocence. "I'm sure I don't know what you mean."

Maggie snorted inelegantly. "Who told you?"

Jade didn't respond right away and, unless Maggie missed her guess, her friend was trying to decide which sibling to throw under the bus. Several of them could have been the source of the gossip: Knox, Claudia, or even Thorne himself. *Although if Thorne had told his sister, it wasn't really gossip*, she mused. The baby was just as much his news as hers.

"I stopped by Claudia's boutique yesterday—apparently I just missed you and Thorne. She was practically dancing in excitement."

"I see," said Maggie, smiling at the thought.

"To be fair, she did try to keep the news to herself. But once Leonor and Josh showed up, she couldn't hold it in any longer."

"Leonor was there?"

Jade nodded. "Yeah. She and Josh were scouting wedding locations. By the way, have you seen Leonor's ring?"

Maggie shook her head. "I bet it's beautiful, though."

"It is," Jade confirmed. "But I think it's way too big to be practical."

Maggie laughed. "Your sister doesn't work with her hands the way you do. I doubt it will get in her way." For a brief second, Maggie felt a pang of longing for a ring of her own. She knew Thorne wasn't the type to propose with a huge diamond, but part of her wondered what kind of ring he would pick out. *Doesn't matter*, she told herself, brushing the question aside. She would drive herself crazy if she focused on hypothetical situations instead of reality.

"You're probably right," Jade said. "But back to you. Is it true?"

Maggie hesitated for a heartbeat. Jade was Thorne's sister; shouldn't she hear the news from him first? But she just as quickly reconsidered. Jade was more than a client, she was her friend, and it would be nice to tell someone who would be happy for her. "It's true," she confirmed. "Rose isn't the only one who's expecting around here."

Jade let out a small squeal and launched herself at Maggie, grabbing her and hugging her tightly. "I'm so excited for you! Claudia said you're due in November, is that right?"

Maggie nodded and laughed as Jade came in for another hug. "How are you feeling?" she asked, glancing up and down Maggie's body. "You look great!"

"Thanks." She appreciated the compliment, and knew Jade wasn't just telling her that to be polite. "I'm tired, but mostly okay. My stomach gets a little queasy now and then, but it's nothing too bad. At least not yet."

Jade's eyes practically glowed with excitement. "You're going to be a mom." Her voice was tinged with awe. "Can you believe it?"

Yes, I am. The thought never failed to fill Maggie with joy. Despite her worries about her abilities as a mother, the fact that she was going to have a baby still made her almost giddy with anticipation. She couldn't wait to meet the little one growing inside her.

"I'm still adjusting," Maggie admitted. "Some moments, it doesn't seem real."

"I can imagine." Jade raked her fingers through Rose's mane, skillfully detangling the strands of hair. "I was pretty shocked when Claudia told me. I had no idea you and Thorne were even an item."

"We, uh, aren't. Not really." Maggie felt her face heat and was grateful for the dim lighting in this portion of the barn. "It was kind of a onetime thing."

Jade's jaw dropped. "Are you serious? What happened?"

"I don't know if you remember, but we had a big storm roll through here in February."

Jade nodded. "Yeah. The winds knocked down a few fence panels and spooked my horses."

"Well, I was out here doing Mac's books. My car wouldn't start, so I called a tow and was all set to wait. Thorne saw me sitting in my car, and he invited me inside for dinner. And…well…"

"Okay," Jade said. "But you've had a crush on Thorne for forever. Why didn't it last?"

"You knew about that?" Maggie's stomach dropped. She'd thought she'd done a good job of keeping her feelings under wraps, but apparently she had broadcast them for all the world to see.

"Only because you're my friend," Jade assured her. "I saw the look on your face once, after Thorne had passed by. That's how I figured it out."

Maggie nodded, relieved to know she hadn't been pathetically obvious after all. "After that night, Thorne pulled away. At first, he kept giving me excuses as to why he couldn't see me or go out with me. He took longer and longer to respond to my calls. Eventually, I got a clue and stopped trying to talk to him."

"What the hell?" Jade crossed her arms and frowned. "That doesn't sound like Thorne. Mac raised us better than that." She looked ready to storm out of the barn in search of her brother, her expression making it clear she wanted to give him a piece of her mind.

Maggie's heart warmed to see Jade ready to defend her, even against her own brother. "He said he was trying to protect me. That he was worried about what people would think of me if they knew we were together. He claimed he didn't want Livia's reputation to stain mine."

Jade snorted. "That's about the dumbest thing I've ever heard. Men can be so pig-headed. Did I tell you about my boyfriend?"

Maggie shook her head. "I don't think so—I didn't even know you had one." Guilt bloomed in her chest. Had she been so wrapped up in her own problems she'd missed this new development in her friend's life?

Jade waved her hand. "I don't. Not anymore. He broke it off after Livia escaped. Said he didn't want to be involved with my family and its problems."

"I'm so sorry." Maggie's heart clenched for her friend. How unfair for Jade! "On the bright side, it sounds like you're better off without him. A man that would leave you over something like that is not someone who deserves you."

"Thanks," Jade said, smiling briefly. "It hurt at first, but I'm over it now. But my point is that Thorne isn't the only ridiculous man out there."

"That's for sure."

Rose whickered softly, as if to add her agreement. Maggie and Jade both laughed, and Maggie reached out to pat the horse's cheek.

"It sounds like things are improving between you two, though," Jade observed. "Has Thorne come to his senses?"

"Not exactly," Maggie said. "He asked me to stay with him because he's worried someone is trying to hurt me." She told Jade about the snakes in Mac's office. "So you see," she finished, "he wants me close because he's worried about the baby, not because he has feelings for me."

Jade put her hand on Maggie's shoulder. "I'm so sorry," she said quietly, her voice full of sympathy. "My brother is an idiot if he doesn't realize how wonderful you are."

Maggie swallowed past the sudden lump in her throat. "Thanks," she said. "It's hard, because I still have feelings for him. But I'm learning to manage them. I want this baby to know its father, so I'm going to have to find a way to be around Thorne without letting my emotions get in the way."

Jade pulled her in for a hug, this embrace gentle in comparison to her earlier, enthusiastic ones. "Hang in there. You'll get through this."

I hope so, Maggie thought. *I really do.*

Chapter 15

Thorne stood rooted in place, shock locking his muscles so that he couldn't move. Maggie's words swirled around in his brain, playing on a seemingly infinite loop.

He wants me close because he's worried about the baby, not because he has feelings for me... I still have feelings for him...

He hadn't set out to eavesdrop on Maggie and his sister. He'd been pulling weeds next to the barn when he'd heard the women's voices floating out from the open window above him. The idea of Maggie visiting with Rose had made him smile—it was good to know his girls were getting along so well.

At first, he hadn't been able to make out their conversation. It was just a light, lilting hum in the air, a nice accompaniment to offset the drudgery of his task.

But then the wind had shifted a bit, and Maggie's words had come through loud and clear.

Dad was right, he thought. The confirmation of his father's statement filled him with both relief and sadness. Relief, because now he knew what was truly bothering Maggie. But his heart ached to know that she really thought he didn't care about her for herself.

Not that he could blame her. He'd been so worried about keeping her safe from Livia and her goons, he hadn't taken the time to convey his true feelings. He'd tried to change after Mac had pointed out his mistake, but clearly he'd been too subtle in his efforts to convince Maggie he wanted her for her own sake.

He had to do better. She deserved more. And his child deserved parents who were happy together, not two people who kept each other at arm's length.

Thorne stood and brushed the dirt from his knees. Determination welled in his chest, edged with a faint twinge of guilt for having eavesdropped on what was clearly meant to be a private conversation. Should he tell her what he'd heard? Or would it be better for him to redouble his efforts without Maggie knowing he'd heard her confession to Jade?

No. He dismissed the latter option almost as soon as the thought entered his head. If he and Maggie were going to build a relationship, it had to be based on honesty and trust. And while keeping this a secret would spare them both an awkward conversation, it was not going to help them move forward in the long run.

His mind made up, Thorne reached down and scooped up the bag of weeds, then set off around the side of the barn. He and Maggie needed to talk, and he wasn't going to put this conversation off any longer.

* * *

"I can't believe you actually talked Mac into updating his records!" Jade shook her head, a smile playing at the corners of her mouth. "You know that's a sign of just how much he likes you, right?"

Maggie laughed. "To be honest, I think he just felt sorry for me, knowing I was stuck in Thorne's apartment with nothing to do. I think he figured working on his office would keep me out of trouble."

"And has it?"

"For the most part, yes. Except for the snakes, but that wasn't really my fault."

"True. I have to say, I don't know how you can handle all this excitement—first your car, then the baby and the—" Jade broke off, and a second later, Maggie heard the sound of heavy footsteps that had distracted her friend. They both turned to look, and Maggie's heart leaped into her throat when she caught sight of Thorne headed their way.

"I think that's my cue," Jade whispered, winking at Maggie before facing her brother. "Hey, you," she said. "I was going to come say hi after I checked on Yellow Rose. But I got a little distracted." She slung her arm around Maggie's shoulders and pulled her in for a half hug.

Thorne smiled at his sister. "No problem," he said easily. "She's better company, I'm sure."

"Most definitely," Jade agreed. "Rose is looking good. I think this baby will make an appearance next week, for sure."

"Uh-huh," Thorne said absently. He nodded at his sister's observation, but his eyes never left Maggie's face. She fought the urge to squirm a little under his scrutiny. Why was he watching her so closely? There was an element of conviction in his expression she'd never seen before, like he was a man on a mission.

And she was his target.

Her stomach fluttered and she found herself wishing they were alone. As much as she enjoyed Jade's company, she could tell Thorne had something to say and she knew he wasn't going to talk in front of an audience.

"I should get going," Jade said, her glance darting between Maggie and Thorne. "I need to say hi to Mac, and then I should get back to my own horses."

"Thanks for stopping by," Thorne said. The words were polite, but his tone made it clear he was ready for his sister to leave.

Jade laughed softly, apparently undeterred by his dismissal. "My pleasure, brother. Call me when Rose goes into labor. I'll come by to help."

"Sure thing."

Maggie tore her gaze away from Thorne's face and offered Jade a smile. "It was great to see you."

"You, too." Jade hugged her gently. "I'll come visit you again soon, now that I know you're here." Her eyes darted over to Thorne and she grinned. "It's important for us girls to stick together."

"Absolutely."

Jade gave Rose a farewell pat on the nose, then turned and started down the central aisle of the barn, headed for the big open doors at the opposite end. Maggie and Thorne watched her go, the silence building between them as Jade's form grew smaller.

What's going on? she wondered. Did he have bad news for her? She instinctively reached for Rose, her nerves calming as soon as she touched the horse. Hopefully she could convince Thorne to talk here, so she could stay by Rose. She drew comfort from the horse's presence, which was something Thorne, of all people, should understand.

He waited until Jade had left the barn before turning back to face her. His broad shoulders rose and fell as he took a deep breath, and Maggie realized he was nervous. *That* was interesting; Thorne always seemed so unflappable. What could possibly be affecting him?

"I need to say something to you, and I'd like for you to listen while I get it all out. Can you do that for me, please?"

Maggie nodded mutely.

"I heard you talking to Jade just now. I was working outside, and your voices carried through the open window."

Maggie's body went cold, then flushed hot as she realized Thorne had overheard her confession to Jade. *He's here because he feels sorry for me*, she realized, her stomach roiling with embarrassment. *He's going to try to let me down easy.*

She curled her fingers into Rose's mane and looked down, unable to meet his gaze. She didn't want to see the sympathy in his eyes, or else she would burst into tears and mortify herself further.

Thorne's touch was gentle as he placed his hand on her face, cupping her cheek. His skin smelled like earth and grass, like spring itself. *He's been working in the dirt*, said a remote part of her brain, as if that mattered right now. "Maggie." His voice was husky with emotion. "Oh, Maggie. I've been such an idiot." He took a step closer, charging the air between them with the heat from his body. Maggie's heart thumped hard as her body celebrated his proximity, even as her heart continued to break.

"I know I'm not the best communicator," he said wryly. "That's something I'm trying to improve, especially where you're concerned. But after hearing what you said to Jade, I realize I have a lot more work to do."

Thorne trailed his fingers along the curve of her jaw, down to her chin. He gently lifted her head until she met his eyes, and the emotion she saw in his light brown gaze made her catch her breath.

"I am so sorry I ever made you feel like I only care about the baby. It breaks my heart to know you think you don't matter to me. You do, Maggie. You're the only woman I've ever felt so strongly about. And I know I made a mess of things earlier, but you have to know that wasn't because I don't care about you. It sounds crazy, but I screwed things up between us because I care about you too much."

His words washed over her, so unexpected that she struggled to keep up with what he was saying. It was almost too good to be true, but his expression was so sincere, so open, that Maggie couldn't help but believe he was being honest.

"I want you," he said simply. "Not just because of the baby. I've wanted you ever since I first laid eyes on you. But I was too much of a coward to do anything, and then after we shared that night together, I let my fear get in the way. I'm not going to make that mistake again."

His hands were warm on her arms, his touch simultaneously urgent and gentle. She could feel the leashed energy in his grip, the power he was holding in check so as not to hurt her. "I want us to be a family. You and me, for now. And eventually, the three of us." He reached out to touch the swell of her belly, hidden under the large shirt she wore. "I don't deserve you, or this baby. But I swear to you, on everything I hold dear, I will do whatever it takes to prove my feelings for you."

Maggie blinked hard, trying to clear her eyes of the stinging tears that threatened to fall. Part of her couldn't believe this was happening, that Thorne truly had feelings for her. She'd spent so much effort trying to convince her heart to get over him—she'd never expected this turn of events.

Claudia was right after all, she thought, shaking her head at the way things had turned out.

Thorne's face fell, and Maggie realized he had mistaken her gesture for rejection. She grabbed his arm before he could withdraw. There had been too much miscommunication between them, too many missed signals. She wasn't going to let it happen again.

"Claudia told me she thought you cared for me," she explained. "I didn't believe her. I guess I should have."

He relaxed, the tension leaving his body with his breath. "Does this mean you'll give me a chance?"

Maggie nodded, unable to contain the smile spreading across her face. "Yes. We've wasted too much time already. I don't want to waste any more."

"I was hoping you'd say that." Thorne stepped closer, nudging her legs apart until he stood between them. He looked down at her face, his eyes flicking from her lips to her nose, her eyebrows to her cheekbones. It was as if he was trying to catalog her features, to imprint them in his mind. Maggie took the opportunity to study him in return, her gaze tracing the slope of his nose, the wind-roughened skin of his cheeks and the dark shadow of stubble along his jaw. He was so beautiful, so graceful. Just like the horses he loved.

And he's mine, she marveled. The urge to touch him rose in her chest, and she realized with a spurt of joy that she didn't have to restrain herself. Thorne cared for her, the same way she did for him. She could touch him, kiss him, and he would welcome it.

She lifted her hand and placed it flat on his chest, directly above his heart. It beat steady and sure against her palm, a visceral sensation that grounded her in this moment, to this man. The misery and heartache that had wrapped her in a cocoon of melancholy dissolved away, leaving her exposed and able to soak up Thorne's presence and the pledge he'd made to her and their baby. In a way, this was a rebirth for them. A new start to their relationship, a chance to get it right. Not just for the baby, but for them, as well.

The whinny of a horse drifted in through the open window, and Rose nickered softly in response. Her nose brushed against Maggie's shoulder as she shook her head, nudging her closer to Thorne.

The contact made Maggie wobble on the stool, but Thorne placed his hands on her shoulders, steadying her before she slipped off. "I forgot we have an audience," he said wryly.

"And a determined one at that," Maggie said. Rose was hungry again, as evidenced by her insistent exploration of Maggie's hair, her neck, back and any other part within reach.

"Rose," Thorne chided. It was obvious he was trying to be stern, but the affection in his tone ruined the effect.

Maggie giggled and he turned to look at her, his expression quizzical. "What's so funny?"

"I just realized I'm probably going to be the disciplinarian when it comes to parenting."

He raised one eyebrow and tilted his head to the side. "What makes you say that?"

"Please. You try to act tough, but you're such a softie where she's concerned." Maggie nodded at Rose, who remained unfazed by Thorne's admonishment. "Do you really think you'll be able to tell your child no?"

He rubbed his nose with his index finger, appearing to consider the question. "Well…" He shifted his weight and scuffed at the dirt with the toe of one boot. "Anything is possible, right?" His smile was pure masculine charm, and Maggie couldn't help but laugh.

Thorne laid his hands on her hips and moved closer, his eyes warm with affection. "I love the sound of your laugh," he said, his voice husky. "It's been too long since I've heard it."

Maggie swallowed, suddenly very aware of his proximity. Goose bumps appeared on the exposed skin of her arms, and the fine hairs at the back of her neck stood on end with anticipation. The rustling of Rose's movements faded to insignificance as Maggie's senses blocked out everything that wasn't related to the man in front of her.

His breath was warm on her cheek and smelled faintly of mint, likely from some long-ago discarded piece of gum. He was so close she could see the flecks of gold in his light brown eyes and the beat of his pulse in the hollow of his neck. His Adam's apple bobbed as he swallowed, and his tongue darted out to moisten his lips.

"Maggie." Her name was a whisper in the still air. "Please... I need to kiss you."

"Yes."

He dropped his head, his lips claiming hers while the word still hung between them. He explored her mouth with a leisurely finesse, as if he had all the time in the world to devote to the task at hand. Maggie gripped his shoulders as the world spun around her, the barn orbiting the pair of them with dizzying speed.

A frisson of unease sparked in the recesses of her brain, cutting through the intoxicating feeling of Thorne's embrace. Something was wrong, but she couldn't quite put her finger on what...

Rose neighed, and even Maggie could detect the note of alarm in her vocalization. Thorne jerked back, eyeing the horse with concern. Maggie tightened her grip on his arm, needing him to stay put. Vertigo clouded her senses, and she feared if he moved away she would fall off the tall stool.

Thorne turned his focus back to her, and his eyes widened. "Are you okay?"

Maggie took a deep breath to clear her head, but the air burned her nostrils. "Do you smell that?" Were the pregnancy hormones wreaking havoc with her sense of smell, or was that really—?

"Smoke," Thorne confirmed grimly. "I think the barn is on fire."

Chapter 16

"Fire?" Maggie echoed blankly. "But how—?"

Thorne gripped her arms and pulled her off the stool to stand in front of him. He shared her confusion, but now was not the time to worry about how the fire had started. He had to get Maggie and Rose to safety before the place burned down around them.

Rose tossed her head and squealed. He had to get her out of here before she hurt herself; if she started to throw herself at the walls in a bid to escape, she might also lose the foal.

Maggie reached for the horse, but Rose was too scared to respond. Thorne bent and scooped Maggie up, pulling her away from Rose's bared teeth and sharp hooves.

He headed down the main aisle of the barn, squinting to see through the growing haze of smoke.

"Thorne!" Maggie twisted in his arms, reaching for the horse. "We can't leave her!"

"I'm not," he replied. The smoke burned his throat, making it hard to talk. The light from the barn entrance was just a dull glow now, growing dimmer by the second. If he didn't move fast, he wouldn't be able to find his way out.

Cries of alarm sounded outside as people began to notice the smoke pouring out of the barn. Thorne's head spun and his vision grew dark around the edges, but he pushed on, ignoring the burning protest of his lungs. Maggie coughed in his arms, her body jerking spasmodically against his chest.

Hang on, he thought.

The yell of voices grew louder, and Thorne thought he heard his name. Then Mac was there, his hands sure and strong as he gripped Thorne's shoulders. He lifted Maggie and yelled for Thorne to follow him out, then turned and made for the exit.

Thorne took a step after his father, needing a breath of fresh air before he went back for Rose. But just then, the horse let out an ear-piercing scream and he heard the unmistakable *thud* of a body slamming into a stall door. Rose was panicking. He couldn't leave her.

He tried to shout after Mac, but his father had already disappeared behind the billows of thick gray smoke. Thorne headed back for the horse, hoping he wasn't too late. Fortunately, all the other animals were out in the pasture. Rose was the only one left in the barn.

The air was a little better by Rose's stall, thanks to the cracked window high in the wall. Thorne reached up and pushed it all the way open, then stood on his tiptoes and pressed his face to the gap, sucking in a deep breath of fresh air. His head cleared a bit, the sickening swimming sensation receding just enough that he thought he might be able to function.

With one last gasp, Thorne turned from the window and reached out for Rose. She tossed her head, the whites of her eyes visible even in the gloom of the smoke. She stamped at the ground and threw herself against the door of her stall. The boards creaked under the strain—if she kept this up, the door would splinter and she'd impale herself on the shards. He had to get her under control, and quickly.

Thorne tugged off his shirt and draped it over Rose's eyes. She stilled instantly, but he could feel the fine tremblings of her muscles and knew she wouldn't remain calm for long. Keeping one hand on the ends of his shirt to hold it in place, Thorne fumbled with the latch on the stall door. The lack of visibility made the task harder than it should be—the smoke was chokingly thick, and tears flooded his eyes and streamed down his face, blurring what little he could see.

Finally, he freed the latch and pulled the door open. As if sensing her imminent freedom, Rose jerked forward, very nearly knocking him down in her haste to get out of the stall. Thorne hung on to the ends of his shirt for dear life as Rose took off, apparently smelling the exit despite the overwhelming stench of fire.

He was grateful for her urgency—it might be the only thing that got him out of there alive. It was becoming more difficult to breathe, and the air in the barn felt like an oven. He heard the sizzle and pop of wood and realized the whole place was melting around him.

A shower of sparks fell from the ceiling, bits of

bright heat that singed his hair and undershirt where they landed. Rose squealed in pain, and he heard the echoing answer of voices, straining to rise over the growing roar of the flames. The barn had never seemed so large before, but now it stretched out before him, an endless length he feared he might not be able to cross.

He sensed, rather than saw, the approach of bodies in the gloom. Hands descended on him, coming from all sides. They gripped his shirt, his arms, even the back of his belt. Thorne surrendered to their grip and allowed himself to be carried, trusting they would see to Rose, as well.

They burst into the courtyard and Thorne dropped his head, the sun blindingly bright after the thick, black smoke of the barn. He sucked in a breath, his chest so tight he felt like it must be about to burst open.

Someone pushed him to the ground, urging him to lie flat. He tried to wave them off, but he couldn't suck in enough oxygen to power his muscles.

"Maggie." He tried to say her name, but it came out as a croak. He cracked open his eyes, peering through the narrow slits of his swollen lids to search for her. From his vantage point on the ground he saw a sea of jean-clad legs milling around, ranch hands and employees darting here and there as they tried to clear space around the barn. The wail of sirens sounded above the din, steadily growing louder.

"Thorne!"

He turned in the direction of the voice, his heart thumping hard. "Maggie?" He sat up and reached out for her, his vision still too blurry to be trusted.

She grabbed his hand and then she was in his arms, her body pressed against his, whole and safe. He felt the swell of her belly against his stomach and wrapped his arms around her, relief flooding him. She had made it out. *They* had made it out.

"Rose?"

"Mac has her. She's fine," Maggie said. Her hand felt cool on his cheek and he turned into her touch. "Just rest now," she said. "We're all okay." She moved out of his arms and knelt by him, smoothing her hand over his forehead in a soothing caress.

Thorne nodded and lay back, the adrenaline draining from his muscles and anchoring him to the ground like the roots of a tree. The fire still raged behind him, and he realized with a sense of utter detachment that the supply building and his apartment were probably not going to survive. But he was too drained to care.

Maggie and the baby were safe, along with Rose and her foal. It was enough for now.

The wooden surface of Mac's kitchen table gleamed in the late afternoon sun, a homey, welcoming sight that was absurdly comforting after the destruction of the day. Maggie smoothed her hand across the top, feeling the small nicks and scratches that had accumulated over the years. How many times had Thorne or his siblings sat here, working on homework or eating an after school snack? She closed her eyes, picturing it all too well—the kids gathered round, laughing and talking, enjoying this oasis from the craziness of life with Livia. From everything she'd heard, Mac's house had served as both respite and refuge for Thorne and his siblings.

It was a role that continued to this day.

"Are you sure you're all right?" Knox bent at the

waist to peer at Thorne, his expression skeptical as he considered his brother's haggard appearance.

Thorne regarded Knox with bloodshot eyes, his gaze steady despite his evident fatigue. "I'm fine." A faint wheeze accompanied his words, a testament to all the smoke he'd inhaled in the barn.

"You don't sound fine," Knox said.

Maggie considered telling Knox not to bother—she'd already had this argument with Thorne, and he'd refused to go to the hospital, claiming it was unnecessary. He had allowed the paramedics to administer oxygen, but he'd brushed off their advice to go to the emergency room. He was determined to remain at the ranch, and no amount of talking from her or from Mac had changed his mind.

"Please," she'd said, practically begging him to go. His face was covered in soot, and there were raw patches on his skin where he'd been burned. But there was a fierce glint in his eyes and she'd realized that despite his injuries, Thorne remained unbroken.

"I can't," he'd said. His voice was so hoarse her throat ached in sympathy with every word he spoke. "Everyone and everything I care about is here. If they take me to the hospital, I'll be too far away."

"I'll go with you."

He'd smiled, his lip cracking with it. "And Mac? And Rose? I can't leave her behind—she's still scared. I want to be close if she goes into labor."

"You're going to catch the foal?" Maggie had said, placing her hand on his cheek. "You can barely stand up."

"I'll use your stool," he'd said, undeterred.

Now he sat at his father's kitchen table, elbows

propped on the surface as he dismissed his brother's concern. "Don't worry about it. The only thing that matters is that no one was hurt." He reached over for Maggie's hand, giving it a squeeze.

Knox straightened and took the chair across from Thorne. "True. I'm sorry about your apartment, though."

Thorne shrugged. "It's just stuff. And not that much of it at that."

Mac snorted softly. "I guess that's one way to find the silver lining."

"Do we know what caused the fire?" Thorne glanced at Mac. "The barn isn't that old, so the wiring shouldn't be a problem. And I haven't noticed any damage that might cause a spark to escape."

Mac frowned. "I haven't seen anything like that, either. But it's possible I missed it. Maybe rodents got into the walls and chewed through the wires?"

"Or maybe," Knox said darkly, "this wasn't an accident after all."

Thorne and Mac fell silent and Maggie realized Knox had stated what everyone was thinking. She wasn't surprised, a fact that should have bothered her. But she'd grown used to living in the shadow of an unknown threat over the past few days. Part of her had been expecting another strike, and it was almost a relief to have it behind her.

One thing was certain: the person behind these attacks was growing bolder. And while the first two episodes had specifically targeted Maggie, the fire made no such discrimination.

Her stomach twisted at the knowledge that Mac had lost his barn and Thorne his home because someone was trying to hurt her. She knew it wasn't her fault, but she still felt guilty about it. None of this would have happened if she hadn't been staying at the ranch.

"I'm so sorry," she whispered.

All three men turned to look at her, their expressions ranging from incredulity to dismay. "I hope you only mean that in the general sense," Mac said gently. "Because this is most definitely not your fault."

"I know," she said. "But I can't help thinking that if I wasn't here—"

"Stop it." Thorne's broken voice sliced right through her words. "I will not have you blaming yourself for the deranged actions of another. Besides, I need you by my side. I don't care if the world crumbles around us, as long as you're with me."

His declaration made her heart sing and Maggie swallowed hard, touched by his words. It wasn't just the display of emotion that meant a lot to her—it was the fact Thorne had made such a public statement of his feelings for her. He was normally a quiet, private man, so this simple act was tantamount to shouting from the rooftops.

Mac and Knox exchanged a knowing look. Then Knox turned back and cleared his throat. "Thorne is right," he said. "You're not to blame. In fact, I'm starting to think you might not be the target at all."

"What makes you say that?" Mac slid a cup of coffee in front of Thorne and sat in the last empty chair. "It was her car that exploded, and she was the one to find the snakes in my office."

"True," said Knox. "But who else was nearby when those things happened?"

"Thorne," Maggie said, grasping the implications at once.

Thorne shook his head. "That doesn't make any sense. My presence was just a coincidence. Surely if someone were really after me, they'd target me directly."

"Maybe not," said Mac. "Perhaps whoever is doing this is trying to be cagey about it. They want us to think Maggie is in danger so you don't think about your own safety."

Thorne opened his mouth to argue, but Maggie jumped in before he had a chance to say anything. "Think about it," she said. "Whoever set the barn on fire today had to know that you wouldn't leave until all the horses were out. You risked your life to save Rose, and you could have easily died."

"She's right," Knox said. "Everyone knows how much you love the horses. The arsonist was probably counting on your heroics, thinking your death would look like an accident."

A chill slid down the valley of Maggie's spine as she realized just how close Thorne had come to death today. She reached for his hand, needing to feel the reassurance of his warm flesh and solid bones.

"I suppose that's possible," Thorne said slowly.

"It's exactly the kind of thing Livia would do," Mac said, shaking his head in evident disgust.

"Do the authorities still think she's in Vegas?" Thorne said. "You told me earlier she'd been spotted on hotel security footage."

"Ah, no," Knox said. He ran a hand through his hair, mussing the short brown strands. "They took a closer look at the tapes, and some things about the woman didn't ring true. The local police got involved, and it turns out the woman in the footage was hired as a decoy."

"Do they know who hired her?" Mac asked.

Knox shook his head. "They're still tracing that back. Whoever contacted her made sure to leave a lot of false trails and dead ends, so it's a difficult investigation."

"But the important thing is that Livia isn't in Vegas, and probably never was," Thorne said. He turned to face Maggie, his expression miserable. "Here I thought I was keeping you safe by having you stay close. But it looks like I put you in even more danger."

"Stop it," she said, giving his hand a squeeze. "Don't think like that."

"I should have realized it from the beginning. It never did make sense for someone to target you," Thorne said, shaking his head. "I figured Livia was trying to hurt you to get to me, but I should have known that approach was too subtle for her."

"She always did have a flair for the dramatic," Mac commented.

"I think you should go stay with your parents for a while, at least until we get things figured out here."

Thorne's words hit her like a slap. "You can't be serious." After all that talk of needing her by his side, he wanted her to leave at the first sign of trouble?

"Maggie, I don't want you around me right now." He squeezed her hand, as if to soften the blow of his words. "Livia isn't going to stop until she's caught or I'm dead. We've been lucky so far. Your injuries have been relatively minor. But our luck is going to run out eventually, and I can't take a chance with your safety. Or the baby's."

His worries made sense, but Maggie still didn't like the idea of leaving him to face the danger alone. "You just said you didn't care if the world fell apart around us, as long as we're together."

"Yes, but—"

"Don't you think I feel the same way about you?"

Thorne's mouth snapped shut, so she pressed her advantage. "If our roles were reversed, and I was the one in danger, would you leave me for the sake of your own safety?"

"No. But you're carrying our child. And as much as I want to be selfish and keep you by my side, I'd never forgive myself if something happened to either one of you."

"But what if we're playing into Livia's hands? What if she wants us to separate so she can target me without you nearby?"

Thorne frowned, apparently considering the possibility.

"Think about it," she said. "When my car exploded you were there to pull me away from the wreckage. You got me out of Mac's office before the snakes had a chance to strike. And you carried me out of the barn. Each time, you've been close enough to help me. And even though I might not be her primary target, Livia has got to know by now that you want to keep me safe. If you send me away, who's to say she won't take the opportunity to come after me?"

"She's right," Knox said. "I know you don't want to hear it, little brother, but I don't think the two of you should split up right now. There's still too much we don't know about this situation, and we don't want to do anything that might make things worse. I know I'd feel better if you both stayed close, at least until we figure out who's behind all this."

"Yeah, well I'm not really sure how we're going to do that, seeing as how my place is currently a smoldering wreck."

"You can stay with me," Knox offered.

"No." Thorne's refusal was instantaneous. "I appreciate the offer, but your family has been through enough already. I'm not going to put Allison and Cody at further risk—your son has been through enough already. Plus, you and Allison are practically still newlyweds. She's a great woman, but I doubt she wants a pair of roommates while you two are still setting up house."

"We'll stay at my place," Maggie said. She would miss seeing Rose and Mac every day, but it was the only possible solution.

Knox frowned. "I don't like the idea of you two off by yourselves…"

"And I can't leave Rose," Thorne added. "Not when she's so close to foaling."

"You'll stay here." Mac's tone was commanding and final. "There's plenty of room for you both, and I can keep an eye out while you two lie low for a few days." He nodded at Thorne. "I'll put Rose in the old barn, and you'll be at hand when she goes into labor. But I don't want you doing anything else, is that clear? You are to stay inside and rest. Don't make yourself a target."

Thorne wrinkled his nose. "You really expect me to stay in bed all day? I'll go out of my mind!"

"No, you won't," Maggie said, unable to contain her smile. It was a little petty, she knew, but part of her was happy that Thorne was going to get a small taste of what her life had been like recently. "If you're nice to me, I'll share my crossword puzzles with you."

Chapter 17

Thorne followed his father down the hall, treading a familiar path back to his childhood room. Mac opened the door and stood to the side so Maggie could pass by. Thorne stopped at the doorway, surveying the space that was at once familiar and strange.

It didn't look the same, of course. Mac had long ago taken down his movie posters and boxed up his shelves of model cars. His colorful collection of horse show ribbons no longer hung in rows on the wall. But Thorne still remembered the nights he'd spent here. It had always been a special treat to stay with Mac, and his father had made sure Thorne had a space to call his own. Livia hadn't let Thorne or his siblings display any kind of personalization in their rooms at her house, but Mac had been happy to hang pictures and paint the walls, giving him the kind of fun retreat every little boy deserved.

"Looks a little different now, doesn't it?" Mac said.

Thorne nodded, taking in the soft gray walls, the midnight blue bedspread and the sheer curtains that softened the late afternoon sun streaming in through the large window. The place looked serene and peaceful, a refuge from the noise and dirt of the ranch.

"I like what you've done with the place," Thorne quipped.

Mac smiled and clapped his hand on Thorne's shoulder. "All your stuff is in boxes in the attic, just waiting for you to claim."

"Thanks, Dad." His tone was sarcastic, but Thorne was touched that Mac had saved all the bric-a-brac from his childhood. Livia would have never thought to preserve any of her children's memories like that. "Think you can store them a little longer until I get a new place?"

"I imagine that can be arranged." Mac stepped back into the hall, his hand sliding off Thorne's shoulder. "You remember where the bathroom is. There are clean towels and new toothbrushes in the cabinet. I'll let you two get settled for now." He nodded at Maggie, who smiled sweetly at him.

"Thank you so much," she said. "This is so generous of you."

Mac snorted. "Nonsense. You're family. I'm not going to leave y'all on your own at a time like this." He nodded at Thorne. "Take a few hours to wash up and rest. I've got to go back to the barn and start the cleanup. I'll come back with food later." He started to leave, but Thorne couldn't let him walk away just yet.

"Dad."

Mac stopped halfway down the hall. "Yes?"

Thorne walked back to his father and pulled him in for a hug. "Thanks," he said quietly, the words catching in his throat. "You saved my life today."

He felt a hitch against his chest as Mac caught his breath. "You never have to thank me for that." His dad gave him a squeeze, then stepped back and rubbed his nose with the side of his hand, blinking rapidly. "I'll leave you two alone. Try to take it easy."

Thorne nodded and Mac turned and headed back down the hall. A few seconds later, he heard the front door shut as Mac left.

He glanced back at the doorway to his old room. During his teenage years, he would have given anything to have a pretty girl waiting for him in there. The fact that Maggie was here now was almost too good to be true.

His stomach fluttered with sudden nerves. They were alone, for the first time in hours. And even though it hadn't been that long since their conversation in the barn, it felt like a lifetime ago.

His mind whirred with possibilities. The idea of picking things up where they'd left off in the barn was deeply appealing, but Thorne wasn't sure he had the energy for much more than crawling into bed and pulling the covers over his head. His lungs ached with every breath and his muscles were stiff with fatigue.

Thorne started down the hall, but another thought made him pause. Perhaps Maggie wasn't interested in resuming anything physical right now. Maybe she just wanted to talk.

That was fine, too, he decided. His brain felt sluggish and foggy, likely the aftereffects of all the smoke he'd inhaled. But he would force himself to rally. If she wanted to talk all night, that's what he'd do. Anything to preserve and strengthen the fragile connection they'd formed before being so dangerously interrupted.

He took a deep breath, wincing a little at the protest in his chest. Then he crossed the remaining steps to the door, determined to follow Maggie's lead.

He needn't have worried. She lay on her side, her knees bent and her back curved, her body unconsciously cradling their unborn baby. Her blond hair spread out in a golden fan behind her head, smooth and glossy. She was facing the door, turned away from the light of the window, and he could see her features, relaxed and peaceful in sleep.

A rush of love filled him, and he pressed a fist to his heart, rubbing at the sudden ache behind his breastbone. God, she was so perfect! She was beauty and light and life, everything that was good and pure in his world. He'd been such a fool to let his fears rule his head; now that he'd been graced with a second chance, he wasn't going to make that mistake again.

Thorne walked softly into the room, grateful that the carpet muffled the sound of his boots. He didn't want to wake her—she needed the rest probably even more than he did.

He sat in the armchair in the corner and tugged off his boots. It took a little effort, as the new leather hadn't molded to his body yet. He set them aside and stood, silently debating his next move. He was desperate to shed his dirty, soot-covered clothes. But how would Maggie respond if she woke up to find him undressed next to her? She might not appreciate him taking such liberties, especially when this connection between them was still so new. And the last thing he wanted was for her to mistake his intentions as to their physical relationship.

Thorne settled for unbuckling his belt and pulling it free of the loops. Then he pulled the hem of his shirt out and unbuttoned his jeans.

He lowered himself to the bed, trying to keep his movements gentle so as not to disturb Maggie's sleep. A groan nearly escaped him as he stretched out fully, his body relaxing into the soft embrace of the mattress. He lay there for a moment, staring at the ceiling, the muscles in his arms and legs randomly twitching in testament to their earlier strain. Maggie's breathing was steady and sure next to him, a comforting, almost hypnotic sound.

He thought about touching her, just a quick caress to assure himself that she was really there, that this wasn't some kind of hallucination brought on by oxygen deprivation. But his arms felt so heavy, as if they'd been glued to the bed. He settled for turning his head, her golden hair filling his vision as he surrendered to the restorative depths of sleep.

Maggie came awake slowly, opening her eyes to a world of gray. Her heart jumped into her throat and for a terrifying instant, she thought the smoke in her dreams had followed her back to reality. She sniffed cautiously and relief washed over her as she realized the pearlescent glow of the room was due to the early evening light slanting through the sheer dove-colored curtains.

She lay there for a moment, taking stock of things. She wasn't sure how long she'd been asleep, but she didn't feel particularly rested. Her dreams had been full of chaos and turmoil, the roar of fire and the shrill whinnies of horses. She'd spent most of the dream running, trying to escape from the thick, choking smoke that purled around her limbs, pulling at her clothes and hair. Thorne had been there with her, but she hadn't been able to see him. He'd remained obscured, and no matter how fast she ran he was always just out of reach.

It didn't take a rocket scientist to interpret *that* dream. And given the events of the last few days, was it any wonder she was having nightmares?

She rubbed her eyes, wincing a little as the irritated tissue burned in response to her touch. Her skin smelled like ash and soot, and a fine grit covered her body. Time to shower; she really hadn't meant to fall asleep without cleaning up first, but the bed had been so comfortable… She'd wanted to stay awake until Thorne returned, but while the spirit had been willing, the flesh had been weak.

She stretched, arching her back off the mattress. A movement to her right caught her eye, and she glanced over to find Thorne watching her, his light brown eyes warm and his lips curved in a half smile.

"Hi," he said, his voice husky with smoke and sleep.

"Hi." Her stomach fluttered at the sight of him lying next to her. How many times had she fantasized about this very moment? How many times over the past few months had she woken up alone, the pillow beside her cold in the morning light? Seeing him now was like a dream come to life, and she was half-afraid to blink, lest he vanish without warning.

"How are you feeling?"

She considered the question for a second as she mentally surveyed her body, checking for any new aches and pains. "I'm okay," she said, a little surprised to find it was true. "What about you? You're the one who carried me out and then went back in for Rose. You've got to be sore."

"A little," he admitted. "But I feel a lot better now that I got some sleep."

Maggie reached out and touched her fingertip to a smudge of soot on his cheek. "You look a little worse for wear."

He responded by trailing his hand down her arm. A pleasant shiver followed his touch, and her skin stippled with goose bumps. "I hate to break it to you," he murmured, "but you're looking a bit rough around the edges, as well."

"I guess we could both use a shower."

He smiled. "Yep. Why don't you go ahead? I'm going to call Mac and check on things, and maybe find something for us to eat in the kitchen."

"You're sure you don't mind?" Maggie was desperate to be clean again, but Thorne had to be feeling even worse. She could wait a bit longer if he wanted to go first...

"Not at all," he said. He climbed out of bed and stretched, the movement shifting the hem of his shirt. Maggie caught a tantalizing glimpse of soot-darkened skin over toned muscle and her body flushed, a wave of warmth spreading through her limbs. Her skin tingled with the memory of his touches in the barn, and she wondered briefly if they would get a chance to pick up where they'd left off...

If Thorne noticed her reaction, he didn't show it. He walked around the bed and extended his hand as she pushed herself into a sitting position. Maggie slid her hand into his, shivering slightly at the raspy feel of his calluses against the skin of her palm.

He tugged gently, helping her stand. He kept hold of her hand as he led her down the hall, stopping at the bathroom door. "Mac always has fresh towels in the linen closet. I'll be in the kitchen if you need me." He lifted her hand to his lips and pressed a soft kiss to her knuckles. "Take your time."

Thorne turned and started down the hall. Maggie's heart lurched as she watched him leave—she didn't want to be alone. Not right now, after this most recent attempt on their lives.

"Wait." She called out before she could second-guess the impulse.

Thorne stopped and turned back, one eyebrow arched in question. "Is everything all right?"

Maggie paused for second as she conducted a quick, yet agonizing, mental debate. She had two choices: tell Thorne she was fine and watch him walk away, or call him back.

He wasn't leaving her, not really. She was just being overly sensitive, thanks to recent events. If she let him go, they could resume their conversation from the barn after they had both showered and eaten, when things were more normal.

Or she could ask him to stay.

It was a possibility that both thrilled and terrified her in equal measures. If Thorne accepted her invitation, it would usher in a new chapter in their relationship. She was ready to reconnect with Thorne on a physical and emotional level; she craved it, in fact, needing the reassurances that only physical touch could provide. But she didn't want to rush him into anything.

While his kiss in the barn had been full of passion, Thorne might prefer to pick things up again at a more romantic time.

The safe option would be to wave him off, to tell him she was fine and have him continue on his way. But if recent events had taught her anything, it was that there were no guarantees in life. It would be nice to make love with Thorne on a blanket under the stars, after a private, candlelit dinner. But they might not ever get that chance. And if she didn't take every opportunity to be with him, she knew she would regret it.

"I—I want you to stay. With me," she added, feeling her cheeks heat.

"Oh." He sounded surprised, as if that was the last thing he'd expected to hear.

"We don't have to do anything," she said, feeling a little self-conscious at having this conversation in the middle of Mac's hallway. "I just want to be by you. Is that all right?"

"Oh, Maggie," Thorne said, his voice husky. He walked toward her, his eyes bright with emotion. "That's the best news I've heard in a long time."

Chapter 18

Thorne followed Maggie into the bathroom, his heart tripping against his breastbone as they stepped into the small space. He knew this was a big step forward for them, and he wanted to make sure everything was perfect.

He hadn't really thought of a bathroom as romantic before, but maybe he could fix that. He glanced around, taking it all in. Mac's redecorating hadn't stopped with Thorne's old bedroom—the bathroom had gotten an overhaul, as well.

White subway tiles extended up from the edges of the bathtub, clean and crisp against the soft green walls that reminded him of spring grass. A long, white marble counter extended down the wall, and a cluster of candles sat on a silver tray. Perfect.

Thorne turned to Maggie, inspiration taking root

in his mind. "Can you give me a minute?" he said. He opened one of the cabinets under the counter and pulled out a fluffy towel, which he handed to her. "Why don't you go back to the room and trade your clothes for this? I'll get the bath going."

"Okay." Her expression was openly curious, but she turned and left without protest.

"I won't take long," he called after her. He shut the bathroom door quietly and flipped on the water, then crouched and started digging through the cabinets. Towels—yes, they would need those. He set them by the tub and continued his search. Matches, surely there were matches somewhere… Ah, yes, there in the corner. He slapped them on the counter as well, then grabbed a small bottle of what he hoped was soap.

He sniffed experimentally, and was rewarded by a floral scent. Not his usual preference, but he was willing to make an exception. Thorne added a generous dollop to the running water, smiling as a rich lather formed. His was looking forward to seeing Maggie in nothing but bubbles.

Now for the candles. He lit a match, but paused before touching the flame to the wick. It was clear the candles had never been used before—his father had probably put them there only for decoration, not to be functional. "Sorry, Dad," he muttered. He made a mental note to buy Mac new candles and tossed the spent match in the trash.

He shut off the water just as a soft knock sounded at the door, and he opened it to find Maggie standing in the hall, clutching the towel around her torso. "I waited as long as I could," she said, smiling shyly.

"Come in." Thorne took a step back so she could

enter. She brushed past him as she walked toward the tub, and he heard a soft hitch in her breathing when she caught sight of the bubbles.

"Oh, my," she whispered. She glanced at the candles flickering on the counter, then at the pile of towels he'd placed by the tub. "You've been busy."

Pleasure bloomed in his chest at her reaction. Maggie deserved so much more, but he was happy she liked what he had managed to throw together.

"Can I help you into the bath?"

She glanced from the water to him and back again, biting her lower lip. "Aren't you going to get in as well?"

"Later," he said, taking her hand. Maggie looked like she wanted to say something, but she allowed him to lead her to the edge of the tub. With only a second's hesitation, she released her grip on the towel, setting it free to land in a puddle at her feet.

It took every ounce of his self-control to help her into the tub, when what Thorne really wanted to do was stare at the gorgeous display of Maggie's pale skin and beautiful curves. He took a mental snapshot of her body as she sank into the water, comparing the image to his memory of her from their night together. Her body had changed a lot, thanks to the pregnancy. Her breasts were fuller and her hips appeared wider. And then there was the roundness of her belly, an arch he ached to caress with his hands.

Soon, he told himself, taking a deep breath. This was about Maggie, what she wanted. He was going to follow her lead and let her set the pace.

Thorne knelt and reached for the sponge on the side of the tub. He dipped it into the warm water and applied some of the soap, then took Maggie's hand and lifted her arm out of the water. Moving slowly, he rubbed the sponge over her skin, washing away the soot and the stench of smoke.

He repeated the process for her other arm, then her legs. Maggie leaned back, her gaze hooded as she silently watched him.

Thorne let her foot slip through his grasp and reached for her shoulder, gently pulling her forward so he could wash her back. It was getting harder and harder for him to control his reactions—he'd meant for the bath to be a relaxing experience for Maggie, but touching her like this, his hands sliding over her warm, naked skin, was almost too much to bear. His inner caveman wanted to haul her out of the tub and carry her to bed so he could slake his lust with her body. He quashed the urge, but his growing arousal clawed at the edges of his composure, a wild beast demanding to be set free.

His hands shook as he started to wash Maggie's shoulders, the sponge skipping over sections of her skin as he moved. He swallowed hard as he soaped the swells of her breasts and nearly groaned when her nipples puckered in response to his attentions.

Maggie made a soft sound and shifted, her hips lifting off the bottom of the tub as he dragged the sponge across her breasts again. He glanced up at her face, wanting to see her reaction.

Her eyes were closed, her brows drawn together in a slight frown as if she was concentrating. Her lips were parted slightly, and he could tell by the way she moved in the water that she had given herself over to feeling, to the sensations he was triggering in her body.

He touched her again, this time with his hand instead of the sponge. She gasped and jerked up, seeking more of his touch.

"Sensitive spot?" He recalled she had enjoyed this before, as well. Apparently, the pregnancy had served to heighten some of her responses.

"Yes," she said, her voice sounding strangled.

Thorne smiled in satisfaction, his own arousal heightening as he focused on giving Maggie pleasure. He might not be good with words, but he could show Maggie how much he loved her by his actions. And after tonight, he wanted there to be no doubts left in her mind as to his intentions.

He ran his hands over her body, pressing here, trailing featherlight touches there. Maggie's responses were totally uninhibited, her reactions telling him as clearly as any words what she enjoyed and wanted.

Thorne was only too happy to oblige.

It was only a matter of minutes before she grabbed his arm, her fingernails digging into his skin as her whole body tensed, her back arching like a drawn bow. Then she sank into the water with a shudder and a sigh, her muscles going lax with her release.

Thorne shifted to smooth the hair back from her face and pressed soft kisses to her closed eyelids, her nose, her cheeks. She was so beautiful, her skin flushed from both the bath and her passion. If he lived to be a hundred years old, he'd never grow tired of seeing her like this.

He cupped the gentle swell of her belly, the firm roundness fitting perfectly into his palms. Could the baby feel his touch? Or was it too early for that? In his mind's eye, he pictured a tiny, perfectly formed child, floating peacefully in the warm waters of its sac. It was a powerful image, and he felt both energized and humbled thinking about the miraculous process taking place under his touch.

Maggie's hands landed on his, her skin soft and warm. Thorne glanced up to find her watching him, a look of unguarded love on her face. "Pretty special, isn't it?"

He nodded, not trusting his voice. He didn't think he could adequately describe the emotions building in his chest and the thoughts whirring through his mind. The sense of wonder he felt when he looked at her, when he touched her like this. How fascinating he found it all, the way a baby was forming, hidden and quiet inside her body. The magnitude of love he felt for this little person he hadn't even met yet. His desire—no, his *need*—to do right by his child. His joy at knowing Maggie was his, that she wanted to be with him as much as he wanted to be with her. And the faint sense of terror that he was going to do something to screw it all up.

Thorne swallowed hard. "I don't have the words," he said simply.

Maggie smiled and reached up to touch his cheek. "You don't need them," she said softly. "Your actions are enough."

He turned his head and kissed her palm, gratitude building in his chest along with a sense of relief. She understood, and she didn't hold his lack of pretty phrases against him. It was yet another reason why he loved her, as if he needed one.

They stayed like that for a few minutes, silently communing over the miracle they had created. Then

Maggie stretched and sat up. "I thought you said you were going to join me."

Thorne eyed the tub and shook his head. "I want to, but there's no way we'll both fit. There's not enough room for the two of us."

"That's okay." Maggie reached for one of the towels, casting him a mischievous glance. "You can have it all to yourself."

She stood, sending water cascading over and off her body. It landed on him in cold, annoying drips, but he kept his focus on her. "What do you mean?" He wrapped her in the towel, rubbing the thick fabric against her skin to keep her warm. He knew he needed to clean up, but he didn't want to leave her. Not after what they'd just shared.

Maggie leaned over and reached for the faucet, cranking on the tap again. A new froth of bubbles foamed at the influx of water, and steam curled into the air. "I mean," she said, tugging at the hem of his shirt until he was forced to lift his arms. "It's your turn for a bath."

She started on his jeans next, tugging the zipper down in one smooth motion. He caught his breath as her fingers grazed him through the cotton of his boxers, the sensitive tissue already stirring to attention. He knew she was simply trying to help him out of his clothes so he could clean up, but his body wasn't capable of such discernment.

He placed his hands on her wrists, gently intercepting her hands. "Let me." If she kept touching him, he was going to embarrass himself. "Do you want to get dressed while I wash up?" She was bound to be getting cold, and he didn't want her to feel any kind of discomfort, especially if he could do something about it.

"No."

His jeans dropped to the floor and he paused, the implications of her response sinking in. His body flushed hot and his skin tingled as he recognized the shifting currents of power in the room. Maggie had started out at his mercy, but now it seemed she was intent on taking control.

She ran her gaze over his body, her eyes tracing his shoulders, his stomach, his thighs. She took her time, surveying him thoroughly, and he fought the urge to squirm, feeling the weight of her regard like a touch. Her lips curved in a smile of feminine satisfaction, as if she knew exactly the effect she was having on him. And why wouldn't she? His body's response wasn't exactly subtle...

"Get in."

Thorne smiled to himself, enjoying the note of command in her tone. It seemed his Maggie had a bit of an authoritative streak. Good; that would make things more interesting.

He sank into the warm water, his muscles relaxing even as his arousal seemed to intensify. Maggie's hands landed on his shoulders, guiding him until he was leaning against the back of the tub, his legs stretched out before him, knees bent to accommodate the small space.

"Close your eyes," she instructed.

He hesitated a second, reluctant to lose his view of Maggie's face. But then her fingers wrapped around him, and the resulting jolt of pleasure sent his eyes rolling back in his head.

* * *

Maggie couldn't help but smile as Thorne let out a low moan of pleasure. She ran her fingers up and down his length experimentally, playing with this newfound power she possessed.

His reaction didn't disappoint. His body tensed, muscles cording and rippling under the water. An electric thrill raced through her limbs at the realization she was capable of affecting him so drastically with such a simple touch.

She spent the next several moments exploring his body, giving her hands free rein to roam across his broad shoulders, taut abdomen and the vulnerable flesh between his legs. Thorne encouraged her, using his big hands to guide her movements over his soap-slippery skin. His voice was husky as he whispered to her, his words ranging from instructions to garbled exclamations of pleasure.

Maggie was an eager student, filing away his reactions as she learned just how he liked to be touched. She ran her index finger along the curve of his collarbone, making him shiver. She leaned forward and bit his earlobe, her hand finding his erection again. He gasped and arched his back, the water sloshing in the tub as he moved.

It was both exciting and sexy as hell to see this powerful man unravel before her eyes and to know that she was the cause. Her own arousal intensified as she watched him move, felt the warmth of his skin and the quivering tension in his muscles. She was half tempted to ditch her towel and climb into the tub with him, logistics be damned.

Thorne must have read her mind because he suddenly gripped her wrist, stilling her hand in midcaress. His eyes popped open, blazing with need.

"I can't stand this much longer," he said, the words clipped. "Are you going to put me out of my misery?" His hips shifted in an instinctive thrust that made his meaning perfectly clear, and Maggie laughed softly.

"Of course."

She stood, intending to climb in with him. But Thorne held up his hand, stopping her before she could throw her leg over the side of the tub. "Not here," he said. "I want you in a bed so I can do this properly."

Her stomach flip-flopped at the promise in his voice, and a shiver of anticipation ran through her. He rose from the bath, water and soap suds sluicing down the solid planes of his body as he moved. Maggie's gaze caught on a droplet of water, and she traced its path from his shoulder, across his chest and down the ridges of his stomach until it was lost in the hair on his muscled thigh. Her mouth went dry as she took in the magnitude of him, standing so close in the small space. The sight of him was overwhelming in the best way, all his masculine power making her feel decidedly feminine in comparison.

Thorne stepped carefully from the tub, his gaze never leaving hers as he reached for a towel. This close, she could feel the heat coming off his body, a testament to both the warmth of the bath and his arousal.

"The way you're looking at me now makes me want to toss you over my shoulder and carry you down the hall." His voice was a deep rumble that she felt as much as heard.

Maggie swallowed, her mouth suddenly dry. "I don't think that would be very comfortable for either of us."

He raised one eyebrow with a suggestive smile. "Maybe not. But I'm sure I can come up with an alternative." He swiped the towel across his chest, then dropped it on the bath mat. His long fingers nimbly pulled the edge of her towel free, and a second later it joined its fellow on the floor. Then he reached for her hands and lifted them up and around his neck.

"Hold on," he whispered. He bent at the knee and grabbed her waist, lifting her up until they were eye level. Maggie's stomach lurched at the sudden change in position, and she instinctively wrapped her legs around his hips.

Thorne hummed as her bottom made contact with his erection. "Perfect," he said, his voice hot in her ear. He started walking, pausing only to pull open the bathroom door. Maggie felt a flash of self-consciousness as the cool air of the hall hit her flushed skin. What if Mac was home? They hadn't exactly been paying attention to the outside world while they were in the bathroom. Had he come back with the promised food yet? She'd never live it down if Mac saw her clutching his son, the pair of them naked as jaybirds.

She was just about to say something to Thorne when he stopped in the hall and pivoted so her back was against the wall. He kissed her, claiming her mouth with an urgency that was all-consuming. Maggie lost herself in the kiss, her thoughts fragmenting until she was no longer certain what she'd been worried about in the first place.

Thorne broke the kiss a moment later. "Sorry," he said, sounding a little breathless. "I just needed to kiss you and I couldn't wait another second."

Maggie smiled and cupped his face. "That's fine by me. You can kiss me anytime you want."

Thorne let out a low rumbling growl and leaned forward to nip her shoulder. A shiver ran through her and she sucked in a breath. "Be careful," he said, pulling her away from the wall and turning to resume the journey to his bedroom. "I'm going to have to take you up on that offer."

As he pushed open the door, Maggie was hit with a strong sense of déjà vu. It took her a second to figure out why, but as Thorne laid her gently on the bed, realization struck: this was the same way their encounter had started all those months ago, right down to the way he'd carried her to his room.

She let out a little laugh at the cosmic coincidence and Thorne paused over her, his eyebrow arched in question. "Does this seem familiar to you?" she asked, smiling up at him.

He considered the question, and Maggie could tell the moment the pin dropped for him, as well. His expression cleared, and his mouth formed a small O of surprise. "It does," he confirmed. His hand slid to her belly, his touch warm and knowing.

Maggie expected him to follow her down to the bed, but Thorne remained standing, his eyes roaming over her body. There was no judgment in his gaze, but his perusal made her feel suddenly shy. The pregnancy had triggered a lot of changes in her body, and Thorne was getting an up close and personal look at every stretch mark and bulge.

She moved her hands to her stomach, trying to hide the dark vertical line that bisected her belly. But Thorne shook his head and circled her wrists with his fingers.

He gently pulled her hands away, revealing her body to him once more.

"Let me look at you," he said softly. "Please."

He released her hands, giving her a choice. Maggie let them drop to her sides, feeling a little scared but also excited to share the outward signs of the baby with Thorne.

At first, he simply looked at her. She lay still, resisting the temptation to squirm as he studied her. His expression was curious, as if he was comparing her present features to the ones from his memory. And why wouldn't he? She looked different, that was for sure. It was only natural he'd notice.

His fingertip grazed the silvery lines of the stretch marks on her hips and belly, tracing each one from end to end. His eyes shone with what might have been wonder, and he bent to press a soft kiss to her lips.

"Beautiful," he whispered against her mouth. "So beautiful."

Her skin warmed at the compliment, the last of her worries fading into insignificance in the face of his declaration. She threaded her hands behind his neck and welcomed his return into her heart and into her body.

Chapter 19

Thorne woke just before dawn. It was still dark outside, but the faint glow from the window next to the bed told him the day wasn't far off.

He was halfway out of bed before he remembered he didn't have to tend to the horses this morning. Mac had told him in no uncertain terms yesterday that he wanted Thorne to rest for a few days. But even though Thorne knew the other stable hands could take care of all the chores, he still felt guilty for lying about when there was work to be done.

He leaned back on the bed with a sigh, wincing as his lungs ached in protest. Maybe it wouldn't hurt him to rest a bit after all…

He closed his eyes, wishing he could go back to sleep. But his lingering fatigue from yesterday's excitement was no match for years of habit. For a moment, he considered getting up and starting the day; he might not be able to help with the horses, but there was still plenty to do on the ranch.

Maggie stirred next to him, and all thoughts of leaving the bed fled his mind. Work could wait. The woman he loved was lying warm and naked next to him—he'd be a fool to willingly leave her. Besides, he didn't want her to wake up alone so soon after making love. There would be many mornings in their future when he'd have to leave before the sun came up. This didn't have to be one of them.

Thorne carefully pulled her close, snugging her against his side where she belonged. He could definitely get used to waking up like this…

But could Maggie?

The thought struck like a bolt of lightning, shattering his sense of peace. Worry slammed down on him, making his stomach roil and his heart race. What if Maggie didn't want this kind of life?

Thorne had assumed now that he and Maggie were together they would live here on the ranch. Maggie could move her office to one of the outbuildings, and the baby would grow up around the horses, playing under the wide blue sky and counting fireflies at dusk. He'd always thought he would raise his children in the country, away from the noise and grit of the city. But he realized now that Maggie might not feel the same way.

She lived in Shadow Creek and was totally unused to the rhythms of a working ranch. And while she'd been staying here for a bit, he'd seen her face in unguarded moments and knew she wasn't happy. Lately, he'd noticed the lines of strain around her eyes and mouth, the pale cast to her skin. Part of it was likely due to the physical stresses of the pregnancy and her continued recovery from the effects of the explosion. But now he wondered if perhaps her mood wasn't also affected by living here on the ranch. She undoubtedly missed her own apartment and her life in town. But could she learn to love it here as well?

He wanted to think so. But what if she hated it? What if the smells and sounds of a working ranch were just too unappealing? He couldn't ask her to stay here if she would be miserable. Maggie's state of mind was important to him, and he would do whatever it took to make sure she was happy.

Even if that meant moving.

He swallowed hard, his stomach hollowing out at the thought of leaving the ranch. The horses, the wide-open sky. And Mac. But he'd trade it all if it made Maggie smile. It would be hard, perhaps the most difficult thing he'd ever done. He'd grown up on this land, sometimes with only the horses for friends. But he could adjust to life in town, as long as Maggie was by his side. And he didn't need to worry about his father, as far as the baby was concerned. Mac would definitely be a part of his grandchild's life, no matter where Thorne and Maggie lived. It would be tougher for him to help his dad if he lived somewhere else, but Thorne could make it work.

If he had to.

Maybe it won't come to that. It was possible he was overthinking the situation, since he and Maggie hadn't even talked about living arrangements yet. He was probably just "borrowing trouble," as Mac liked to say. He certainly hoped that was the case. But either way, it was a conversation he and Maggie needed to have, and the sooner the better. Life was only going to get busier from here on out, and he'd prefer they have some time to settle into their new life together before the baby was born.

He glanced at her face, relaxed and peaceful in sleep. It had been almost a year since he'd met her, standing in Mac's office with her hair glowing like spun gold in the afternoon light. He'd been smitten from the start, especially after she'd turned those big blue eyes on him and smiled. She'd offered her hand, and he'd taken it without thinking, remembering a second too late he was dirty from chores. Mac had chided him, but Maggie hadn't seemed to mind.

That was the moment Thorne had lost his heart. But he'd never thought for even a second he had a chance with such a beautiful, composed woman.

I am the luckiest man alive.

He stared down at her, wonder and awe filling his chest as he considered the amazing turn of events in his life. In just a few short months, everything had changed completely. He'd gone from being a shy loner to having the woman he loved by his side, their baby growing safely inside her. He was going to be a father! Sometimes it still didn't feel real, but the proof of it was pressed against his hip, snug and warm.

Thorne wasn't sure what he'd done to deserve Maggie and the baby, but he was going to spend the rest of his life earning her love.

And he couldn't wait to get started.

Mac was up and out of the house while dawn was still just a hint of pink in the eastern sky. He hadn't slept well—he'd tossed and turned most of the night, plagued by images of the barn being consumed by flames. Fortunately, once the dust had settled he'd realized no one had been hurt, but it could have just as easily gone the other way. He couldn't fault Thorne for going back in after Rose, but he didn't like his son taking such dangerous chances. He was going to be a father now, and he couldn't put himself at risk like that. Maggie and the baby would need him.

Mac had given the couple a wide berth last night. Whatever else had happened yesterday, it seemed Thorne and Maggie had turned a corner in their relationship. Mac was happy to see it—he didn't know what had gone wrong between the pair of them, but he liked Maggie and he knew she was good for Thorne. She was the first woman Thorne had shown any kind of serious interest in, and he wanted his son to be happy. He'd spent too much time alone, feeling like an outsider in his own life.

After a quick visit with the horses, Mac saddled his usual mount and rode out to check the perimeter fences. He didn't think there was a breach, but he needed to ride and he might as well do something productive while he was out. He'd always thought better while on the back of a horse, and hopefully this morning would be no exception.

The idea that Livia was targeting Thorne was enough to make his blood run cold. There was no love lost between him and Livia—not now, anyway. After she'd bought the ranch, he'd stayed on initially out of a sense of pride. The land had been in his family for generations. It didn't matter what the bank said; he'd paid for the ranch with his blood, sweat and tears.

But it didn't hurt that Livia was a beautiful woman. He'd noticed her right away; she had that effect on him. There was something electric about her, an alchemy of personality that drew him to her and made him want her.

If only she wasn't a married woman, he'd thought, on more than one occasion. But she was Wes Kingston's wife, and Mac had no interest in breaking up their marriage.

Until that fateful morning in the barn.

He shuddered, feeling the ghost of her touch on his skin. Almost twenty-nine years had passed, but the memory of it still felt fresh.

She'd run into one of the empty stalls, slamming the door behind her with a crash that startled the horses. She hadn't stopped to acknowledge him, and Mac realized she hadn't seen him as she'd raced past. He was content to let her be, but then he'd heard the muffled sound of crying.

His heart twisted as her quiet sobs filled the air. No woman should ever cry like that.

He quietly approached the stall, knowing he was playing with fire. The responsible thing would be to go get Wes. He was her husband, and he should be the one to comfort her.

But Mac couldn't bring himself to leave her when she was so upset.

So he'd carefully opened the stall door and found Livia sitting in the corner, her face buried in her hands.

"You okay?" he said gently.

She jerked and looked up, her tear-filled eyes wide.

"Sorry," Mac said. "I didn't mean to scare you."

"It's okay." Her voice was thick with emotion, but she offered him a watery smile.

Mac took a step inside the stall and let the door swing shut behind him. "What's got you so upset?"

Livia sniffed inelegantly, and he pulled out a well-worn bandana from his pocket. She took it with a nod and dabbed at her eyes and nose.

"It's nothing," she said.

Mac tilted his head to the side. "Doesn't look like nothing to me."

He was on dangerous ground here, and he knew it. The last thing he should do was get more involved with her. But he couldn't help himself. She drew him in, and he wasn't strong enough to resist.

She shook her head. "Wes and I got into a fight."

Warning bells went off in Mac's head, and he looked her over, searching for signs of abuse. Was Wes hurting her? "Did things get physical?"

She shook her head. "No, nothing like that."

Mac relaxed, relieved to know her husband wasn't hurting her. At least not physically.

"I think he's having an affair," she blurted out. Fresh tears welled in her eyes, and she dropped her head again, not bothering to mop them up.

Shock rippled through Mac at the news. Wes was cheating on her? What kind of an idiot was he? Livia was a beautiful, charming woman. Why would Wes want to step out with a mistress when he had such a gorgeous wife waiting in his bed at home?

"I'm so sorry," Mac said. Indignation began to rise in his chest, and he felt angry on her behalf. "He's an ass."

She huffed out a laugh, and he smiled despite the circumstances. "That he is," she murmured.

They stayed there talking for what seemed like

hours, and the more time they spent together, the more Mac's crush intensified.

The relationship between them blossomed over the next few weeks. Livia visited him often in the stables, and he took her riding on several occasions. Any guilt he may have felt over getting so close to a married woman was absolved by Livia's assertion that her husband was cheating on her. Mac figured he was simply giving Livia the appreciation she was so clearly due.

For a few weeks, life was great. He got along well with Livia's children, and the two of them never seemed to run out of things to talk about. It was perfect, everything he'd ever wanted.

The night they'd finally made love had been one of the highlights of his life. He'd held her close in the aftermath, staring up at the stars and feeling like his heart would burst.

And then she told him they were over, and he'd come crashing back down to Earth.

"I can't do this anymore," she said, a few days later. "Wes wants to try to work on our marriage, and I think that's best for my family."

Mac had nodded dumbly, but inside he'd been screaming. His dreams were slipping through his fingers, but he could do nothing to save them. Livia had made her choice, and he couldn't force her to love him.

He'd packed his bags, knowing he couldn't stay and see her every day. It would hurt too much to be reminded of what they'd once shared.

But then she had turned up pregnant.

Mac had known right away it was his, even though she never confirmed it. As soon as he'd found out about the baby he'd known he had to stay. No way could he leave his child. So he'd stuck around, taking a more active role in the lives of her other children. He had fallen in love with them, too, and was glad that he could still be a part of their lives. Fortunately, Livia had turned a mostly blind eye to his involvement. As the years had gone by and he'd realized her true colors, he wondered if perhaps she hadn't cared about his presence, or if she had simply been happy to take advantage of his willingness to step up and actually parent the kids she was content to treat as accessories. But whatever her reason, she'd left him alone.

As soon as Mac had seen the baby, he'd known Thorne was his. There was no doubt in his mind, even if Wes refused to publicly acknowledge it. Mac had taken one look at that baby and fallen head over heels in love. The intensity of his reaction had surprised him; he'd thought the pain caused by Livia's rejection would overshadow any paternal affection he might have felt for the wee one. But his love for Thorne had burned away his anguish, cleaning out disappointment and sense of rejection that had been festering inside him. Mac would never fully get over the choice Livia had made. But he couldn't totally regret their actions either, not when Thorne had been the consequence.

He'd never told Thorne the details of his conception. He'd told his son that his relationship with Livia had been a mistake, but he wasn't willing to share more than that. It wouldn't do anyone good to dredge up the past.

He shook his head, trying to clear the fog of memories from his brain. Thinking about Livia always put him in a bad mood. And if she was really targeting

Thorne now that she was out of prison? Well, that was low, even for her.

Mac wasn't sure what he could do to protect his son and his future grandchild. But he wasn't about to sit around and let Livia take potshots at the people he cared about. That woman had already sowed too much chaos and destruction, and Thorne had paid the price many times over for being her son. He deserved some happiness, something pure and untarnished by the evil in Livia's soul.

He wasn't a violent man, but a dark part of Mac wished Livia would appear on the trail in front of him so he could wring her neck. Her specter hung over the lives of her children, and he knew none of them would feel truly safe until she was dead. It broke his heart that the kids had grown up without knowing the joys of a mother's love. He was glad that Knox and Leonor had found someone to share their lives with, and it made his heart sing to see Thorne with Maggie. But he still worried about the other kids, especially Jade. She'd been the one to finally bring her mother down, and she'd earned a target on her back for her efforts. Livia's escape from prison had put all her children on edge, but Mac knew Jade lived in fear that mother would come back to seek revenge for what she viewed as a betrayal.

He made a mental note to ask Knox about the status of the investigation into Livia's whereabouts. Knox still had connections in the Texas Rangers, and maybe they would want to come out and take fingerprints or other evidence from the smoldering remains of his barn. Sheriff Jeffries didn't seem too interested in mounting a forensic investigation, claiming he didn't have the resources to spare. But Mac figured there had to be a few useful clues amid the destruction, maybe even something compelling enough to put Livia away for the rest of her life.

The morning sun was warm on his back and he closed his eyes and basked in the glow for a moment. Despite all the dangers and troubles going on right now, it was shaping up to be a truly beautiful day. Of course, that would make it much harder to convince Thorne to stay in bed and rest...

He crested a low ridge, shaking his head at his son's stubbornness. It was further proof Thorne was his get, as if there was any doubt left.

A small copse of trees lay to the right, the leafy green branches swaying in the breeze. Birdsong floated in the air, the trill of warblers and the whistle of sparrows undercut by the jeering notes from blue jays. He paused for a moment, enjoying the sounds of spring on the ranch. He imagined the birds, flitting from tree to bush, from branch to nest, gathering food and teaching their hatchlings the basics of life.

He glanced over to the left, to a stretch of land left mostly untouched. Grass stalks grew tall and wispy, dancing gracefully in the wind. It was a mesmerizing sight, almost hypnotic in its beauty. Mac felt a sense of peace wash over him as he emptied his mind of thoughts of Livia and focused on the beauty of the land.

His land.

The horse leaned forward, eager to graze on the fresh, tender grass of the field. Mac gave him his head, content to let the animal roam for a few minutes.

They started down the slope, the horse stopping every few paces to grab a mouthful from a particularly tasty clump of green. Mac's gaze caught on the well about fifty yards away. It was an old, hand-dug well, long dried up. He'd boarded it over and took pains to make sure it stayed that way—this stretch of the ranch was fairly isolated, and if anyone were to accidentally fall in, it was unlikely they would still be alive when they were found. He'd replaced the boards with fresh lumber not two months ago, but something about the well seemed off...

Mac stood in the saddle, squinting to get a better look. The shape was different, and he realized with a small jolt that the cover he'd so recently bolted over the top had been removed and was leaning against the stone apron.

He kneed the horse into a trot, his heart kicking into his throat. It was probably just some kids messing around, but he hoped no one had fallen in...

He jumped down from the saddle and rushed over to the edge of the well. He paused a second to brace himself for what he might find, then leaned over to peer down into the dusty depths.

It was empty.

His breath gusted out in a sigh of relief. At least no one was hurt.

He turned to the wood leaning against the stone, annoyance replacing his worry. The cover he'd fashioned out of two-by-fours was intact, undamaged except for a few marks around the edges where someone had pried the wood up using a crowbar. Probably some kind of prank, maybe the work of teenagers on a dare. Either way, he'd have to make another trip out here—he didn't have the tools in his saddlebag to fix this.

Even though he couldn't bolt the cover back down, he still needed to slide it back into place to discourage any would-be daredevils who might come back. Mac slipped his work gloves on and took a grip on the wood, grunting a bit as he heaved it up and onto the lip of the well's opening. He'd deliberately made the cover solid and strong, hoping its weight would help keep it in place.

It took a little elbow grease, but he managed to slide the wood across the well opening. That would do for now. He pulled off his gloves and stepped back, eyeing the cover critically. He'd need new bolts, a few washers, the wrench...

His horse nickered in alarm, and he turned to check on the animal. The grass made for good grazing, but it also provided camouflage for snakes that might be warming themselves in the morning sun. If his horse had startled a rattler, Mac would have bigger problems than a missing well cover.

He was still moving when he caught a flash of movement on the edges of his vision. Then the back of his head exploded in a bright nova of pain and he dropped to the ground, the world going dark.

Chapter 20

Maggie stretched, arching her back as she extended her legs and lifted her arms above her head. Her muscles shifted and pulled, twinging pleasurably as she moved. A few new aches registered, thanks in large part to last night's activities. The memory sent a flush of heat through her limbs, and she relaxed back into the soft embrace of the mattress, images of Thorne flashing through her mind in a sensuous, sexy highlight reel of their night together.

"Good morning."

Thorne's deep voice washed over her like a caress. Maggie turned to find him watching her, his eyes warm and a smile playing at the corners of his lips.

"Morning," she replied, reaching out to cup his cheek. "How'd you sleep?"

He chuckled. "It wasn't my most restful night." He

turned to nip the palm of her hand, sending a shiver up her arm. "But I'm not about to complain."

Maggie rolled onto her side and threw a leg over Thorne's thigh. "You did work pretty hard."

His hand trailed down her stomach, the light touch making her squirm. "You seemed to enjoy yourself," he observed. His hand dipped lower and she gasped, her reply forgotten as Thorne's clever fingers ensured she was well and truly awake.

"You're not playing fair," she said, reaching for him. But Thorne shifted out of her grasp. "I don't think so," he teased. He gathered her wrists with his free hand and raised her arms above her head. Then he guided her onto her back. "I'm in charge this morning."

Maggie relaxed, happy to submit to Thorne's attentions. Every kiss, every stroke, every touch—each one was further proof of his love for her.

Wave after wave of pleasure washed over her until she was drowning in sensation, unable to think or even speak. She held on to Thorne, his presence a solid anchor as the world spun around her.

Her release came quickly, a shuddering burst that made her muscles tremble. She dimly heard Thorne hum with satisfaction and felt the mattress dip as he lay down next to her. His arm snaked around her waist and he pulled her over until she lay flush against him, his body a warm, solid wall against her back.

She wasn't sure how much time passed, but the window glowed brightly with the morning sunshine when Thorne spoke again. "Did you know you snore?"

His question was so unexpected it took Maggie a moment to fully process his words. Indignation rose in her chest and she pulled free from his embrace, rolling over to face him. "I do not!"

"Like a freight train," he said, oblivious to her dismay. "There were a few times I thought you were going to break the windows."

"Thorne!" She pushed his shoulder playfully. "I've never snored in my life."

One dark eyebrow shot up. "I beg to differ," he said solemnly. "I can record it, if you like."

"No, I would not like." She sniffed, her pride feeling a little bruised. "How do you know it was me? Maybe you were hearing your father through the walls."

"Nice try, but it was definitely you." Thorne leaned over and tried to kiss her, but she twisted away. He laughed and reached for her again. "It's actually kind of cute."

"Cute?" She stopped evading him and he pulled her close again.

"Yep," he confirmed, pressing his lips to the tip of her nose. "I got a kick out of hearing such loud sounds come from such a dainty woman."

Maggie snorted inelegantly. "Please. I'm not dainty." She gestured down the length of her body. "I'm pretty much the opposite of dainty right now. All thanks to you," she tacked on, giving him a mock glare.

His grin was full of male pride, beaming and unapologetic. "Damn straight," he said, sliding his hand down to rest on her bump. "You're all mine, Maggie girl. Can't get rid of me now."

"Good thing I don't want to," she replied, placing her hand over his.

"Want some breakfast?"

The suggestion of food made her stomach flutter,

but she put on a brave face. "Maybe just a little something."

Thorne gave her belly a soft pat and climbed out of bed. "Leave it to me. I'll meet you in the kitchen."

Maggie watched him walk away, admiring the view of his toned backside as he moved down the hall. He ducked into the bathroom for a moment, then emerged with a towel wrapped around his waist. "I'll grab something clean for you to wear," he called back. "I'll put it in the bathroom if you want to hop in the shower."

"Thanks," Maggie said. She hated to wash Thorne's touch from her skin, but she did need to get cleaned up. Might as well get started while Thorne was putting breakfast together. She headed for the bathroom and stepped under the warm spray of the shower, memories from the night before keeping her company as she bathed.

She stepped out to find some clothes sitting on the bathroom counter. She smiled at the sight; Thorne must have sneaked in while she was showering. It was one of those small, thoughtful gestures Thorne specialized in, his way of looking after her and showing that he cared.

The shirt and pants obviously belonged to Mac, but they were clean and didn't reek of smoke like her clothes did. The T-shirt was huge but comfortable, the well-worn cotton soft as silk. She eyed the pants apprehensively, but she needn't have worried. Thorne had found her a pair of sweatpants, and while they were a little large, the elastic waist accommodated her bump nicely.

Feeling refreshed, Maggie headed for the kitchen, where the scents of toast and scrambled eggs beckoned enticingly. Thorne turned as she walked into the kitchen and offered her a smile.

"Have a seat," he said, gesturing to a bar stool snugged up against the counter. "I'm almost done here."

Maggie crossed the room, a little disappointed to see Thorne had swapped out the towel for his own set of sweatpants and a T-shirt. *It's still a nice view, though*, she mused as she climbed onto the stool. While Mac's clothes were too big for her, Thorne had the opposite problem. His broad shoulders and muscled arms stretched the fabric of his shirt and the cotton pants left little to her imagination.

Not that she needed to imagine anything after last night. Or this morning, for that matter.

Her body flushed as a wave of heat started in her chest and spread outward, suffusing her limbs and making her feel deliciously aware of Thorne's nearness.

Whoa, she thought, taken aback by her body's response. It hadn't even been an hour since Thorne's good-morning treat, and she was already wanting more.

It's got to be the pregnancy hormones, she decided. That was the only reasonable explanation for this sudden insatiability.

If Thorne was aware of her carnal cravings, he didn't show it. He twisted the knob on the stove and carried the pan over to the counter, where he divided the eggs onto two plates. After adding a few slices of toast, he set one in front of her with a dramatic flourish.

"Bon appétit," he said with a wink.

"Thank you," she said. She forked a bite of eggs into her mouth, hoping they would taste as good as they looked. But the food congealed on her tongue, a gummy mass that nearly made her retch.

She quickly grabbed a napkin and dabbed at her mouth, hoping Thorne didn't notice her discreet attempt to spit out the food.

"Stomach bothering you?" he asked, his tone sympathetic.

"A little," she admitted. "I'm sorry."

"Don't apologize," he said. "Is there anything I can do to help you feel better? Something else I can make for you?"

Maggie shook her head. "I don't think so. I'm going to try the toast. I think that will go down easier." She took a cautious bite, pleased to find her stomach didn't immediately protest the taste.

Thorne watched her, his eyes glued to her face as she chewed and eventually swallowed the toast. "Do you think horses get morning sickness?" she asked, only half joking.

He appeared to consider her question for a moment. "Well, horses can't vomit, so—"

"What?" she blurted out before he could finish. "They can't throw up?" That sounded nice right about now...

Thorne lifted one shoulder and slid his toast onto her plate, then scooped her eggs onto his. "Nope. It's one of their physiological quirks. So to answer your question, they don't get that part of morning sickness. But I have seen a few mares that look a bit off during the early months of pregnancy. Maybe that's their version of it?"

"Maybe so," Maggie murmured, still flabbergasted at the revelation that horses were incapable of doing something that seemed to come so naturally to her right now. What else was different about these creatures that Thorne loved so much?

"Can we go see Rose after this?"

Thorne seemed pleased by her question. "I was hoping you'd want to," he said. "And yes, we definitely can."

"Where did she stay last night? Mac said something about an older barn?"

He nodded. "Yes, it's about a half mile out. I'm sure the workers put all the horses in there for the night."

"That's good," she said, glad to hear Rose hadn't had to spend the night outside. For some reason, the thought of the pregnant mare sleeping under a tree worried her.

"I'm sure she's fine," Thorne said between bites. "She's not due to give birth until next week, so I'm not too worried about her yet."

"Do you think Mac has already checked on her this morning?"

Thorne nodded. "Oh, most definitely. He's been gone since the sun came up."

Maggie eyed him over her toast. "Why do I get the feeling you've been up that long as well?"

He smiled at that. "Guilty as charged."

"You were supposed to get some rest," she chided. And since they hadn't done much sleeping last night, he was probably exhausted.

"Old habits," he said simply. "I woke up and couldn't get back to sleep."

"Why didn't you wake me? I hate to think of you awake and lonely."

"Are you kidding me? You're pregnant with my child and you think I'm going to deprive you of sleep because I woke up early? No way." He shook his head and forked another bite of eggs into his mouth. "Absolutely not," he said, the words muffled. He swallowed and spoke again, his voice gentle. "You need your rest, now more than ever."

"I do appreciate it," she said. "I'm pretty much the opposite of a morning person, so having a baby is going to be a big adjustment."

A strange look crossed Thorne's face, as if she had said something troubling. But before she could ask him if everything was all right, he smiled. "It'll be a change for both of us," he said.

He polished off the last of his breakfast and nodded to her plate. "Is the toast sitting okay?"

Maggie nodded. "I think it's going to stay put."

"Excellent. Would you like more?"

"No, thanks. I'm ready to get going if you are." She was excited to see Rose and check on the horse after yesterday's events, and she could tell Thorne was anxious to see her, as well. And it would be good for Thorne to get outside for a bit. Even though he was supposed to be resting, she had a feeling he wouldn't be able to relax until he had seen for himself that Rose was all right.

Maggie stood and gathered the plates, brushing aside Thorne's protests. "You cooked. I'll clean."

Thorne didn't argue, which told her just how much he was still feeling the effects of the fire. He was trying to act like nothing was wrong, but she could tell he was tired, and she'd seen him wince slightly when taking a deep breath. *His chest must ache from all the smoke*, she realized.

"I was thinking," she said, trying to sound casual as she dried the pan. "I'm still feeling pretty tired from yesterday. Do you think we could come back here and rest for a bit after we check on Rose?" Thorne would never admit he needed a break, but perhaps she could trick him into taking one. If he could say he was only keeping her company, his male pride would be spared.

"Are you sure you're up for going now? I could go by myself if you want to stay here."

Stubborn man, she thought. If she wasn't careful, her plan would backfire before it even got off the ground. "No," she assured him quickly. "I want to see Rose. I have to give her a treat. It's kind of our thing now."

Thorne chuckled. "Far be it from me to interrupt a new tradition." He stood and gallantly offered his arm. Maggie walked over and slid her hand into the crook of his elbow. "Ready, my lady?"

She smiled up at him, her heart expanding with love. "Let's go."

It was midmorning by the time Thorne and Maggie climbed out of the golf cart Mac kept on hand for traveling around the ranch. It was a testament to the ranch's success that Mac had agreed to buy one—even as recently as a few years ago he'd insisted on walking or riding everywhere. But as the operation had expanded, Mac had been forced to admit he sometimes needed to go faster than his feet could carry him. He'd broken down and purchased a couple of golf carts. Thorne hadn't ever thought he'd need to make use of them, but he was grateful to have the option now.

The old barn was smaller than the one that had burned down yesterday, and while Mac would never let a building on his property fall into disrepair, the barn was showing a few signs of age. The paint was a little dull and there were a few cobwebs under the eaves. But it was structurally sound and it would keep the horses safe and dry while the other stable was being rebuilt.

Rose let out a shrill neigh as soon as they walked inside. She shook her head as they approached her stall, snorting her displeasure at the change in accommodations.

"I know, I know," he said, trying not to laugh. "It's just for a little while until we get the other place fixed." In truth, he thought the barn was a total loss. It would probably be faster to rebuild the thing from the ground up, but he hadn't had a chance to talk to Mac about it yet.

"Good morning," Maggie cooed softly. Rose settled down a bit when Maggie touched her nose, and she whinnied in pleasure as Maggie presented her with a shiny ripe apple. Thorne smiled as he watched their reunion. It seemed like Maggie and Rose had formed quite a bond in a short period of time. It was understandable—Rose was easy to love. But Thorne hoped this connection was a sign that Maggie might be willing to live on the ranch after their baby was born.

Thorne opened the stall and stepped inside so he could touch Rose. He ran his hands over her body, checking for small injuries that may have gone overlooked in yesterday's chaos. Even a little nick or burn could cause trouble if it got infected and began to fester. And with Rose so close to her due date, he wanted to make sure she didn't have any issues that might harm her or the foal, or make her delivery more difficult.

Fortunately, he didn't find a mark on her. It was possible the smoke had irritated her nose or even her lungs, but her breathing didn't sound labored and he didn't see any gunk in her nose. He stepped back, a weight lifting off his shoulders as he realized Rose was most likely unaffected by yesterday's adventures.

"Is she okay?" There was a note of concern in Maggie's voice, a testament to her affection for the horse.

He smiled, happy to be able to deliver good news. "I think she's fine. I didn't find anything wrong, and she's acting normal." He ran his hand along her back and down her side. She felt a little warm, but that could be due to her restlessness and the new surroundings. Her belly had changed shape a bit, looking more pendulous than before. Both were signs of impending labor, but since this was Rose's first foaling, he had no way to know if she would foal in a few hours or a few days. He'd just have to keep a close eye on her so he could be ready to assist if needed.

Thorne gave Rose one final pat and stepped out of the stall. He'd just latched the door behind him when a startled shout drew his attention to the barn entrance.

He started for the noise, pausing only to look over his shoulder. "Stay here," he said. The last thing he wanted was for Maggie to leave the relative safety of the building, especially when he had no idea what was going on outside.

He stepped into the yard to find a stable hand reaching for the reins of his father's mount. But Mac was nowhere to be seen.

"What happened?"

The man shook his head. "No idea. Jericho just came running up, saddled and ready to ride. But I could have sworn his stall was empty when I went to do the morning feeds. I figured Mac had already taken him out."

Thorne walked over and placed his hand on the big gelding's nose, stroking softly to calm him. "Where have you been?" he said quietly, worry rising in his chest. His father was an excellent rider. For Jericho to return without him meant something had happened.

"Where's your walkie-talkie?"

The stable hand blinked at him, then nodded. "In my truck. I'll go grab it." He transferred the reins to Thorne and took off, returning a moment later with the device.

"Thorne?" Maggie called to him from the shadows of the barn. "Is everything all right out here?"

He nodded, not wanting to scare her. But his gut twisted in knots at the thought of Mac lying somewhere, injured and unable to ride.

What if it's more serious than that? Maybe his father hadn't fallen or been thrown from Jericho. Maybe the same person who was trying to hurt him had decided to take a shot at Mac, as well.

Thorne's throat burned as bile rose from his stomach, his breakfast eggs threatening to make a reappearance. He swallowed hard, then switched on the walkie-talkie and held it to his mouth. "Mac? Can you read me?"

Come on, Dad. Mac was a stickler for safety, and he'd bought several sets of portable radios, wanting each employee to carry one so they could call for help if necessary. He usually never left on a ride without one of his own, and Thorne hoped his father hadn't forgotten it this morning.

But as the seconds passed with no response, Thorne

began to fear the worst. Surely Mac would have answered by now, if he was able.

"Mac, come in, please. Where are you?"

Static crackled across the line, but Thorne refused to give up.

"We're coming for you, Dad. I'm going to find you."

Chapter 21

Wes Kingston squatted and pulled the walkie-talkie off Mac's belt. He rose, examining it with a speculative look. It squawked to life in his hands.

"We're coming for you, Dad. I'm going to find you."

Mac's heart clenched at the sound of Thorne's voice. But he didn't want his son anywhere near him right now. There was no telling what Wes would do if he saw Thorne.

Wes tossed the radio to the ground near Mac's head. "Answer him."

Mac shook his head, wincing as a lightning bolt of pain seared his brain. "No."

Wes squatted again and pushed the brim of his hat up with one finger. "Answer him," he repeated, an edge to his voice.

"Why? As soon as he hears my voice he'll know something is wrong. Is that what you want?"

"No. I want you to tell him where you are."

Fear washed over Mac in a cold wave as he realized the true goal of Wes's plan. The man wasn't afraid of getting caught. He wanted to lure Thorne out here, away from prying eyes and help. Mac eyed the pistol tucked into the holster on Wes's belt. Would he shoot Thorne dead on sight, or merely injure him, playing with him the way a cat toyed with a mouse?

Either way, Mac wasn't going to let his son walk into a trap.

"I won't do it."

"Yes, you will," Wes replied calmly. "Because if you don't, I'm going to shoot you in the head. Then I'm going to head for the barn and strangle that pretty little thing your son has been spending so much time with. And once I've done that, I'm going to kill Thorne and anyone who tries to get in my way." He paused, letting the horror of his words sink in for a moment. "So what's it going to be? The three of us, out here away from innocent people? Or am I going to have to take a little trip to finish things? Either way, this is happening."

Mac didn't doubt for a second that Wes was telling the truth. But there was no guarantee he wouldn't go after Maggie once he had finished with Thorne. Still, it was a chance he had to take—he couldn't risk Maggie's safety, or that of his grandchild. Not to mention the ranch hands working in and around the barn. So many innocent lives...

He reached for the walkie-talkie with a shaking hand and brought it to his mouth. "Thorne? Can you read me?"

Thorne replied almost immediately. "Dad! Where are you? What happened?"

Mac glanced up at Wes, who was watching him dispassionately. He debated telling Thorne the truth, but knew if he did Wes would simply kill him and head for the barn. And Maggie. So he scrambled to come up with a plausible lie.

"I had a little accident. I'm out by the old well. Can you come?"

"Of course. We'll be there right away."

"No, son. Just you." He couldn't stand the thought of Thorne bringing an innocent employee into this mess. "I, uh, I'm kind of embarrassed and I don't want anyone else to see me like this."

"Okay." There was a note of confusion in Thorne's voice, but he didn't argue. "I'll just bring Maggie then. She's dying to see for herself that you're okay."

"No," Mac said forcefully. "Have her stay at the barn. I've noticed some snakes around here, and I don't want to risk her getting bit."

There was a pause, and Mac hoped his real message had gotten through. It was bad enough he had to lure his son to certain danger. He wasn't going to let Maggie and his unborn grandchild walk into a trap, as well.

"I understand," Thorne said. "Sit tight, Dad. I'll be there soon."

Mac lowered his hand, letting the walkie-talkie roll out onto the ground. He stared up at Wes, squinting against the bright rays of the midmorning sun. "Now what?"

"Now we wait."

Thorne clipped the walkie-talkie to his belt and dug his cell phone out of his pocket. He dialed Knox, then turned to the ranch hand who was holding Jericho's reins.

"I need to borrow your truck." Mac's was still parked at his house, but it would take too long for Thorne to go back and get it. "Do you have a gun?"

The man's eyes widened. "There's a pistol under the front seat in a holster."

"Thorne?" Maggie's voice held a note of alarm. "What's going on?"

"Mac's in trouble," he said shortly. She opened her mouth to ask another question, but he held up his hand. "Knox? Yeah, I need you. Mac's hurt, and I think it's the same person who's been targeting me. He's out by the old well—you remember where that is?" At his brother's affirmation, Thorne continued. "I need you to bring your rifle. I'll call you when I'm on my way out there." The beginnings of a plan were forming in his mind, but he needed a few more minutes of thought to work out the details.

He hung up the phone and turned to Maggie. "I have to go help Mac. I need you to stay here and call the police." He tossed her his phone, then turned to the ranch hand.

"You can't go by yourself," she protested. "You don't know what you're walking into!"

"I know my father needs me," he said simply. Adrenaline, fear and anger were a potent swirl in his chest, driving him to do something. There was no way he could simply sit still and wait for the authorities to arrive. Besides, given Bud Jeffries's incompetence and hatred of his family, he couldn't even be sure the police would take his call seriously.

"Thorne!"

He held up a hand, stalling any further objections. "Just a minute, Maggie."

The ranch hand looked like a deer caught in the headlights of an oncoming semi. Thorne cursed silently. Where were the experienced people when he needed them? But he'd just have to make the best of it with this rookie. Maggie took a step back, her voice a low murmur in his ear as she called the police while he issued instructions to the young man.

"Turn Jericho out to pasture. Don't forget to close the gate behind you. Then run back to the old barn and gather as many hands as you can. I want you guys doing patrols of the inner perimeter of the ranch."

The man swallowed, his Adam's apple bobbing like a fishing lure in his thin neck. "Yessir," he said.

"Everyone takes their walkie-talkies," Thorne said. "And everyone who's licensed needs a pistol, just in case." It was possible the situation with Mac was just a distraction, meant to lure people away so the real attack could take place. While Thorne didn't like the thought of sending his people out on patrol armed and jumpy, he didn't want them to be caught defenseless either.

The hand moved to lead Jericho away, but paused when Thorne called after him. "Make sure everyone keeps the safety on." Hopefully that would prevent any accidents.

"Yessir," he called back.

Satisfied he'd done all he could on that front, Thorne turned back to Maggie. "I have to go," he said softly.

She frowned, worry etched on her brow. "Let me come," she said. "I can help if Mac's been hurt."

"No. He said there were snakes around. Now that might be true, but I think he was making a reference to the snakes in his office. He's trying to warn me to keep you away."

Maggie sighed, sounding like the weight of the world was on her shoulders. "Finc. I'll stay behind, but only because I'm pregnant. If I didn't have this baby to worry about, I'd be going with you, no matter what Mac says."

A surge of relief made Thorne smile, despite the circumstances. "I know," he said. "And I love you for it. But right now I need you to stay inside, out of sight. I don't know if this is the opening move to a larger attack. Whatever happens, I don't want you to be an easy target."

She nodded. "Please be careful."

"Always." He leaned down and pressed a hard kiss to her mouth. "I'll be coming back to you soon. I promise."

He took the phone from her hand and started for the truck, his heart feeling torn in two. He couldn't leave his father, but it gutted him to walk away from Maggie and the baby when he didn't know what danger they faced.

I hope I'm making the right choice. If he lost Maggie because he was trying to save Mac, it would kill him.

The thought made him pause behind the wheel of the truck, indecision threatening to paralyze him. Was it right for him to risk two lives in the service of saving one? Or should he stay here with his future and trust that Knox would find Mac in time?

The more he thought about it, the more his certainty waned. There was no good choice here—whatever he decided, he was damned. It was just a matter of figuring out what choice he could best live with…

A sharp tap on the window made him jump. He turned to find Maggie standing there, her expression full of compassion. "Go," she said, loudly enough that he could hear her through the glass. "We'll be fine."

He nodded, tears stinging his eyes. "I love you," he said, raising his voice so she could hear the words.

"I love you, too," she said.

Thorne swallowed and put the truck in gear, dialing the phone with his free hand. He bounced down the road, his eyes glued to the image of Maggie in the rearview mirror, growing smaller with each passing second.

I'm coming back, he promised silently. *Please stay safe*.

Maggie walked back into the barn, her emotions swirling like a summer storm. Worry for Mac and for Thorne were foremost in her mind, but she couldn't ignore the bubbly feeling in her stomach thanks to Thorne's confession of love. She hadn't doubted his feelings for her, but it was nice to finally hear him say those three words.

Too bad it was under such dire circumstances.

She approached Rose's stall slowly, not wanting to startle the horse. The animal seemed agitated this morning, probably due to the fire yesterday and her new surroundings. Maggie wanted to give her comfort, but since she and Rose were still getting to know each other, she didn't know how her overtures would be received. And since Thorne wasn't around to smooth the way, she thought it was best if she gave Rose a wide berth, at least until things settled down again.

Rose whinnied as she approached, evidently smelling her presence. Maggie walked up to the stall door and peeked inside, expecting to find the horse in the same spot she'd been in moments before.

But Rose was pacing the confines of the stall, rubbing her sides up against the walls as if she itched. She called out to Maggie as soon as she saw her, and the plaintive note in her neigh made Maggie's heart crack. The animal was clearly in distress, but Maggie had no idea what to do.

She watched in horror as Rose lifted one of her back legs and kicked at her pendulous belly. "Oh, no! Please don't do that," Maggie begged. But Rose ignored her and continued pacing and kicking, her distress clearly growing.

All of a sudden, Rose knelt and listed to her side until she was lying on the floor. Maggie heard a distinct "pop" and then a gush of fluid hit the floor of the stall. An earthy, slightly sweet tang filled the air, not unlike the scent of freshly mowed hay.

"Rose," Maggie said slowly, panic rising in her chest. "Please tell me you just peed yourself."

But no matter how strongly Maggie wanted to deny it, she couldn't escape the truth. Rose was in labor.

And she was going to have to deal with it by herself.

Chapter 22

Thorne drove as slowly as he dared, wanting to give Knox time to arrive and get into position. He wasn't quite sure what he would find when he arrived at the old well, but he didn't want to face it alone.

He left the gravel road and drove into the tall grasses, using the copse of trees as a landmark to guide his trajectory. After cresting a low hill he spotted the well in the distance, little more than a bump in the field.

Thorne maneuvered the truck closer, wanting to park by the well to minimize the distance Mac had to travel to get inside the vehicle. He wasn't sure what condition his father was in, but hopefully he could still walk...

He pulled to a stop and took a second to study the scene before him. Mac was on the ground, propped against the stone skirt of the well. Wes Kingston, his former stepfather, stood over him, his gun pointed at Mac's head. The look of determination in Wes's eyes made Thorne's heart skip a beat. This was a man who was prepared to do violence. There would be no reasoning with him.

Thorne opened the door of the truck and slowly slid out, careful to keep his hands up and visible so as not to give Wes an excuse to pull the trigger.

"Look who finally showed up," Wes remarked, shifting his weight slightly.

Thorne glanced at his father. There was a dark stain on the collar of his shirt, and the way he squinted made Thorne think he was in pain. He scanned his father's body, but didn't see signs of any other injuries. That was good, but Thorne still didn't relax. Mac might be relatively unharmed now, but it would take only one bullet to end his life.

"What's going on here, Wes?" Thorne tried to keep his tone casual, but inside he was practically vibrating with adrenaline and anger. He never would have guessed that his onetime stepfather was in league with Livia, especially after the way she'd cheated on him and then publicly humiliated him during their divorce.

"It's rather obvious, don't you think?" Wes replied. "But then again, you always were a little slow."

Thorne ignored the jab. "I'm guessing you're the one who's behind all the recent excitement?"

Wes's jaw tightened, as if he was unhappy about something. "Things didn't work out the way I'd hoped. But I'm still going to come out on top." He cocked the gun, and Thorne's heart froze.

"Just a second," he said quickly, stepping forward.

"It's obvious you want to kill me and Mac. But just tell me why. Why are you working with Livia after all the pain she caused you?"

Wes stared at him a moment, his features twisted in confusion. Then he laughed, a harsh, barking sound that cut through the air and silenced the ambient birdsong. "You think I'm working for that bitch?" He sounded genuinely amused, and for a second, Thorne thought this was all some kind of elaborate prank. "No," Wes continued. "I wouldn't piss on her if she was on fire."

"Then what—?"

"I'm using her," Wes said, as if this should explain everything. "Now that she's out of jail, I can kill Mac and you, his son, and blame Livia for it." He cocked his head to the side, studying Thorne for a moment. "Did you really think I was going to let that go? That I would just forgive and forget the fact that this man—" he kicked Mac hard in the legs, causing him to groan "—slept with my wife?"

"But you hate Livia," Thorne said, trying to wrap his brain around the delusions driving Wes. Why take out his anger on Mac for something that happened almost thirty years ago, especially when whatever love Wes had once had for Livia had long ago turned to hate?

"Yes, I do," Wes agreed. "That's why I'm going to enjoy framing her for murder." He pointed the gun at Mac's head again, and Thorne realized the time for talking was over.

He sucked in a breath and tensed his muscles, preparing to charge at Wes. Hopefully he could knock the man off balance and cause his shot to go wide. But he was standing so very close to Mac…

Just as Thorne pushed forward, a shot rang out. He dropped to his knees, expecting to find Mac's limp body on the ground. But his father stared back at him, his eyes wide and his expression shocked.

Wes let out a low moan, and Mac and Thorne turned as one to see the man sink onto his knees, a rapidly growing bloodstain blossoming on his chest. Wes looked at them with wild, panicked eyes and tried to lift his arm to aim the gun he still held. Thorne launched himself at the man, knocking him onto his back and wrestling the gun free. He passed it to Mac, then turned back to Wes and applied pressure to his wound, trying to staunch the flow of blood.

After a few moments Thorne heard the sound of footsteps approach. "You took your sweet time," he observed.

"Had to give him a chance to change his mind," Knox said. "Is he still alive?"

"So far," Thorne replied. "Let's hope the ambulance gets here soon."

Knox squatted by Mac and the pair started talking. Thorne listened as his father told Knox everything that had happened, from his early morning ride to finding the cover off the well and getting hit on the back of the head.

"The next thing I knew, I opened my eyes and he was standing over me," Mac said.

"Thank God he didn't shoot you outright," Thorne said.

Mac's eyes filled with tears as he looked at Thorne. "I almost wish he had," he said. "I hated luring you out here, knowing this man intended to do you harm. I only did it because he threatened to kill Maggie and the ranch hands if I didn't cooperate."

"Dad, you don't have to apologize," Thorne said. He wanted to hug his father, but he didn't want to stain him with Wes's blood. "Believe me, I know you were only doing what you thought was right. Besides, I picked up on your warning. Maggie's back at the barn with Rose, and I have the hands doing patrols of the inner perimeter, just to make sure we have no other surprises."

"That was smart thinking," Mac said quietly. "I'm glad you kept your head."

"Calling me wasn't a bad move, either," Knox observed.

"I'm just glad your shooting skills aren't too rusty," Thorne said with a grin. "Otherwise, I'd be the one on the ground now."

The faint whine of an ambulance sounded in the distance, and Thorne gave a mental sigh of relief. He couldn't wait to turn Wes over to the proper authorities and get Mac checked out. He'd left Maggie alone for far too long, and he wanted to get back to her and share the good news that the threat hanging over their heads was now gone. He smiled at the thought, imagining her reaction. They could finally start their life together, free from fear.

He couldn't wait.

Maggie had never been more terrified in her life.

The car bomb had been scary. The snakes in Mac's office had given her chills. And yesterday's fire had lived on in her nightmares. But they all paled in comparison to the events unfolding before her now.

There was no denying Rose was in labor. She was heaving and groaning, working herself into a lather as she tried to give birth to her foal. Maggie was no expert, but it was clear something was wrong. She'd seen a foot appear, only to disappear again a second later. This pattern had been going on for the last quarter of an hour, and Rose was growing weaker by the moment.

Maggie wanted desperately to help her, but she had no idea of what to do. After Rose's water had broken, Maggie had tried to find someone—*anyone*—to help. But she didn't have her cell phone and none of the ranch hands answered her cries. The place was like a ghost town. So Maggie had returned to the stall, wanting to offer the comfort of her presence, if nothing else.

"Maggie?"

Her head whipped around at the sound of her name, and she nearly wept with relief. "Jade! Oh, thank God you're here!" She ran toward her friend and grabbed her by the hand, then started pulling her back to the stall.

"What's going on? Are you okay?" Jade stopped when she saw Rose on the ground. "Oh," she said, her tone changing from concerned to professional. "How long has she been like this?"

Jade slipped into the stall, moving carefully around Rose. The horse let out a pained whinny and Jade placed a hand on her heaving side. "I know, sweetheart. I know."

"I'm not sure. Her water broke maybe thirty minutes ago? There's been a foot coming out and sliding back in for about fifteen minutes. I tried to go for help, but no one is here." Maggie stopped, realizing she was babbling."

Jade merely nodded and rolled up her shirtsleeves.

"Okay. Sounds like a bit of obstructed labor. Let's see if we can help her out." She knelt by Rose's tail to take a look, then rose and pulled her phone from her pocket. She passed it to Maggie. "Call the vet. Speed dial number three. Tell him we have a maiden mare trying to foal, and it looks like the baby isn't positioned correctly."

Maggie's hands shook as she brought the phone to her ear. She relayed Jade's instructions while her friend pulled on Rose's halter, tugging and coaxing until the horse had no choice but to stand.

"He said he'd be here in twenty minutes." Jade shook her head at this news, and Maggie's heart sank. "That's not good enough?"

"No," Jade said shortly. "We have five minutes, maybe ten, to get this foal out if we want it and Rose to survive."

Maggie cursed silently, despair settling over her like a second skin. It was bad enough Thorne was putting himself in danger to save Mac. He'd never forgive himself if Rose died because he hadn't been there when she'd tried to give birth.

She had to do something to help. Even if their efforts turned out to be in vain, Maggie had to be able to say she'd tried to save them.

"What can I do?"

Jade glanced at her, nodding in approval at the question. "Open the stall door. We need to make her walk."

Maggie did as she was told, throwing the door wide so Jade could lead a reluctant Rose into the main aisle of the barn. "Now help me encourage her," Jade said. "She wants to lie back down and push, but we can't let her do that yet."

"Okay." Maggie put her hand on Rose's neck and began to talk to the horse, urging her to keep moving. "Why are we making her do this?"

"I think the foal is in the wrong position. If we can get Rose to move enough, it might shift the baby enough so it can be born."

"And if this doesn't work? Is there something else we can try?"

Jade didn't reply, but the tight set of her mouth told Maggie everything she needed to know.

Maggie turned back to Rose, her stomach in knots. "Come on, girl. You can do this. You *have* to do this."

They marched her up and down the aisle for several minutes, until Rose planted her feet and refused to budge another inch. "Okay, mama," Jade said soothingly. "You can lay back down now."

Rose allowed them to lead her back into the stall, where she promptly knelt and leaned over onto her side. Jade knelt by the horse's tail and gestured for Maggie to join her. "Hold her tail out of the way, will you?"

Maggie gathered up the coarse strands of hair and pulled them out of the way. She watched in fascination and fear as Rose's belly heaved with a contraction. Her breath caught in her chest as one foot began to emerge...

"Come on," Jade whispered. "Please, Rose, come on."

Maggie found herself leaning forward, as if she could help the horse through sheer force of will. As she watched, more of the first foot emerged, followed by a second hoof, and a few seconds later, what looked like a nose.

"Yes!" Jade exclaimed in a loud whisper. "That's it, girl! Keep going."

Maggie's body sagged with relief and she nearly lost her grip on the tail. Rose continued to push and, within a couple of minutes, the rest of the foal's body had been delivered.

Jade sprang into action then, tearing away the white membrane covering the baby and gently manipulating the umbilical cord so that it was away from Rose's hooves. The foal lay on the straw, limp and stunned, but as Maggie watched its sides heaved as it drew its first breaths.

She sank onto her bottom, heedless of the mess surrounding her. "Good job, Rose," she said softly, patting the mare's hip gently.

Jade gripped the foal and rotated the baby so that it sat on its chest with its feet forward. Rose sniffed at the foal with interest and began to nuzzle and nibble at its slick coat.

Maggie sat motionless, entranced by the vision of mother and baby meeting for the first time. Now that the ordeal was over she felt hollowed out and exhausted, her body and emotions almost numb from the intensity of the experience.

"What do we do now?" she whispered to Jade.

"Nothing," Jade said with a smile. "We need to clean her up, but that can wait a few minutes while they get acquainted." She turned to look at Maggie and her eyes widened in surprise. "Looks like we need to get you cleaned up, as well."

Maggie looked down, registering the gore around her for the first time. The sweatpants were likely ruined beyond saving, and they clung wetly to her body as she got to her feet. Jade offered her a hand, helping her to walk across the slick hay. "I can't have you falling," she said lightly. "Thorne will be upset enough that he missed the foaling. He'd kill me if I let you get hurt, too."

"I'm just glad you were here," Maggie said. A shadow of her initial terror passed over her and she shuddered. "If you hadn't showed up when you did, Rose probably would have died."

"You can thank Thorne for that," Jade replied. "He called me and told me to get out here right away. He wanted me to keep you company."

"Oh," Maggie said, at a loss for words. Leave it to Thorne to worry about her while he was in the midst of saving his father. It was just like the man to try to take care of everyone in his life, no matter the circumstances.

A flash of love warmed her chest, followed closely by a shot of fear. Thorne had been gone for a while now. Had he found Mac? More importantly, were they both safe?

"What's going on?" Jade asked. "Thorne said he didn't have time to explain. He sounded stressed, so I didn't press the subject. But I was hoping you could tell me."

Maggie opened her mouth to do just that but was interrupted by Jade's phone. "Speak of the devil," Jade said. Maggie heart leaped into her throat—that must be Thorne! She fisted her hands by her side to keep from snatching the phone away from her friend, but she didn't hesitate to lean forward in an attempt to overhear the conversation.

"Hello?" Jade listened for a moment, then held the phone out to her. "He wants to talk to you."

Maggie didn't waste any time. "Thorne? Are you okay? What happened?"

His deep voice was the most beautiful sound she'd ever heard. "I'm fine. Mac is fine. Knox made it here in time and the threat is gone."

Her muscles threatened to give out and she gripped the edge of the stall door. "That's good," she said, emotion clogging her voice. "I'm glad to hear that."

"Maggie, what's wrong?" He sounded alarmed, and she realized he thought she was hurt.

"Nothing, everything's fine. Your sister and I had a little adventure while you were gone, that's all."

"Are you okay? Is Jade?" he said urgently.

"We're both fine," she assured him. "Rose decided to have her baby while you were gone."

"Oh, damn," he said softly. "I was hoping to be there. Did it go smoothly?"

Maggie couldn't help but laugh. "Well, not exactly. But Jade got here just in time."

"Put her back on for me, will you?"

Maggie passed the phone to Jade, who took it with a slight frown.

"Uh-huh," Jade said. "Yes, I did that. Yes, the foal is sitting normally and breathing fine. No, I didn't break the cord." She rolled her eyes at Maggie and shook her head. "This isn't my first rodeo, Thorne. The vet is on his way—he'll check them both over, but for now, stop worrying."

She thrust the phone back into Maggie's hands. "You talk to him. I'm going to go flag down the vet." She walked away, muttering to herself.

"I think you made her mad," she said.

"She'll get over it," Thorne replied. "I just need to make sure all my girls are safe."

"We are," Maggie confirmed. "But I, for one, will feel much better when I see you again."

"I'll be there soon," he said. "Can you wait a little longer?"

Maggie smiled, picturing his face. "I'll wait for you forever, if that's what it takes."

Epilogue

Mac's house. Two weeks later...

"Congratulations again!" Knox said, pulling Maggie against his broad chest for a hug. "I can't wait to have you as a sister-in-law!"

"Thank you," Maggie said, smiling up at him. Thorne had told her how Knox had fired the shot that kept Wes from killing Mac. She'd always liked Knox Colton, but the fact that he'd saved Mac and Thorne from certain death had tipped that like over into love. She turned to his new wife, Allison, and stepped close to hug her. "I'm so glad you could make it."

"Wouldn't miss it," Allison said. "Not only are we thrilled to welcome you to the family, but this guy is dying to see the new foal." She ruffled Cody's hair affectionately as the boy bounced on his heels.

"I heard you delivered it," he said excitedly. "Was it gross? Was it really messy?"

Maggie laughed. "Your aunt Jade gets most of the credit, but I was there, yes. And yes, it was pretty messy."

Cody grinned, his blue eyes twinkling. "Cool." Then he darted away, making a beeline for the table of hors d'oeuvres. Knox followed with a knowing sigh, trailing in his son's wake.

"So how are you feeling?" Allison asked. She eyed Maggie up and down, taking in the deep purple of her dress. "You look amazing—I love your dress. It's the perfect outfit for your engagement party."

"Thanks," Maggie said, smiling at the compliment. She nodded at Claudia, who was standing a few feet away talking to Jade. "It's one of Claudia's designs. She made me a few maternity dresses as prototypes for a new line she's thinking about launching."

"The girl has talent, that much is clear," Allison said. "But you're the reason the outfit really shines. You're practically glowing, and it can't all be from the pregnancy hormones." She leaned forward a bit, a smile playing at the corners of her mouth. "Are you going to show me the ring, or do I have to beg you to see it?"

"Oh! I thought you'd already seen it!" Maggie held out her hand for inspection, and Allison clasped her fingers, turning her hand this way and that as she oohed and ahhed.

Maggie smiled at her reaction. Thorne had proposed a few days ago, and she hadn't taken the ring off since then. She knew she'd have to eventually, but it was still so new she couldn't bear to part with it, even for a moment.

The large pearl gleamed warm and lustrous in the afternoon light streaming in from the window. Green sparks flashed from the halo of emeralds surrounding the stone as Allison moved her hand. She touched the braided gold band with her fingertip, humming to herself. "It's gorgeous!" she said. "I just love it!"

"Me, too," Maggie replied, grinning. She'd once wondered what kind of ring Thorne would choose if he ever proposed to a woman. Now she knew, and it exceeded her wildest dreams.

The man in question sidled over and put his arm around her shoulders. "My ears are burning."

"They should be," Allison said. She gestured toward Maggie's ring. "You did a fabulous job."

"Well, I do try," he said modestly.

"So are y'all going to live here, or will you be moving to the city?"

"We're staying here," Maggie said. She wrapped her arm around Thorne's waist and gave him a squeeze. Maggie knew he was worried about how she'd take to life on the ranch, but she'd explained to him in no uncertain terms that her home was with him, wherever that may be. Ranching and horses were in his blood, and she wasn't about to ask him to give that up. Besides, she rather liked the idea of their baby growing up on the ranch.

"Aren't you afraid you'll get bored?" Thorne had asked her. "Life out here is very different from what you're used to."

Maggie had laughed. In her short time on the ranch, she'd been anything but bored. "I'm ready for a change," she'd said. "Besides, I have to keep an eye on Rose and her little one. I'd miss them if I wasn't around all the time."

"Is that the only reason you want to stay?" He'd looked down, appearing suddenly shy.

Maggie had tipped his chin up with her finger until he met her eyes. "Thorne Colton," she'd said. "You know I love you. And that means I love all of you—the total package. This ranch and these horses are a part of you. I could no sooner take you away from that than fly to the moon."

His eyes had filled with emotion and he'd embraced her, his relief palpable. "We can try it out for a while, see if you like it," he'd said. "And if you don't, we'll move into town. I just want you to be happy."

"Stay with me, then," she'd said. "That's all I need."

"We're building a house not far from Mac's," Thorne said now, pulling Maggie's thoughts back to the present conversation. "The foundation has just been poured. We're hoping it'll be ready before the baby arrives."

"I can't wait to see it," Allison said. There was a crash from the direction of the table, followed by a startled yelp. Allison winced. "Please excuse me," she said. "I believe that's my cue."

Thorne and Maggie watched her walk over to a contrite-looking Cody, who was standing over a dropped plate of food. "Think our little one will have that much energy?" she whispered.

He snorted. "Oh, yeah. Most definitely."

A knock sounded on the door behind him. Maggie glanced up to see Thorne's frown. "Are we expecting anyone else?" As far as she knew, everyone was here. Knox and Allison were helping Cody clean up his mess, Claudia and Jade were talking in the corner with her parents, and Leonor and her fiancé, Joshua, were talking to Mac.

"Not as far as I know," he replied. He moved to the door and Maggie followed.

Thorne opened the door and froze, his body going stiff as he saw who was on the other side. Maggie glanced over, bracing herself for the worst.

But the man that stood on the welcome mat didn't appear threatening. He was tall and muscular, with close-cropped dark brown hair. He wore a patch over his right eye, giving him a rakish, almost piratical, air. A few angry-looking red lines extended beyond the patch, but they didn't detract from his looks. He was a handsome man, one who probably turned a lot of female heads.

Thorne's breath gusted out. "River!" He took a step forward and threw his arms around the man, hugging him tightly. His half brother looked a little stunned, as if he hadn't been expecting this reaction.

"It's good to see you," he said. His voice was gravelly, and Maggie got the impression he didn't do much talking.

Thorne released his grip and leaned back, giving River some space. "Where have you been? We'd heard you'd retired from the Marine Corps, but we didn't know where you were."

"Yeah," River said ruefully. "Turns out I'm too banged up to fight anymore." He gingerly touched the patch over his eye. "Thought I'd come home for a while, but I stopped by Austin first to see Wes while he waits for his trial to start."

"Are you okay?" It had to have been difficult for his brother to see his father behind bars.

River smiled, the expression transforming his face. "I'm better than okay. Turns out, Wes doesn't actually think he's my father. Can you believe it?"

Surprise rippled through Thorne, followed quickly by acceptance. "Unfortunately, yeah. Livia didn't lack for lovers."

River nodded. "That was my reaction, too. I'm getting a DNA test done to confirm it, but hopefully I'll get lucky and have at least one parent who isn't a criminal."

"I'll keep my fingers crossed."

River turned to Maggie. "We're being rude. I apologize, ma'am."

"Hello," she said.

Thorne shook his head. "I'm sorry. I forgot myself. River, this is Maggie, my fiancée. Maggie, this is River. He's my brother."

River's eye widened at the word *fiancée*, but he offered his hand for her to shake. "Pleasure to meet you, Miss." He cast a look at Thorne. "I'm glad to see you've found someone."

"You and me both," Thorne said. "Come inside— your timing is actually perfect. We're having our engagement party. The family is all here."

River shook his head and took a step back, almost as if he was afraid of joining them. "Oh, no. I can't."

Thorne frowned. "Why not?"

River shuffled his feet, clearly uncomfortable. "I came here to apologize to Mac. For what Wes did. But I'll come back later. I don't want to interrupt your party."

"Nonsense," Thorne said. "Don't go. Everyone will be so excited to see you."

River hesitated, and Maggie could tell he wanted to

run. "Please stay," she said. She reached out and laid her hand on his arm. "Just for a few minutes, at least."

He nodded slowly, and Thorne and Maggie stepped out of the way so he could enter the house. "Only for a moment," he murmured as he brushed past them.

Thorne walked his brother into the den while Maggie stayed behind to close the door. She waited a moment while Thorne announced River's arrival, smiling as the Colton siblings shrieked with joy and surprise to see him again.

Thorne caught her eye and hung back as River was pulled into the room. He walked over to slip his arms around her waist. "Thank you for that," he said softly.

"For what?"

"For convincing him to stay. We've all been worried about him. Hopefully he'll be in Shadow Creek for a while. I think he needs help."

"Then we'll make sure he gets it," she said.

Thorne shook his head. "You are too good to me," he said, dropping his head to kiss her softly.

Their embrace was interrupted a moment later by Cody, who danced around them like a puppy. "Uncle Thorne! Can we go see the baby horse now? Uncle River said he wants to see it, too."

Thorne laughed and nodded. "Okay. Just let me get your aunt Maggie something to drink. Then I'll take you both."

"I want to come with you," she said.

"Are you sure?" He slipped his hand into hers. "You wouldn't rather rest a bit?"

Maggie shook her head. "Nope. I'm sticking with you, cowboy. Now and forever."

"Forever sounds good to me." Thorne lifted her left

hand and pressed a kiss to her ring. Then he grinned, a twinkle entering his light brown eyes. "All right. Let's try to get those new boots of yours broken in."

* * * * *

*If you loved this novel,
don't miss the next thrilling romance in
the* COLTONS OF SHADOW CREEK *series:*
COLD CASE COLTON
*by Addison Fox,
available in June 2017
from Mills & Boon Romantic Suspense!*

*And check out these suspenseful titles in
Lara Lacombe's* DOCTORS IN DANGER *series:*

*DR. DO-OR-DIE
ENTICED BY THE OPERATIVE*

Available now from Mills & Boon Romantic Suspense!

MILLS & BOON®

INTRIGUE
Romantic Suspense

A SEDUCTIVE COMBINATION OF DANGER AND DESIRE

MILLS & BOON®
are delighted to support
World Book Night

Georgie Lee

The Secret Marriage Pact

World
Book Night
23 April 2017

World Book Night is run by The Reading Agency and is a national celebration of reading and books which takes place on 23 April every year. To find out more visit worldbooknight.org.

**THE
READING
AGENCY**

www.millsandboon.co.uk

30517_2